WHEEL OF FORTUNE

WHEEL OF FORTUNE
A Western Trio

MAX BRAND®

SAGEBRUSH
Large Print Westerns

First published in Great Britain by ISIS Publishing Ltd
First published in the United States by
The Golden West Literary Agency

Published in Large Print 2009 by ISIS Publishing Ltd.,
7 Centremead, Osney Mead, Oxford OX2 0ES
United Kingdom
by arrangement with
Golden West Literary Agency

British Library Cataloguing in Publication Data
Brand, Max, 1892–1944
    Wheel of fortune: a western trio. – Large print ed. –
    (Sagebrush western series)
    1. Western stories
    2. Large type books
    I. Title II. Brand, Max, 1892–1944. Chick's fall
    III. Brand, Max, 1892–1944. Speedy's bargain
    813.5'2 [FS]

ISBN 978–0–7531–8248–2 (hb)

Printed and bound in Great Britain by
T. J. International Ltd., Padstow, Cornwall

Table of Contents

CHICK'S FALL

"Chick's Fall" was one of twenty-two short novels written by Frederick Faust that were published in 1924. In addition twelve serials also appeared that year. The story was published in the November 15th issue of Street & Smith's *Western Story Magazine* under Faust's Max Brand byline. "Every man has his price," so the saying goes, and in this tale Sheriff Chick Marvin, an honest man, finds out what price could buy his dishonesty.

CHAPTER
ONE

When the news of the Holcombe robbery was brought to the sheriff, he was sound asleep, at the end of a thirty-six hour ride. But he was in the saddle in five minutes. He sent his horse over the nine miles to Holcombe so fast that the poor beast was staggering and foaming at the end of the journey.

In Holcombe, the sheriff spent fifteen minutes finding the one man who could give a sensible story of the robbery; he gave five minutes more to hearing that story. Then he changed horses, taking a fast animal belonging to the banker who had just been ruined by the calamity.

They could not have gone down the valley from Holcombe. It was fairly certain that they had gone up toward the hills. So Sheriff Chick Marvin loosed the reins and fled straight up to the higher country. Then he reached the place where the valley forked, and, before he made a choice of the ways, he dismounted from his horse, loosened the girths, and sat himself down beneath the skeleton shade of a Spanish dagger to think matters over. His mind was thick with fatigue. Therefore he rolled a cigarette and smoked it rapidly, and under that mild narcotic his brain cleared.

He had no doubt as to who had committed the robbery. The neatness of the job, the precision and the speed with which it had been executed, pointed to Corrigan again. That worthy had operated too many times and too successfully in the sheriff's county for the latter to have any doubt as to his methods. He was a canny man, was Lew Corrigan. The bank robberies attributed to him were in the scores, yet he had been apprehended only once, and, when mugged for the rogues' gallery, a copy of the picture had at once been sent for by Sheriff Chick Marvin. The picture revealed a squat-built man with long, swaggering arms as he walked, a broad face, small bright eyes, and something ape-like in his entire makeup. He must be very rich from his loot if he saved even a tithe of it, but thieves usually have the ability to get rid of their funds, and Lew Corrigan seemed to be no exception to that rule. Nothing but constant pressure from poverty could have forced him to such steady exertion to make more money. Yet what he did with his money was most strange. Some said that he was financed and his operations all directed by some mastermind that remained in the background.

The sheriff cared very little for such reflections. What he wanted was the person of Mr. Corrigan with bracelets of steel linking his capable hands together. And, if he could gain that end, the sheriff would willingly have sacrificed a year or even five years of his life. For he was only thirty, and at thirty years seem cheap things. He was the youngest sheriff, in fact, that the county had ever seen. And yet he had already been sheriff for no less than eight long years. He had become, at thirty, a landmark of the community as distinctly taken for granted as the mountains or the desert itself. No one would have dreamed of running against young Chick Marvin for the office. No one would have dreamed of voting for any other person. He had done a number of great things. He had found the underground system along which the Chinese were brought north from Mexico, across the Rio Grande. Young Marvin had cut the thread of that traffic squarely across, and for that important service he could show letters from a United States marshal, and the governors of three states, giving him unstinted praise.

Yet his whole career had begun and been founded upon an accident. When, in his twenty-second year, with no more knowledge of gunfighting than a thousand other cow waddies, he had faced the terrible Les Devine, the gun of Les had hung in the holster. It was due to the fact that the gun was new and Les had not had time to file away the front sight. At any rate, upon that accident the fame of Marvin had been built — that and what followed. For he had explained calmly and earnestly exactly what had happened and why it was that he was alive and Les Devine dead. But the older citizens of the community would not listen. Such a deed coupled with such modesty was enough to convince them that they had found a man. Many men were discontented with Sandy Pillsbury as sheriff, and at the next election Marvin was put up and elected.

He was the most astonished man in the county, but he straightway set about making himself worthy of the great position — for such it seemed to him. He practiced three hours a day with guns; he studied all that was known about the criminals of the county; when he took a trail, he followed it like a ferret, than which there is nothing more terribly tenacious. The result was that in his first year he made only two important captures, but those were important indeed. He had followed one man across five states. He had ridden 1,000 miles after the second. And he had brought both men home alive, after their wounds were cured. Such labors had their reward — the more so because he never boasted. It seemed to him that two arrests were a very small achievement for a year in office, but other men felt differently about it. And wrongdoers decided that it was distinctly unprofitable to operate in a community where the sheriff thought nothing of clinging to one trail for three months at a time.

His game grew with the passing of time. During each of the eight years he was ceaselessly working, his lean, ugly face became furrowed with marks of care. Smiles rarely came upon his lips, and in his eyes there was a far-off, wistful look as though he were hunting for that time when all evil-doing should cease in his county. And, like all men who have before them a goal that is impossible of attainment, he grew more humble. All other things passed out of his life. There was no play. There were no cards or drinking parties. And women did not enter his life. In the apprehension of criminals he grew as methodical as a clerk in an office. And, indeed, he kept careful records of everything he saw or heard that might help him. He watched not only suspicious characters, but the friends of the suspicious. And thus it was that while a crime might be committed in his county with impunity, he generally caught the criminal the second time.

Only Lew Corrigan descended from time to time upon his district, struck his blow, and departed unharmed, until some one said: "Does Marvin *want* to catch him?"

That was repeated to Marvin, as all evil things are sure to come back to the ears that they will sting most sharply, and he put that cruel suspicion away in his heart never to be forgotten. And so it was that, sitting under the gaunt shade of the Spanish dagger, he revolved his thoughts most earnestly. In the meantime, precious moments were slipping from him. Every second lost at the beginning of a chase means minutes, hours, days, weeks, even months at the end of the trail. The sheriff knew all of this perfectly. He was in no doubt about the necessity of haste, but he knew that blind hurry has never yet caught any fox like Lew Corrigan.

He considered the trails. He knew every mile of them, every twist and turn, for his mind was full of well-charted courses, like a book of minute maps. The right-hand way was no doubt the most likely one. It twisted across the hills and then cast a long, straight loop across the San Mateo Valley. Then it drove straight up to the higher mountains, climbing fast. The left-hand trail kept for a longer time through the foothills. It was not so much traveled. It was not half so fast as the right-hand path. Its advantage lay only in that the grades that it climbed were more gradual — a thing of moment only to a man mounted upon a weary horse, or a fast animal without great strength. But this was not true of Lew Corrigan. He was sure to be mounted upon the best horseflesh that money could buy. Always, between his knees, he had a bit of four-hoofed lightning that could flash away through the hills and flaunt across the desert, two miles to a cow pony's one.

At this thought the sheriff looked to his own horse, a lumpish head, a small ugly eye, a tangle of mane, a wisp of a ragged tail. In short, a caricature of a horse, but the sheriff looked not so much at the twisted body as at the fine legs — and the meanness in the eye of the brute was at least equaled by its courage. This was his means of conveyance, to pit against the high-blooded horses of the outlaws. But in such ugly mustangs as these the sheriff put his trust. The soul of a man, it is said, is revealed in the horses he loves, and the sheriff had no use for showy horseflesh. He neither loved nor hated horses. They were simply machines that got him from point to point through difficult country. He could not imagine mourning greatly for anything about a horse except its stout legs. He took his horses for granted, as other men take their shoes, feeling no gratitude to the sole leather that saves their skin from the stones. But his preference for the mustang breed was a thing of character only. A dozen times fine horses had been proffered to him by various ranchers; a dozen times he had tried out the animals and sent them back. They looked like thrilling pictures, but they worried the sheriff. When he was in the saddle on the back of one of those lovely creatures, he felt as Maria, the cook, would feel in a Paris gown. Marvin was like his mustang, made for work, not for show, with no beauty in his lean, sun-dried body, but a great deal of serviceableness.

At last, going over all the details in his estimate of the two trails, he hit on the deciding factor. If he did not know much about Lew Corrigan, he *did* know a little, here and there, about those who favored the safe-cracker. And this information, which he had gathered with the greatest difficulty, was of use to him now.

The left-hand trail wound through tossing hills, continually, to be sure, but at one point it came close to the ranch house of Sam Dervitt. And there was just a trace of a suspicion in the mind of the sheriff that Sam Dervitt might be a friend of the outlaw. At least, this chance was enough to decide him. He settled the heavy sombrero on his head and rose into the full blast of the sun, feeling its heat sink like hot water through the back of his shirt, scorching his shoulder blades. The leather of the saddle was almost too warm to touch — even the coat of the mustang would have stung a tender hand.

There was little wind. Now and again it came in a languid wave, not cooling, but simply washing new floods of heat about him. All was heat — all was heat and light. It was the interior of an oven. All the hills, all of the greater and more distant mountains were brightly veiled with waves of shimmering mist — sheer power of the sun's light. And the sky was a faded thing from which the blue had been burned, leaving only a pale concave filled with the blaze of the sun.

The sheriff did not complain. He did not grow nervous. He did not sigh for better or for cooler lands. When a whirlwind took up a handful of mingled sand and grit and powdered cactus refuse and sifted it in his face and down his neck, he merely tightened his bandanna a little more and smiled earnestly into the distance.

He complained no more of this fiery furnace than the salamander complained of breathing flame. It was the natural element of the sheriff; it was all he knew in this world.

So he went on patiently up the trail, through the fire of the sun, with the mustang dog-trotting over the level, and swinging into a rolling canter down every slope, with the reins hanging slack, and the slender form of the sheriff drooping in the saddle, for he was one of those men who cannot be graceful.

CHAPTER
TWO

He came to Sam Dervitt's place at dusk and waited among the hills until the night was black. He found a tiny spring that gave drink to himself and to the mustang; for supper he had two biscuits, hard as iron, which he munched. But the quality of the food that he ate never seemed to make any difference to the sheriff.

When the full dark lay across the land, when the stars were burning their brightest and their lowest, he left the horse standing with thrown reins, and advanced on the house. 100 yards from the place, he saw the form of a horseman loom at one side. Chick Marvin dropped flat upon the ground and waited, nursing the butt of his revolver in his steady right hand.

Just above him the horseman loomed against the stars, but it was not what the sheriff wanted. It was a bare-legged boy riding a cow pony without a saddle, clucking to it, and thumping it with his heels. He continued past the sheriff and turned again, making a slow circle around the house. When he noted that, the heart of the sheriff grew warm in him. Sam Dervitt had posted his boy on that horse to ride guard on the house; what, therefore, was Sam Dervitt guarding?

The sheriff rose to his feet and hurried on; he paused again beside the wall of the house, and there he waited, while the young rider again loomed in view and went steadily on the circle of his beat. In the meantime, Sheriff Marvin was "seeing" with his ears, drinking in all that he could hear from the house. There was nothing, at first, except the sound of the voice of Sam Dervitt, telling how he had beaten Hugh Miller in a horse trade. His narration was interrupted by the admiring comments of his wife.

"I says . . . 'There she stands, Hugh. Look her over and make up your mind for yourself.'

" 'Is she sound?' says Hugh.

" 'Hugh,' says I, 'I ain't aimin' to tell an old hand like yourself what a hoss might be. I reckon you know hossflesh better than I do.'

"That sort of tickled him . . . he scratched his chin and walked around her. 'I'll give her a canter,' says he."

"How did she act, Sam?" asked the nasal voice of Mrs. Dervitt.

"She didn't let down none at all. I was holdin' my breath for fear of it, but it ain't till she's warmed up a bit that that hoof goes bad on her. He comes back teasin' her with the bits, and she puts up her head mighty high and proud.

" 'She's got a good feel,' says he. 'What's makin' you want to get rid of her?'

" 'She's a daisy,' says I, 'but she ain't up to my weight. You can see for yourself. She ain't cut out for a fat man like me. That's why I want your hoss.'

" 'How much boot?' says he.

" 'Why,' says I, speaking sort of slow and careful, 'I'll let you have the mare if you give me the brown hoss and twenty-five dollars.' "

"Sam!" cried his wife. "You don't mean that you said that?"

"He let out a holler you could've heard over here, pretty nigh.

" 'Twenty-five dollars?' says he. 'I pay *you* boot? No, sir, I'll take the boot myself!'

"I looks him steady in the eye.

" 'Hugh,' said I, 'do I look as plumb simple as all that? That mare is something that's right. Put her to a good stud and she'll give you a foal that'll be pretty nigh a racer!'

"He blinks a bit and I seen that I'd got him.

" 'Look here,' says I, 'I'll show you that I ain't no hog. Gimme ten dollars and the gelding and we'll call it quits. I got to have a hoss that'll carry me better'n she does. Take a gent ordinary sized, like you, and she'll work with you as good as any hoss that you could ask. But I need something strong under me.'

"He figgered for a minute and then he says . . ."

The sheriff reached the doorway and peered in. There sat Sam with his red, swollen face wreathed with smiles as he narrated his rascality; his wife, with her little glittering eyes, looked like a bird of prey as she gloated over the story. They had finished their supper. Their bare, grimy elbows were resting on the oilcloth that covered the table; Sam's pipe was between his teeth, but he talked slowly around it.

And there was no token of a stranger in the house, no sign of Lew Corrigan. The glance of the sheriff went like lightning from place to place — the table, marking that only two plates had been laid there — the wall, where the bridles hung — and there his glance lingered.

Two of those bridles were blackened with perspiration. Who had been using the second one? Mrs. Dervitt, perhaps, had been out. She rode like a man, freely and fearlessly. Or it might be the boy, although the chances were decidedly that he was using his own bridle now. Upon that second bridle the sheriff's glance lingered wistfully. But there was nothing to be made of it. It was as like the others as a pea out of the same pod.

However, he decided to act upon that small hint. He slipped around the house to the rear, keeping close to the wall. He could never tell when the boy, in his steady rounds, might have a glimpse of him against the wall of the house; it was only that the attention of the youngster was probably fixed upon the outer regions that had kept the sheriff from observation before this, perhaps. Sitting under the kitchen window, he pulled off his boots and laid down hat, gun belt, and holster. Only the Colt itself was in his hand as he stood up and watched the boy trot his horse past at a little distance, a black silhouette against the stars.

No doubt he would grow up like his father, a cunning rascal, a shrewd and a deadly fighter, a familiar of all the evil-doers in the county. And yet, granting a slight change in environment, might not young Dervitt come to as fine and clean a manhood as any boy? The sheriff thought of his nephew, Harry. So clean-eyed and straight-minded a boy, it seemed, could never have a wrong thought. Yet, if Harry had such a man as Dervitt for a father, he would be corrupted in a month. There would be no such influence in his life, heaven be praised. Poor Jack Marvin was as poor as poor could be; every month was a struggle to keep from utter ruin, but there was no more honest man in the world. And that strong, fine spirit had pervaded the boy, insensibly, and made him like a grown man in quiet dignity and in poise.

This went through the mind of the sheriff as he stood in the shadow of the cabin, for his brother's family was never long out of his thoughts. His life, indeed, fell into two sharply divided halves. On the one hand he was the sheriff; on the other hand he was the brother of Jack Marvin, the uncle of young Harry, the brother-in-law of hard-working Bess. It was of them that he dreamed, for them that he hoped. He gave them his savings.

He brushed this tenderness away, turned, seized the low-hanging edge of the roof, and swung himself on top of the shed that served as kitchen room in that cramped little house. He made toward the single window of the attic room, going carefully, lest his weight should start a creaking that would alarm those in the house.

He had his hand on the edge of the window when he heard a shrill cry from the outer night, piercing his mind like a slender shaft of light.

"Look out! They's someone on the roof . . ."

Inside the attic room, there was an instant stir — like the sliding of a startled snake through dry leaves, while the voice of Sam Dervitt, beneath, exploded in a great oath.

The sheriff set his teeth. He was caught in a position at once horribly humiliating and fearfully dangerous. He could he shot with impunity if he were found, and there was no doubt that he would be found. If he tried to flee, he would have to make off in stockinged feet across the ground strewn with cactus points, poisonous and sharp as the fangs of snakes. They could not fail to catch him, and, having caught him, they could do with him what they would. The law protects acts of violence when they are at the expense of night prowlers.

This went through his mind before the cry of the boy had died, while the rustle in the attic room was barely beginning. And he knew what he must do. He leaped for the little window, not to clamber through it, but as a swimmer dives into deep water. He was halfway through before a nail caught in his trousers with a noisy rip, and checked him, leaving him hanging, sprawling. At the same instant, a voice snarled, a gun spoke, a bullet moaned past him, and by the flash he saw the brutal face of Lew Corrigan in a corner of the room, contorted with hate.

The next instant the sheriff had twisted himself free, but he fell flat on his face and the second shot merely caught the loose flap of his shirt above his shoulders and twitched at it. Now, on the stairs, began the thunder of the feet of Sam Dervitt, rushing to the rescue with mighty oaths. Then Marvin, stretching forth his long arm, fired at the shadow. There was a cry of pain; the shadow dissolved and turned in a twisting heap on the floor while Sam Dervitt came raging into the doorway.

"Keep back, Dervitt," said the sheriff. "This is Sheriff Marvin."

"You damned rat catcher!" yelled Dervitt. "I'll . . ."

"Steady," said the sheriff, "or I'll shoot you through the head like a pig, which dog-gone me if you ain't one. Now light a match for me while you throw down your gun. Lemme hear it drop."

There was a breath of pause, and then the metal *crash* of the gun on the floor. The door banged downstairs; the voice of the boy shrilled: "Ma, what's goin' on?"

"Shut up that fool brat!" thundered Sam Dervitt. "What in the devil have you got ag'in' me, Sheriff Marvin?"

"Light a match and lemme see what I got," said the sheriff.

The match was lighted and revealed Lew Corrigan, one hand clasped to his body where the blood was welling out, and the other stretching toward the gun that Sam Dervitt had flung down upon the floor. The sheriff kicked the gun out of reach.

"Get your wife, Sam," he commanded.

CHAPTER
THREE

Four weeks went by, and the sheriff was still in the house of Sam Dervitt. During those weeks, he was not once out of sight of Lew Corrigan. During those weeks, Lew lay flat on his back, begging fate to blast his foe with lightning, cursing at the world, and waiting.

"You'll never take me out of this here house," he told the sheriff defiantly.

"How come?" said the sheriff, who was always willing to hear a criminal's opinions about anything, at any time, and at any length.

But Lew Corrigan merely winked and grinned at the other in a sly and repulsive way that was peculiarly his own expression.

"I'll tell you when the time comes," he said. "We'll fool you like we fooled you about the loot. You couldn't find the cash I robbed the bank of because I didn't bring it here with me. I had it transferred on the way to insure its safety in case you got on my trail. Well, we've fooled you and . . . and we'll fool you again."

But afterward, when his patience began to be rubbed transparent, he was heard to groan: "Damn their hearts, they'll never be here."

"No matter who comes," said Chick Marvin, "they ain't much chance that I'll let you go, old-timer."

Corrigan turned his head and sneered broadly. "The devil, man," he said. "When they get through with you, you'll be glad to let 'em have me."

"They're fighters, eh? Lion eaters, eh?" inquired the sheriff mildly.

"Son," said the outlaw, "guns ain't the only things to fight with."

"No," reflected the sheriff. "I've seen some handy Mexicans with knives, but the best that I ever seen was a little dago. He done this." He pointed to a white scar, a ragged mark in the brow of his forehead. He continued: "Dog-gone me if that little rat didn't throw a knife fifty feet and do that."

"What happened then?" asked Corrigan curiously.

"The blood sort of blinded me," said the sheriff, "but I managed to wipe it out of my eyes."

The yegg grew contemplative for a moment. "You shot him?" he said.

"I figgered on hitting him in the shoulder. But I was a bit wild," he said plaintively. "He only lived about ten minutes."

"Well," said the wounded man, "it ain't guns nor knives that I'm talkin' about, bo. When these pals of mine come, they'll slam you with somethin' that ain't ever hit you before."

"Like what?" asked Marvin.

But the other grinned and shrugged his shoulders. It seemed to the sheriff that the man on the bed was regarding him from a vast distance, with amusement, with the contempt of a superior wisdom so great that the sheriff could never plumb it. Others had affected him in the same fashion, but none so much as Corrigan.

In the meantime, that terrible watch went on. He commanded Sam Dervitt to go to town and let it be known that the sheriff wanted help to take Corrigan to jail. But Sam Dervitt discovered that he had on hand work that must be done at once. And when the sheriff demanded that the boy be sent, it was said that the boy had already been dismissed on an errand. After that, Marvin gave up. He dared not leave his prisoner. If he did, wounded though Corrigan was, he was sure to be transported to some secure hiding place. And, in the meantime, a thousand dangers surrounded Marvin. Sam Dervitt was ever near, blunt, evil of face. And Mrs. Sam hovered like a hawk in the background.

During the first week, by a certain tenseness in the atmosphere, Marvin knew that they were contemplating an attack by force. And, every day and night, he admitted Mrs. Dervitt only, and she could enter the room to bring food, and for no other purpose. At night, when he drowsed a little in the chair beside the bed, he barricaded the door and the windows and tied the wounded man in his bed.

On the eighth or the ninth day there was a change in manner. A certain surety and indifference sounded in the voices of Mrs. Dervitt and her husband. She came in with breakfast and asked for an opportunity to speak with the prisoner privately. The sheriff hesitated, but he was not one to take unnecessary advantages. He withdrew to the corner of the room, keeping a hawk eye upon them to make sure that nothing was given to the outlaw by his hostess. But all that he could make out passing between them were a few murmured words and one black look of piercing intensity fixed upon Mrs. Dervitt by the prisoner.

After she left, Corrigan lay for a long time quietly, staring at the ceiling. Afterward, he remembered breakfast and ate it. Still later in the day, he complained of fever and general sickness, and, when lunch was brought, he refused to touch it.

"You better eat, Lew," said Mrs. Dervitt, staring at him out of her little bright eyes. "You can't hold up and keep strong when you ain't eatin'."

"Lemme be!" snapped out Corrigan. "I know how I feel."

The sheriff laid his hand on the forehead of the prisoner. It was, in fact, burning hot. He took the pulse of the man. It was strong but quite rapid and, it seemed to the inexpert finger tip of Marvin, a little irregular.

"This here friend of yours is sick," he said. "Will you call in a doctor, Missus Dervitt?"

"Will you be that bad that you need a doctor, Lew?" asked Mrs. Dervitt, without a shade of emotion in her face.

"Damn the doctors!" growled out the other, and turned his face to the wall.

"You men are all like that," said Mrs. Dervitt to the sheriff. And she left the room while Chick Marvin sat down to his lunch.

He had a fork load of meat at his lips when a thought slid through his mind like the silently, twisting body of a snake. Towzer, the dog, was sniffing beneath the door, and the sheriff opened it and called the brute in. It looked at the plate of victuals with a quiver of eagerness, shaking its lean body. It was an ugly brute, half coyote, half town cur, with the disagreeable features of both, but wise as Solomon himself.

"Here, pup," said the sheriff, "help yourself." He extended the plate.

The mongrel leaped at it; the green fire of gluttony was in its eyes as it dreamed of a filled maw for the first time in weeks, or since the Rafferty's calf had been cut down by a passing timber wolf and most of the body left for dogs and coyotes. But with its slavering jaws about to close on the food, it winced and shrank as though under the stroke of a whip. Twice it shrank away; twice it came again for the plate of food, but although it slobbered over Mrs. Dervitt's cooking, it would not touch those provisions, and at last it shrank into a corner of the room and lay there shuddering with hunger and with hatred while it snarled at the man.

Then Chick Marvin sat down and rolled a smoke. He cast a side glance at Lew Corrigan lying on the bed, and he found that Corrigan had turned a covert head and was watching the sheriff with an eye of ominous fire. It was all clear to Marvin now. But he waited until he had finished his smoke before he went to the door and called Mrs. Dervitt.

She answered at once. "What's the matter? What's the matter? Want more water? That's that fish . . . it's so mighty salty."

Even the sheriff's strong nerves quaked a little at this, and he turned pale. "I'd like to speak to you, personal," he said.

Presently he saw Mrs. Dervitt coming up the stairs, her lean face turned to a sickly pallor, her eyes staring. Upon the sheriff she fixed a curious, half-horrified regard.

"You don't have to look at me so queer, Missus Dervitt," said the sheriff. "I ain't so thirsty as all that. All that I want you to do is to take a bite of this here food before I eat . . ."

"Ah . . . heaven!" gasped out Mrs. Dervitt. She had no more self-control than this. But, breaking down at once, she cringed before the man of the law.

"But what might be ailin' with you, Missus Dervitt?" asked the sheriff, as cold and as steady as ever. "Your dog wouldn't eat this here lunch, and now you seem sort of scared at the idea. What's the matter? Ain't it too good for me?"

She tried to speak, but only made a rattling deep in her throat. The voice of the outlaw broke in upon them.

"Let it lie, honey. Don't start tryin' to talk him out of his hunch. He's tumbled. That's all. Even a fool sometimes gets the right idea."

As for the sheriff, he was a little too sick in body and in soul to make any threat against Mrs. Sam Dervitt. He sank into a chair and sat there for a long time, turning the matter back and forth through his brain. It was not only the affair of the woman and her husband and the wounded outlaw. It was that their attitudes were significant of other attitudes. 10,000 men and women, perhaps, would take his life if they could, and take it without remorse. This affair of the poisoning was merely suggestive.

He had taken it for granted, always, that his life could not be long. Living as he did, he was almost certain to be snuffed out before his time. He, who plays forever with fire, must at last be burned. But a quick-stinging death from a bullet had been his imagining of the end. This was far otherwise — far otherwise. To die like a poisoned rat in a stranger's house, to be watched with curious, exultant eyes as he lay in a death agony — that was a death too horrible!

What had he done to bring upon himself such mortal hatred? That answer was too simple to escape him. He was a bloodhound. He was the foot and the tooth of red justice. And, whereas he had always looked upon himself as the simplest and the gentlest of men, he began to see how it was that others could behold in him a bloody hand of vengeance and wish for nothing but his destruction. He was so filled with this thought that he never so much as mentioned to Mrs. Sam Dervitt her attempt upon his life through poison. But, thereafter, when she brought food into the room, he always waited until she had tasted each dish, no matter what it might be.

A grim silence fell over the house on the heels of this event. The sheriff, knowing that the prisoner had planned the poisoning with the woman, and that the whispered words had been to warn Lew Corrigan to touch no food at supper time, found it hard to leave the subject untouched with the outlaw. He broke out, at last, one day when Corrigan's wound was almost healed enough to endure travel on horseback. "Corrigan," he said, "I dunno that I understand a gent like you . . . you can shoot straight with a gun, but still you'd hit around a corner with poison and knock out a gent when he didn't have no chance ag'in' you?"

"Why not?" asked Corrigan with astonishing frankness. "If I want you killed, what difference does it make to me how I get you dead? Fair play, you say? The devil, man, only fools and cowards believe in that stuff. What counts is bein' left alive with the goods. The other birds have got bumped off. You're alone on deck. That's what counts. The gent that brings the ship in is the gent that gets the scare-heads, not him that done the hero act in the middle of the sea and was sewed up and dropped overboard afterward. Nope, Sheriff, if I could be sure of killin' you by lyin' behind a log, wouldn't I be a fool to stand out in the sun and give *you* a crack at me?"

The sheriff did not answer. He was beginning to see what he had never been able to convince himself of before, which was that there are two classes of men — those who live by and understand the right, and those who detest and scorn what other men love.

This lesson he wrote quietly into his heart, never to be forgotten.

It was a scant week after that, that he moved Corrigan to town.

CHAPTER
FOUR

He did that simple thing with a feeling of the most consummate anxiety, for the outlaw had insisted so often that he would never be taken into town that the sheriff himself had begun to fear that he must be right. It appeared to be a black day for Corrigan. He made the journey to town in a glowering silence, with Sam Dervitt driving the buckboard and the sheriff cantering behind on the mustang. And, on the way, nothing whatever happened.

For the sheriff, it was the greatest moment of his life, next to the first election day which had given him office, when he saw Lew Corrigan locked behind the steel bars of the jail. He could not help saying in some exultation: "Well, Corrigan, here we are. I guess your friends ain't troubled themselves much about you, yet."

Corrigan turned to him with his broad face swollen with passion. "What's a jail to them?" he said. "Do you think a few steel bars makes any difference to them? Not a bit. They'll have me out of here in a jiffy. That's all!"

This, of course, was pure braggadocio, decided the sheriff, and he rode home with his head high in the air.

Half a dozen people stopped him here and there. It was always the same story.

"We didn't worry none," they all said. "Seein' you was gone a month, we knowed that you'd come back with Corrigan . . . and there he is. I reckon that old man Holcombe will be pretty pleased."

"Did that robbery break the bank?" asked the sheriff of the first man who spoke to him in this fashion.

"Sure it didn't. Old man Holcombe dug down in his pocket and made up everything. Didn't even worry him a minute, I guess. He's mighty rich."

Home for Corrigan was his brother's house. It stood just a mile out from the town, a bleak little shack on the slope of a hill, without a single tree to veil its worn nakedness from the eye of the world. However, to the sheriff it was the happiest spot in the world, for to him it was home. He sent the mustang forward, therefore, at a round gallop, unsaddled at the shed, turned the horse loose in the pasture, and hurried into the house.

They were at the supper table, Bess behind the coffee pot, Jack at the farther side of the table, and Harry between. Opposite Harry, a fourth place was laid. No matter how long the sheriff was absent, that table was never laid without a chair for him. He noted this fact now with a leap of the heart that never failed. Yet he had paid high for this attention. Out of his salary he had always contributed more to the upkeep of the family than had poor Jack, toiling on that wretched ranch with his handful of cows.

They were all up from their places in a minute to receive him, and, when he sat down at the table, he had

27

to tell all the story. And he told it from beginning to end. In other places he was a taciturn man, but here he could unlock his heart. Yet he noticed, before he was more than halfway through, that he had only one whole-hearted listener, and this was the boy, who drank it all in, agape with joy. But Jack and Bess were staring into the distance, smiling faintly, with half of their attention elsewhere. So he stumbled hastily through the rest of the story, then he sat by the stove and smoked while Bess cleaned the dishes.

It was not until Harry had gone to bed that he put the question that had been growing heavier and heavier in his inmost heart.

"Jack, what's wrong?"

"Nothin'," said Jack. "Not a thing. Why d'you ask?"

"I seen by your look that there was trouble. What is it?"

"It's too bad for tellin'," said Jack. "The way it happened . . ."

"Hush, dear," said the wife. "You ain't gonna spoil Chick's first night at home?"

"You're right," said Jack, and nodded gloomily.

He was like his brother in features, but more worn, more weary, and ten years of added age had streaked his hair with gray. He was a beaten man; he had been a beaten man for many a year.

"Look here," said the sheriff. "D'you think it's gonna make me sleep any better to know that there's trouble but not be able to figger out just what it is?"

"That's right," muttered Jack. "Well, Chick, I'm done, and that's an end of it."

"The end?" said the sheriff. "Why, man, ain't you got your land and your cows, no matter how many debts you got?"

"I got the debts, God knows," said Jack. "And I got the land. But I ain't got the cows no more, old-timer."

A stifled sob from Bess put a period to that sentence. The sheriff, from the corner of his eye, saw that she was crying as she leaned above the pan of dishwater, making blind motions with her hands but accomplishing nothing.

"Blackleg," muttered Jack. "It done the work pretty slick and pretty smooth, I tell you."

The sheriff paused in the making of a cigarette, then resumed it and lighted his smoke before he said briefly: "How many?"

"Left?"

"Dead?"

"Easier to tell you how many are left. The old brindled cow that Harry's been milkin' . . . she's left. That's why we got fresh milk on the table. And that Hereford bull, he's still with us."

"Go on," said the sheriff.

"Go on with what?"

"The others that are left."

"I'm finished, Chick."

It raised the sheriff half out of his chair. Then he sank back with a sigh. Poor Bess was weeping openly, leaning against the wall, her face covered with her apron. Then the sheriff went to her and put his arm around her work-bowed shoulders.

"Look here, Bess . . . ," he began.

"It's the plumb finish of everything," moaned Bess. "All these here years of workin' and worryin' are done."

"You got Jack, still."

"His heart is broke, Chick."

"You got Harry."

"That's what kills me, thinkin' about him. Where's his schoolin' gonna come out? He'd ought to go to high school this comin' year."

"Well, I'll see to it that he does go there."

"Oh, Chick, if you could!"

"Why can't I?"

"Because of me!" broke in his brother sternly. "Harry'll stay right here and help me work out of the hell that we've dropped into. Same as I helped to work my old man out of the hell that *he* dropped into!"

"Steady up, Jack. It ain't so bad as all that."

"It's worse than you know, old-timer. They're closin' in on me for cash now."

"The bank?"

"Yep."

"Not after the way they been keepin' you along all these years. They wouldn't hit you now that you're down."

"I says something like that to old Curran. He shook his head at me. He says . . . 'We ain't a charitable institution, Mister Marvin. So long as you was able to pay your interest and had the right amount of security behind you, we could let our principal ride along. But now it is a different matter. Very different, I assure you. We have to have that money. But we're not gonna rush you. You got a month to turn around and get hold of it.'"

This quotation left the room full of a stunned silence. Then the sheriff said softly: "How much might it be, Jack?"

"Not much. After that last fifteen hundred I got, only about eight thousand nine hundred and fifty-two dollars. That's all." He said it with the carelessness of despair.

"Nine thousand dollars!" breathed the sheriff, almost reverently. "Old man, how come it to run away up like that on you?"

"By runnin' short each year. I kept the boy in school. I tried to keep him dressed decent. Heaven knows that we ain't spent much on ourselves. But they ain't a livin' on this here place. It's too small ... it's too poor. I can see that now. We been waiting for a big rise in prices ... a big herd of cows. Well, we'll never get it. I can see it all pretty clear."

So could the sheriff, now that he looked back over the years. The little ranch had never been a sane proposition. It was a profitable possibility only as a small section of a great ranch. It was not big enough or rich enough to repay the intense labor of his brother. And his own money had been poured fruitlessly into it, like water into a desert.

"All right," said the sheriff. "I got to sleep on this here. Tomorrow maybe I'll have an idea. Maybe the bank'll offer a reward. That might help."

He went up to bed; Bess came after he was stretched between the sheets. She sat down and fumbled for his hand and took it in hot, trembling fingers.

"Dear Chick," she said, "it ain't the ranch, it ain't Harry that bothers me most. It's Jack. He's sitting in his room with one boot pulled off and the other left on. I tell him to get to bed. He grunts and don't do nothin'. Chick, he's gonna go crazy. He's bustin' down. Oh, God help you to help us!"

So she went away, and the sheriff lay rigidly all night, staring like one who strives to see a light where there is nothing but blank night ahead. Once he was roused by a shrill cry. Then he heard the quick voice of Bess soothing her husband, who had roused with a nightmare. To the sheriff, it was like the thrust of a spur into his tender flesh.

CHAPTER
FIVE

He had a letter from the Holcombe bank waiting for him at his office when he went to it the next morning. It was written in the small, cramped hand of Mr. Frank Holcombe himself, each letter drawn out with a sort of trembling care, indicative of the character of that old but militant spirit. It read:

My Dear Sheriff Marvin: Word has just come to me of your fine achievement. I sit down at once to write to you to express my intense satisfaction. There was so long a silence that I feared the rogue Corrigan, if you were right in your first guess as to the name of the criminal, had escaped once more from a tardy justice, but I understand that you have run him down, closed with him in fight, beaten him, held him captive in a hostile house until his wound healed, and then that you have brought him back triumphantly, alive.

This is a splendid achievement! How many men, satisfied with what they had done, would have ended the life of the villain with a second bullet and ridden home content, but you did not rest, Sheriff Marvin, until you saw him placed behind the bars. There is every hope that a confession on his part will now unravel the mysteries of many crimes; and above all, standing before his judge and his jury to be condemned, Corrigan will become an example to every loose-minded young man in the country, showing that even the keenest wits and the greatest resolution cannot save a persevering scoundrel from ruin in the end.

For our own part, we feel that more than half the sting of the recent loss which he inflicted upon us has been remedied by his capture and the prospect of his immediate punishment. I enclose my check, in the name of the bank, for $1,000, not to repay you for your exertions, which have been priceless, but as a token of our esteem.

Yours most faithfully,
Francis Tolliver Holcombe

He stared at that signature for some time. He drew out the check and considered it, also. How many a time that signature had been found beneath a letter that brought an announcement of ruin to him who received it. How many times, also, that signature had meant the withdrawal of large sums. It was cash — it was a name of gold. And as for the $1,000, it was the largest sum that he had ever been able to call his own at any one time. But this, at the present moment, was nothing to him.

For it fell $8,000 short of his need. Neither did the praise in the letter, extravagant praise, indeed, from that hard-hearted old man, melt the spirit of the sheriff or lift his heart with pride. Nothing existed for him except the troubles of his brother.

He went to see his captive in the jail and found that building already surrounded by more than five dozen curious visitors, not counting women and children. They set up a clamor when they saw the sheriff, for Charlie Guernsey, his jailer, had refused them admittance. They expected better luck from the amiable sheriff. He brushed through them and stood on the little porch at the head of the steps. Such an audience would have embarrassed him at any other time, but with such inward agony of spirit he found himself calm and grave before them.

"Gents," he said, looking over their faces, "I guess that I know why you're here. You want to see Corrigan. Well, gents, I'd like to please you. But I can't. It ain't that I don't want to please you, but the trouble is that I dunno that I got a good reason for torturin' Corrigan. You figger that them that bust open banks at night and take out thousands of dollars and bust gents that they never seen before . . . you figger that they got no sensitiveness. But I tell you, friends, that I'd as soon put Corrigan on top of a pile of dry wood and touch a match to it as I'd turn everybody loose to go in and stare at him and point him out and shake their heads at him. I guess that's final!"

He went into the jail, leaving a murmur of discontent outside. He found Corrigan totally unsubdued by his present situation. So much so that he almost regretted his speech to the crowd. Lew Corrigan was made comfortable upon his cot with his blankets wadded under his head for a higher pillow. He was smoking a cigarette and reading the newspaper, over the edge of which he peered at his visitor, with a bold, bright eye.

"Are you pretty comfortable?" asked the sheriff.

"You'd be worried a pile if I wasn't?" said Corrigan sneeringly.

"It ain't my aim to beat a hoss after I got a rope on him," said the sheriff mildly, "no matter how long it's took me to catch him."

Corrigan stared at him. "Well," he said, "I dunno what you mean by that, exactly. But you lemme be. I'll take care of myself. I ain't gonna be more'n three or four days here before I'm free."

"This here," said the sheriff, "is tool-proof steel. I reckon it'll hold you for a while."

Corrigan shrugged his thick shoulders. "My friends," he said, "have got keys that fit every lock." And he returned, straightway, to the reading of his sheet.

The sheriff went back to his office. Corrigan had been a great event the day before. He was only a small spot of brightness in the black spot of this gloomy day. At the office he was waited for by a stranger, a dapper little man with alert eyes and a brisk, courteous manner.

"You're Sheriff Marvin?" he asked

"I'm him."

"My own name," said the stranger, "does not matter. I have only to tell you that I'm a friend of Lew Corrigan, who is in trouble, as you know, at the present moment. I shall not trouble you with talk. I merely wish to leave this letter with you for your consideration. I shall call tomorrow to get a reply. No, on second thought, I'll call this afternoon."

With that, he handed an envelope to the sheriff and walked out of the room. The sheriff regarded the letter with some curiosity. It was a long envelope, and the paper on which the letter was written seemed to be of a peculiarly soft, limp nature, crushing like a sponge under the pressure of the fingers. He opened the envelope and shook forth into his waiting hand a neat sheaf of bills, secured with a brown-paper wrapper. They were all five-hundreds — ten of them! Here, between thumb and forefinger, he held $5,000!

He put them back into the envelope with a smile. This, after all, was the simple explanation of the mysterious confidence of Corrigan. This was the key that would fit any door. The friends upon whom he depended so entirely were, no doubt, those hidden partners who benefited by his crimes, who planned and prepared the way for them, and who took the lion's share of the profits of his daring adventures. They could not afford to surrender so readily, one who had been such a great source of income to them. And in this knowledge, the criminal had rested content, assured that they would put forth great efforts to save him.

How little, then, he knew the man with whom he had to deal. For the thought of selling himself was to the sheriff as horrible and as strange as the thought of taking poison. Worse, far worse — for poison could only touch the body, but this was a matter of the immortal soul!

37

He put the letter into his pocket, with all of its eloquent contents, and then turned his mind back to the troubles of his brother. He knew that Bess was right. This last blow, coming on top of the many troubles that had overwhelmed his life, was apt to unhinge the simple brain of Jack. Never a resourceful fellow, always fitted rather to keep his nose to the grindstone and peg away blindly at the work before him, Jack should never have risen above the position of a common cowhand, in which he had once excelled. But the necessity of providing for a family had been too much; he had been forced to work for greater returns. Now he was confronted by undeserved ruin, unless, indeed, stupidity is a crime that deserves the cruelest punishment.

He turned back to the heaped-up correspondence that had accumulated during his prolonged absence. There were letters apprising him that various criminals had been traveling in his direction; there was a heap of notices of various kinds concerning the latest crimes. He could set his mind upon them only dimly. For the main current of his thoughts could not be long under way on any subject without making a quick wreckage on the reef of the troubles of Jack Marvin. And the bright face of Harry looked in upon his mind many and many a time. What would become of that restless young intelligence cut off from any adequate education and forced back, an unwilling recruit in the ranks of the cow waddies? And then, with a keen thrill of horror, the idea came to him — that $5,000, added to the $1,000 that he had already received from Mr. Holcombe, would almost be enough to extricate his brother from all of his troubles.

He jumped from his chair and hurried out into the open, as if he felt that the temptation would dissipate more quickly in the honest sunshine. But the thought was still nagging him when he went inside again. Do what he would, it remained with him until he told himself calmly, that $6,000 was still an unreachable distance from $9,000.

And he was at this point when, sharp at noon, the dapper little form of Lew Corrigan's friend appeared once more in his doorway.

"This here letter . . . ," began the sheriff.

"Ah," said the stranger gravely, "I hope that you have been able to digest the contents?"

"Sure," replied Chick Marvin, grinning. "You can take it back. I dunno that line of talk is any good to me."

"Ah," said the other. He started a little, and looked at the ugly, thin face of Chick Marvin a little more closely.

"Well," he said at last, "if we have not expressed our ideas dearly in that first letter, I am authorized to let you have this second one."

He dropped another envelope, a blood brother of the first, upon the sheriff's desk.

"It ain't no good," said Chick Marvin calmly. "It don't matter if there was to be a million . . ."

"Words?" said the stranger. "Certainly not. We aim at crispness, always. Please read that second letter by the light of the first. I shall be back in an hour to have your reply." He turned on his heel and was off quickly, walking down the boardwalk with a quick, springy stride.

The sheriff, with a grunt, tore open the second envelope. Not, he told himself, for any good reason, but merely out of curiosity to see how high these rascals prized the services of the safe-cracker. He counted out the money in five hundreds again. $2,500. In addition to the $5,000, he now had in his hands a snug little fortune to the tune of $7,500, to which if he added the $1,000 from Holcombe, he had in his possession enough, within a few hundreds, to meet the whole need of his brother.

He could feel his brain reel. And then a sort of sense of foredoom struck upon him. Somewhere, at some time, a man had said: "Every man has his price." He had often smiled at that, feeling that he, at least, could never be touched by the hunger for money. But now he was beset by a dizziness, a weakness. Here, in the very touch of his finger tips, was salvation for Jack.

He gathered all his strength, thrust the pair of envelopes into the drawer of his desk, and went out onto the little verandah that fronted his tiny office building. The town was at lunch. All loud out-of-door noises had ceased. But from the houses on either side and across the street, he caught the subdued murmur of the voices of those who sat at tables — clearly heard voices that, if he strove to make the effort, he could identify. The sun was riding in the center of the sky, but still it would gather fiercer strength through the next three hours, making every strip of shade a blessing.

Even now, through the heat mist, the mountains were withdrawn to a dim blueness.

All was quiet, all was dreaming peace. And out of that quiet a great feeling of lonely weakness passed over the sheriff. For there was no one in the whole world to whom he could confide his sorrows.

CHAPTER
SIX

The *clicking* hoofs of a horse brought a rider into view around the next turn of the old street, which had been laid out five generations before by the feet of cattle straying back from the river to the upland pastures. Then he saw Harry Marvin hurrying toward him on the little pinto. He flung himself from the back of the horse and ran to his uncle.

"Uncle Chick," he gasped out, "Ma wants you to come out right quick if you can. Dad . . ."

"What about him?"

"He tried . . . ," and the boy choked again.

"Well?"

"Uncle Chick," breathed Harry Marvin, "I found him out in the barn leaning by the manger, puttin' his gun to his head."

"Lord," whispered the sheriff.

He heard nothing more for a moment as the boy continued, for the horror of that news had turned all his senses numb, as though the gun had been placed to his own head.

Then he heard the boy continuing: "I managed to get it away from him. I tried to talk to him. He didn't seem to know what I was sayin'. Then he let me lead him back to the house like a boy. He had a sort of funny look . . . like he didn't know where he was. I left him settin' peaceful in the kitchen, starin' at mother and sayin' nothin'. Uncle Chick, come out quick . . . we need you terrible bad. Terrible bad!"

The sheriff rubbed his stiff fingers over his face and felt his blood begin to circulate again. "Didn't he say nothin'?" he said at last.

"Only one thing, a good many times over . . . he says . . . 'They're sort of closin' in on me. They ain't a way out!' "

"There's got to be a way out!" groaned the sheriff. "You go back, son, and don't you ever leave him. I ain't comin' until I come with help. Now run along."

Harry nodded, leaped onto the back of the pinto, and scurried down the street at full speed. He left the sheriff suddenly and more hideously alone than before. For there was nothing that could give him shelter from the leveled gun of his thoughts. Poor Jack had attempted suicide — Jack of all men, the mildest and the best! Even he had attempted to leave the sinking ship like a scared rat, while his wife and his child could fight it out with beggary.

Tears swam into the eyes of the sheriff. He winked them out again. He walked up and down, drawing down great breaths until he could breathe easily once more. It was lunch time, yet he could not have endured the sight of food, and this was a strange condition indeed for him.

Then, very suddenly, before a full hour could have elapsed, it seemed, the stranger came back, walking jauntily, whistling a little monotonous tune as he came. "Very well," he said to the sheriff. "I see that you have found our second letter more convincing. Am I wrong?"

And the sheriff said simply: "I got to have five hundred more."

"Certainly," said the stranger, smiling, and held forth his hand. Into the palm of the sheriff dropped a single crumpled piece of paper — that was $500 more. The price was paid.

"As for the time when Corrigan is to go free . . . ," began the stranger.

"Tonight."

"There is no hurry, of course. We don't want to draw suspicion on you, but at the same time we wish to assure you that this very kind act of co-operation . . ."

The sheriff stared at him in a mute admiration. He had always wondered how any man could have the brazen effrontery to offer a bribe to another, and under what language the offer could be transacted. But the words flowed freely from the tongue of this adept. He showed neither scorn nor surprise, but a sort of honest pleasure, like that of any businessman when a transaction has been concluded to his satisfaction.

"I ain't a talkin' man," said the sheriff huskily. "I'll turn him loose tonight. And . . . I hope to heaven that we don't have to see each other ever again. But," he added savagely, "if I ever come onto Corrigan ag'in, I'm gonna make sure of him."

The stranger nodded in his bright, cheerful way. "Of course," he said. "You're an honest man, Marvin. I understand that your brother is in trouble. Well, I'll say good bye." And he was off down the street again.

The sheriff watched him with a chilly sense of awe. This was the personification of the devil, entering his life and leaving it again, and automatically some of the banker's letter flowed through his memory.

The very thing for which he had been thanked and paid he was now about to undo, and the bitterest shame stung poor Chick Marvin. In the meantime, to drive some of those pangs out of his mind, he could take the money to Jack Marvin. That, certainly, should be a panacea for his present sickness of mind. He went out to the mustang that stood, as usual, head down, in the shed beside the little office building. The saddle was already on. There needed only a tug at the girths, then he was on the back of the little horse.

Out onto the street he trotted when — "Hello, Chick!" — came from the sidewalk, and he saw the last person in the world who he wished to see at that moment. It was Sally Deacon with her arm akimbo and her head tilted to one side, smiling at him. It was she and she alone who made him realize that, in spite of the drabness of his existence, he was not an old man. For, after all, he was only ten years older than she, and to be a mere ten years older than the very spirit of youth is really not so very ancient.

Ten years had been a great deal, indeed, when he was fifteen and she was five. And, when he had first taken the oath of office, she had been a barefooted youngster of twelve who shook her red pigtail of hair and shouted at him through her cupped hands. It was she who, out of regard for his solemn air that seldom left him, christened him The Undertaker, a name through which he had since become famous. The Undertaker, indeed, to many a brilliant young gunfighter's hopes, or rising safe-cracker. The name was bestowed on him now, half with awe and half in compliment. But, some three years since, he had looked at Sally, on a day, and found that she was a woman. She was seventeen, and the angles of lean-bodied girlhood were beginning to soften into a lithe beauty. Not that she was really beautiful — she had only a pretty face — but she was beautifully young, beautifully contented with the world. Men could talk with her as they talked with one another, with just one stinging little shade of difference that made a prickling of pleasure run through their blood.

On that day, three years ago, she had sung out to him: "I'm going to take The Undertaker to a dance. Will you come along with me, Mister Sheriff?"

He had stared at her, agape, then grinned feebly and passed on.

Afterward, she came to his office and sat on the window sill. "I've got a bet that I can get you to a dance," she said with a boyish frankness. "You ought to let me win, stingy."

"I ain't a dancin' man," he said feebly.

"I'll teach you in five minutes."

"I'm too old," said the sheriff mildly.

"You?" she said, and then she bent back her head and laughed joyously. "Jiminy, Mister Marvin, you ain't so mighty old. You ain't no older than you feel, and I'll make you feel young."

"Run along," said the sheriff, and turned scarlet.

"You're blushin' something awful," she said, craning her neck to observe him more carefully.

At that, he actually began to quake. He would have done anything to get her eyes off his face. "If you'll go along like a good girl," he said, "I'll go to that . . . that dance with you."

And he had gone, to the utter amazement of the town. People chuckled for a week, but their laughter was of a friendly sort.

But, after that, it was tacitly agreed that the sheriff was the property of Sally Deacon. If anyone wanted a favor from him, Sally Deacon was approached. The sheriff felt that his interest was purely paternal.

"I ain't got no kids of my own," he used to say.

And people were too kind-hearted to smile in his face. It went on in this manner from year to year. She was twenty, now, and at twenty a woman is old enough to be considered seriously by the oldest man in the world. The sheriff had to admit it, and he was troubled by the necessity for that admission. And he thought, now, as he stared at her, so blithe, so young, so regardless of the oven-hot sun, and so unwithered by it, that she was tied with strings of more than flesh to his very heart.

"You ain't seein' folks very clear these days," said Sally to him, as he looked down at her, mechanically touching the brim of his hat.

"I was thinkin' something, Sally," he said.

"You was thinkin' how famous you've growed, all of a sudden," she said. "I guess they'll make you a United States marshal, or something like that, maybe."

"Heaven knows," he said sadly, "that I wasn't thinkin' no good of myself."

It seemed to him that her face lighted. She went out to him and idly caught hold of one of the saddle straps. "Tell me, Chick, did you ever do a *really* wrong thing in your life?"

"A thousand," he said.

"I don't mean stealin' apples. Something really bad?"

A wave of horror rushed across his heart — across his face. "Ah, Sally," he groaned, "yes, yes. Stand back and lemme go on."

She stood back, too dazed to oppose him, and, chief miracle of all, it seemed to the sheriff that there was something really akin to pleasure in her face. But this, of course, could never be true.

CHAPTER
SEVEN

His spirits raised a little when the little house on the hillside looked back at him like an ugly but familiar face. He threw himself out of the saddle and hurried in. Harry met him at the door of the kitchen with trouble in his eyes.

"He's got worse," said Harry in a whisper. "Ma wanted him to go to bed . . . and he went."

The sheriff reached for the door and leaned against it. "To bed? At this time of day?"

"It's terrible hard to believe, but that's just what he done."

The sheriff crossed the room in a stride and opened the door, but there he paused, for he heard a strange sound from the upper part of the house, a broken, suppressed sound of weeping.

"It's Ma," said the boy, his face twisted into an expression of acutest pain. "She's plumb broke up."

The sheriff turned vacantly upon the youngster. "Go call her down," he commanded.

He waited by the window, looking out on the sunburned fields, and listening vaguely to the far-off bellowing of the red bull. A fly was *buzzing* in the warm, heavy air of the kitchen, and the little sound, in the silence that followed the departure of Harry, grew to the importance of thunder.

Then Bess came down to him, red-eyed, with trembling lips. He could not wait or prolong the thing. He simply took out the money and pushed it into her hands.

"Go up," he said, "and count it out to him. Nine thousand dollars, Bess. Go up and count it out to him."

"Ah," she breathed, "what have you done, Chick?"

"Me?" he said, suddenly angry. "Nothing! What should I do? I've brung you nine thousand. You go take it to him, and don't let's have no more talk."

He had never spoken in such a tone in all his life before that moment, far less to a woman, far less to Bess of all people. She blinked like one who had been struck, and then she backed out of the room and he heard her footfall going slowly up the stairs.

And he waited, waited until he heard a sudden cry that rang with joy. There weren't questions; there was no wonder in the mind of Jack. He did not pause to ask where that money had come from. Like all men whose hearts have been broken, he had waited for a miracle, and, behold, the miracle had come!

Now his footfall sounded on the steps. He would come to wring the hands of Chick and call him his savior and bless heaven that any man on earth could have such a brother, but the sheriff did not pause to receive those thanks. He rose and bolted for the door. Down the steps outside he went at a leap, found the mustang, and was in the saddle scurrying away before the door was cast open by Jack.

"Hey, Chick!" he called.

But the sheriff would not turn his head. He rode like one possessed until he reached the top of the hill on the road toward town. There he glanced back to see his brother had run a little distance after him and was still waving and shouting. He saw that, and it gave him no joy. His heart was as heavy as lead. He rode slowly down the farther side of the hill toward the town. This, which he had thought would be the touch of grace to ease him of pain, had cost him more anguish than all the rest. And he felt, indeed, that he could not endure to face his brother again. The price of that brotherhood had been too great. Neither could he face Bess. She had looked too deeply into his soul in the instant during which she had faced him.

When he reached the town, he went back to the office. Behind the business room there was a little cabinet where a cot stood and on which he often slept when he had business that kept him too late in town. Into that room he went now. It was past the mid-afternoon. With appalling speed the evening was growing upon them, and, when the evening had turned black, he must liberate the outlaw, according to his promise.

A hand tapped at the windowpane, and, turning sharply, he saw the face of Sally Deacon outside. He raised the pane. "You'd ought to keep your windows open, a day like this," she told him. "Why, it's like an oven in there!" She stretched in a hand and waved it in the air.

"Have you come for something?" asked the sheriff heavily.

"Sure," she said. "I've come for a talk. What you said a while back was bait for me. I've took the hook. And here I am. Chick, what d'you mean by callin' yourself a bad man?"

He looked back at her hopelessly. It was dawning on him, in these bitter moments, that he loved her, and she felt not unkindly toward him. This truth was coming into his mind at the very moment when he realized that he was further beneath her than the dust in which she stood.

"Who's the worst man you know?" he asked her.

"Lew Corrigan . . . the mean rat!"

"Sally, I'm worse'n him. A pile worse than Lew Corrigan ever could've been."

"Hush!" cried the girl, and she laid a finger on his lips. "Somebody outside of me might hear you say it. And fools will believe anything they hear. Chick. Chick, you ain't jokin' . . . you're serious. What's happened?"

"Would I be tellin' it?"

"For the sake of easin' your heart, Chick. And you'd trust me as much as you'd trust yourself."

"Ah, yes," he said. "Ah, Sally, I'd be trustin' you a thousand times more. But this time I can't tell you. I'd never be able to look you in the face ag'in."

"Wait!" she cried. "It ain't right to talk that way about yourself, clear old kind Chick. It ain't right. Why, Chick, it makes me sad enough to cry to hear you talk like that."

Now the time was come. He knew, with a sudden and a perfect knowledge, that he had merely to go to her and take her in his arms, and in another instant she would have sworn to be his wife, to love him always, and no other man. All of this was in the grip of his fingers. A word would do the thing. And yet he could not stir, he could not touch her with voice or hand, he being what that day had made him.

He said slowly: "Sally, I guess I'd better talk about the weather, or something else that don't matter."

Her answer was most astonishing. For she said gravely: "Chick, you're a terrible baby. All men are!" After which, she left him.

When the evening came, he remembered that he had not eaten for a long time. He went out to supper, and the first person he encountered was the banker, who stopped him — hurried across the street to stop him.

"I've seen Jack," he said. "He brought in the money and said that you'd given it to him. Well, Sheriff, that was a fine thing to do . . . such generosity is very admirable . . . at times. Only I wonder if this was one of the right times. We all have certain duties to ourselves, you know. That money must have represented the savings of your life. It was enough for you to have married on. You could have set yourself up in the cow business, you know, with that much. Instead, you dump it into the hands of Jack. Well, my boy, is Jack worthy of such a trust? The best fellow in the world, of course, but as a businessman . . . a failure. Is it right to keep bolstering him up? We have to find our right levels. The level of Jack is not that of a rancher. Believe me,

53

because I've followed him and I know. No doubt you feel that I have been rather hard on Jack. Not at all. But he simply is not a good venture for me as a businessman. How much less so for you. And if he is ruined a second time, you will be ruined, also. Sheriff, you need to take advice in your business affairs. However, I wouldn't have you different . . . not while you're the sheriff of this county."

He laid an affectionate hand on the shoulder of the sheriff, but Chick Marvin could not look up into his eyes — all he could see was the glistening watch fob that dangled from the vest pocket of the man of money. Then he went on to the hotel to get his supper.

It seemed to have been arranged, all of it, to torture him. He was a little late, and the dining room was full. Every head turned to him. Every pair of eyes bore straight upon him full of speaking admiration. They sang out to him one by one:

"Here comes old Never Say Die!"

"Well, old bulldog!"

"They're playin' tag with jail when they play with you, Chick."

"Old Slow Lightnin'!" cried another.

They were immensely proud of him. He, in a manner of speaking, had put their county on the map. Sheriff Chick Marvin was the most famous man they had ever produced. And because he was so humble, they were able both to admire and love him. Whereas, in our heart of hearts, we are apt to hate most prominent people because they know their prominence, they almost pitied him, forsooth, because he was so mild, so gentle in his greatness. And they referred to him, as often as not, affectionately as "Poor old Chick Marvin." Now he came back from the latest scene of his glory not like a conqueror, but like a laborer from the field. He shrank from their words. He took an obscure seat, and he ate, or tried to eat, what was put before him. Then he sneaked out from the room again.

"Only one thing that scares him. He's afraid of bein' praised."

Such was their sentiment. At that moment, in the height of their love and their devotion, they would have followed him to the door of the devil and back again; they would have trusted their lives and their honors in his efficient hands.

But out of all that atmosphere of affection and of admiration, the sheriff went gloomily back toward the jail, loathing himself like a hideous thing. He went to the jail and met there honest Charlie Guernsey.

"Go on home and have a rest, Charlie," he said. "There ain't no use in you stayin' on here at the jail. I'll tend to things here. I got some business in the office."

So Charlie Guernsey left and the sheriff was alone in his proper domain.

CHAPTER
EIGHT

He went, first, straight into his own little private room. It should have been his office, and, if he had never used it as such, it was because he had always hated to associate himself too closely with the jail. It was a living horror with which he had no sympathy. To hunt down a courageous and cunning criminal, to match one's wits and one's skill with the wits and the fighting craft of a fugitive, had always seemed to him eminently fair, but to lock a man behind steel bars was a hideous atrocity. Rather put out the light in his eyes — far rather. Death at the swift touch of a bullet was preferable.

So he had kept his own office apart from the jail. Now he went into the little room at the jail and found everything thinly covered with that fine-sifted sand of the desert, that kind of dust that penetrates through the smallest crevices and maddens housewives. He pushed back the top of the roller-topped desk, lighted the lamp, blew away the dust, and sat down with his thoughts for a time, for at that moment he was too weak of heart to go on with his task.

There was nothing in the desk except a few mementos of his unlucky predecessor who he had succeeded in this office. He stared down at the time-faded ink stains on the broad blotter. He pulled out a drawer and found in it a rusted gun that he himself had once put there and forgotten. And now he had come to the end of his career of glory. The whole long process of eight years was to be undone by a single act of shame. It sickened, it weakened him, and then he heard a light noise at the closed window. He strode to it and tossed it open. Little Joe Peters was revealed clinging to the window sill, his eyes popping out from his head with fear because he had been caught spying. But the distance from the sill to the ground was too great for him to risk a drop. The sheriff caught him by the nape of the neck, leaned far out, and dropped him from an extended arm. Joe Peters fell to earth with a howl, leaped to his feet, and fled, yelling.

The sheriff looked after him without mirth. For it seemed to him that even a child, looking in upon him at this unclean hour of his life, might have looked into his mind and read what was there of shame. Next he went over to the desk once more, and from another drawer he took out an old assortment of files, once the pride of Pillsbury. Equipped with these and a lantern, he went back to the cells. The light of the lamp shone through half a dozen of the empty little cages and gleamed in parallel lines from the strong steel bars, until it fell upon the broad, ugly face of the outlaw. He stood up and stretched his arms. When he lowered them, he was grinning at the sheriff.

"Well, old son," he said, "I thought that it was about time. Hurry up and unlock the door. I'm achin' to get loose from this hole. It's about time that the boys was rememberin' me. What was my price, anyway?"

The sheriff said not a word. But he remained for a moment turning a wild thought in his brain — to give this scoundrel a gun, and then, on terms of equal vantage, allow him to fight for his life. If the crooks who were behind him strove to expose the deal that they had closed with him, he, as the sheriff and with the weight of his taintless life to help, could sweep away all they said by a simple denial.

He hesitated, and then he knew that he could not do it. No, he knew more than this, that if he took a gun in his hand, that hand would be so unsteady that he would not be able to use it.

"Take a file," he said. "Here's some oil. Don't make no noise. We got to cut through a couple of these here bars."

"And cover you up, eh?" chuckled the outlaw. "Well, I don't mind. You ain't a half bad old-timer. There was some that would've sunk a chunk of lead into me and left me lyin' and rottin' out at old man Dervitt's place. But you didn't. Sure, I'll work for you."

It was not long. Under false pretenses, indeed, that steel had been sold as tool-proof. Those files of the finest steel, hard as ridges of diamond, cut swiftly into the heart of the bars, with the frequent dabs of oil deadening all noise. Two bars were cut through, and the prisoner sidled forth.

"Only one thing left, friend," he said to the sheriff. "I don't want no break away without a little money to help me along. I don't feel none too much like roughin' it through the desert without no coin. Did the boys say where they'd meet me?"

"Nope."

"Do they know when?"

"They know it's tonight."

"Then they'll be waitin'. Look here, old kid, you look sort of sick. Don't be takin' this game too much to heart. It ain't nothin'. A damn' sight better men than you have shoved a bit of the long green into their wallets on the sly."

"Come into the office," said the sheriff huskily. "I'll stake you to a few dollars. My wallet's in there." He turned his back and led the way to the office, where the window shade, which he had drawn after the visitation of Joe Peters, was flapping back and forth a little in the faint night air. When he turned, he found that the eyes of the outlaw were green and bright as the eyes of a beast of prey.

"You turned your back on me," Lew Corrigan said, "sort of hopin' that I'd try to jump you?" His nostrils flared; his face was working with his murdering passion.

The sheriff said not a word. Ah, how bitterly he had hungered for that very thing.

"I knew," said Corrigan. "But it ain't me that'll jump you, old kid. I've seen you work. I'll fight a thousand gents and think nothin' of it. But you're the extra one that proves the rule. I've seen you work, and I'd rather fight poison, damn your slick old skin. Anybody that can see in the dark the way that you can is too good for me with a gun, and I admit it pretty free and easy. But some other time I'll get you . . ."

"Out from behind a bush, eh?" inquired the sheriff.

"I ain't sayin' where. You won't know nothin' about it. You'll be in purgatory so fast your head'll swim. Now, where's the coin?"

The sheriff went to his coat and took out his wallet. "Will twenty do?"

"That's enough. The boys will meet me, anyway. If they don't . . . they'll wish to heaven that they had, before I'm through with 'em." He took the bill, folded it without looking, and slipped it into his trousers pocket.

Even at such a time as this, the sheriff wondered vaguely how anyone could treat so much money with such indifference.

"So long," said the outlaw. "I'll take the back door, I guess?"

"No, the window next to it is unlocked. I saw to that."

"Is it far to the ground?"

"An easy drop for you."

"Good bye, old faithful."

The sheriff raised his hand in a mute gesture of farewell, and the criminal backed through the door. The sheriff, as that door swung to, could hear the swift whirl of the feet of the other as he turned and bolted for the back of the jail. It raised a wild impulse in the sheriff's heart to take up the chase at once. But he checked himself. The work was nearly done, now; he had taken money and bound his honor to this dishonorable act. And, perspiring with agony, digging his finger tips into the palms of his hands, he waited until he heard the sound of the raising of the window. Then, through the quiet air of the night he heard, most distinctly, the muffled *thud* as the feet of the fugitive struck the ground beneath the window.

It was ended. But scarcely ended before something else began. There was a catching of breath at the window of his own room, or at least a sound strangely like a catching of breath. He leaped to the window and brushed the shade aside, and there he found himself looking into the frightened face of Joe Peters once more. Again, he took the boy by the nape of the neck, save that this time he drew him safely into the office itself. But now, indeed, he saw his ruin, for in the terrified face of the boy he saw that the youngster had overheard everything that had passed between sheriff and prisoner.

CHAPTER
NINE

The first thought of the sheriff was the first thought that comes to every cornered rat. But, an instant later, he realized that he had before him a child. His fury left him, but not before Joseph Peters had turned green in an agony of terror, and now, in swift waves of prophecy, the sheriff saw what would happen. The boy would go straight to his father; to his father he would tell all that he had overheard, and tell it with that peculiar vividness that boys sometimes are capable of. And when his father disbelieved the entire wild tale, it would be fortified by the ascertained facts that the famous prisoner was indeed missing, and that, on this very day, the sheriff had presented $9,000 to his brother. Suppose that he were asked to account for that sum of money? How could it be done?

He saw himself, clearly, driven back against a wall, and with a logical mind, the mind of a natural fighter, he accepted the issue. He looked down upon Joe Peters without the slightest malice, and even with a strange feeling for the power of society, which is armed with ten million eyes and ears, all working for the common cause. A child may serve where a king would fail.

He put a hand on the shoulder of the boy. "Joe," he said, "you come back to the window, after all?"

"I only just that minute climbed up . . . I . . . I . . . I was afeard that maybe the shade might blow out and get loose and . . ."

The sheriff wiped a trace of moisture from his upper lip. This was a sufficient proof. In a deadly terror, the boy was attempting to defend himself from danger that he felt would fall upon his head if it were known that he had overheard.

"Well," said the sheriff, "you know who was in the room with me here?"

"Was there somebody in here with you?" asked Joe in a piping voice.

But it was a shade overdone. A very young boy is a very natural actor. But in a pinch, his nerve will sometimes fail him, and all of his magnificent gifts as a liar will be thrown away. They were thrown away now. The face of Joe, so pale that the freckles stood out like spots of rust on a yellow leather background, betrayed too much of his perturbed soul. The sheriff shook his head, but he smiled.

"You don't know who was in here, I guess?" he said.

"No," said the boy. "Sure I don't."

"You lie," the sheriff said coldly.

"Good heavens," whispered Joe, and shrank far back in his chair.

That was enough. He had betrayed himself, and he knew it in an instant.

"I was only guessing," confessed Chick Marvin, "but I guess I hit pretty close to the line. You heard me and Corrigan talkin'?"

"I swear nobody ain't gonna never hear a word of it from me!" cried Joe in a fever of terror and anguish.

"You wouldn't tell a soul?"

"Not a soul."

"Not until you were safely away from me? Why, Joe, you ain't got no call to be so mighty scared of me. I ain't gonna eat you, son."

"Sheriff . . ."

"Hush up, son. You're scared now. I tell you, I ain't gonna do you no harm. D'you think that to keep from havin' the rotten truth knowed about me, I'd put you so's you couldn't never talk no more to nobody?"

The boy shuddered.

"That ain't me, son. Go home to your daddy and tell him. He'll be mighty excited by what he hears. You go home and tell your daddy that the sheriff has took bribe money and has turned Lew Corrigan loose. That's all that you got to say. He'll tend to the rest." He took the boy to the door of the jail and opened it wide.

"Are you gonna let me go?" whispered Joe.

"I sure am. I ain't gonna chase you with no bullet, neither. Look here . . . I left both my guns back in the office."

"Sheriff Marvin . . ."

"Well, kid?"

"What *you* gonna do?"

"What you think?"

"You ain't gonna *kill* yourself?"

"You been readin' books, kid. Real folks don't kill themselves just because they've turned into low-down skunks. It takes sort of a real man to kill himself . . . not a dog-gone bribe-takin' yaller dog. Now you run along. Skat!"

Joe vanished like lightning down the steps. Afterward, the sheriff went slowly about the thing that remained for him to do. He closed the door of the jail, carefully locked it — as though there were anything in it, now, that needed guarding! Then he went back toward his office, still methodically, not in haste. He almost hoped that they would find him, that they would surround him with guns. He would not lift a hand. He would not have to. Multiplied by his reputation, they would fall back from him like dogs before a lion, and they would open fire without even asking him to put up his hands. And that would be the end. He would not fight back. Far, far better to die and have this spoiled life ended.

He went to the shed to get the mustang, but, as he fitted his foot into the stirrup, he saw a pale form in the corner of the shed. It was Sally Deacon. And she would know that he had seen her. Yet he dared not speak. He swung into the saddle. Neither did she speak to him. Perhaps, with a woman's special sense, she had divined that there was disgrace come upon him. So he left her and went off through the thick of the night.

He rode steadily until close to midnight, and there was not a thought in his mind during all of that time, but only a dull numbness occupied all his faculties.

Now and then he found that words were forming in his throat and passing soundlessly through his brain.

This here is the finish. This here is the end.

He rode until the mustang began to stumble. Then he unsaddled the horse in a hollow, hobbled it, and turned in with his blanket. He did not sleep. He lay with his arms thrown wide, his head pressing against a bunch of grass, hardly yet cold with the chill of the night. So he watched the stars. Some of them had names; most were nameless; all were unknown to him. And most were worlds ten thousand times greater than this earth of ours. Someone had told him that. Or had he read it? He could not tell, but he knew that he had been like a star, in his honesty. He had given light to others. He had helped to make the world beautiful and happy as the stars helped to make the night. Now he was blotted out. Evil is not remembered. He would be forgotten. He could see the end very clearly.

He was unfitted for any life except that stern one of manhunting. He could not attempt to flee to some strange land and there live a new life. He did not want a new life. For the land itself was a vital part of him. This smell of alkali, for instance, that the night wind whirled into the air — it might be choking to some, but it was dear to the sheriff, because he knew it and loved it. The somber note of the screech owl was weird and lovely music that he understood. No, there was no existence for him in any other country, no matter how fresh, how rich with grass, how fair with towns and cities. For in other lands there would be no hawks or buzzards in the sky, no crisp, brown hills rolling into a sunpaled heaven, no vast horizons where the heart and the brain were lost in attempting to keep pace with the giant strides of the eye. There would be none of these things in other countries. There would be no Sally Deacon, either. And it seemed to the sheriff, as he lay there, that a melancholy sweetness and softness was in the air that touched his face. His love for her was like love for one who is dead. From her mind, at least, he was gone forever.

In a few weeks they would find him; they would either kill him on the spot or they would capture him and take him back to prison. No, it would be better to die, and he could invite death by firing a single shot over their heads.

A sweet death it would be — a blow, a pang, and the bullet would have done its work. Afterward they would come to look at him and they would note his ugly face and his dull eyes in death and wonder that he could ever have been terrible to the doers of evil.

When he thought of his own ugliness, he smiled again — then sat up with a start, for he found that the stars had paled. The dawn was already beginning. Indeed, the hours had passed with a strange swiftness over his head. He was a little stiff as he rose. But he found that the mustang had not lain down at all. It had dozed for a few moments with legs braced, head hanging. Now it was busy foraging once more. When he swung into the saddle, it had regained heart enough to attempt to pitch him over its head. He chuckled as he swayed to that fence rowing. He knew all of the tricks and the schemes of the wicked old gelding as well as he knew an old song. He could always anticipate what was coming next. In three minutes the horse had bucked the kinks out of his legs and was rocking away across country again.

In the meantime, the east had brightened. The full morning was coming. The misty light of the border time brightened. League upon league the landscape rushed upon his eye. The world was let in upon him. Danger was sweeping closer and closer.

It was a little appalling. It was stimulating, also. And he wondered, as he rode, how long it would be that, with all of his wits, with all of his familiarity with the country, he would be able to hold the hands of the law at bay. He would have no friends to help. All of his friends were honest men. And, being honest men, they were sure to be turned solidly against him when they knew of the cowardly and low thing that he had done. Perhaps a week, perhaps a fortnight would bring him to his last day.

Then, as he rode, he fixed fast upon a single determination. He would do his desperate best to reach Lew Corrigan before the law reached him; he would pay off Lew Corrigan and Corrigan's bribing friends before the law gathered him in.

CHAPTER
TEN

There was a grim pleasure in having a goal other than the mere protection of himself. To get Corrigan, he should land Corrigan's trail. But that was obviously impossible. He was far from town, and it was from the town that he should logically attempt to pick up the steps of the outlaw. There was another way, a long chance and perhaps a foolish one, but he was determined upon it.

He headed straight across the country for the house of Sam Dervitt. The red sun was not two yards from the eastern hilltop, looking like a terrific blossom on the top of a lonely Spanish dagger stalk, when he dismounted and strode up to the open kitchen door of the house. He entered with his gun in his hand and looked down into the startled, savage faces of Dervitt, his boy, and Mrs. Sam.

"You ain't had enough out of us already?" cried the woman. "You got to come back and plague us ag'in! Livin' on free board off of us all them weeks . . . that wasn't enough for you, sheriff Marvin, but you got to come back and try to arrest us . . . maybe both of us! Oh, what'll my poor boy come to? Oh . . ."

"You, there," said the sheriff to Sam Dervitt, who was chewing his lip, thoroughly savage and thoroughly cowed, "stop her howlin'."

It was a new tone in the voice of the sheriff. He had been heard to speak in great emergencies before, but his voice had never been other than gentle. Now there was a ring of iron brutality in it that jerked up the head of Sam Dervitt and sent a shudder through Mrs. Dervitt.

"Hush up, fool," breathed Sam, keeping his fascinated eyes upon the man of the law.

Mrs. Dervitt had already banished her tears.

"What's up, Sheriff?" asked Dervitt, trying to be civil, but unable to keep a snarling whine out of his voice.

"I'll have some breakfast," said the sheriff, and, taking a chair from the corner, and his gun in the other hand, he dragged it up to the table.

"Sure, sure, Mister Marvin," Mrs. Dervitt said. "Sure you're gonna have some breakfast with us. I wouldn't be turnin' me worst enemy away hungry . . ."

It was easy to locate her point of view. When a man has been fed a meal, he cannot very well, in any conscience, do a harm to the lord or the lady of the mansion.

"Go rustle me in some wood, Buddy!" she snapped at her son. "Sam, reach me the side of bacon yonder and hurry up about it."

"Set quiet and easy where you be," the sheriff said in the same brutal tone. "You, young feller, keep away from that there door. They's plenty of wood in that box to keep up the fire for a day or two. And when that wood peters out, we'll eat food raw for a while, I reckon. There's plenty of food, too, by the looks of that sack of cornmeal and that side of bacon. And there's plenty of water in that there tub. Set down, Sam Dervitt, and don't be aimin' to slide around behind my chair, partner. It ain't neither pleasant nor restful to have you behind me."

They sank back in their chairs and gaped at him.

"I dunno that I figger out what's in your head," Sam Dervitt said slowly, "but it ain't hard to see that you got the drop on me, Sheriff. I guess you don't have to explain yourself, unless you want to."

"I ain't feelin' secretive," said the sheriff. "Lew Corrigan is loose ag'in."

"Lew has busted away!" they cried in a chorus of three jarring notes, all in differing pitches.

"He's loose," the sheriff affirmed calmly.

"And you've come here to wait for him?" Mrs. Dervitt said. "Lemme tell you, Sheriff, that you're wastin' your time. He's had bad luck in this here house, and he don't never go back where he's had any trouble. That's his way. He steers clear of trouble and the place where he's ever had trouble. It'll be a funny day when any of us ever lay eyes on the face of Lew Corrigan ag'in." And she sighed and shook her head.

"That'll be some money out of the pocket of Sam, I guess," said the sheriff. "Well, Sam, now that Lew is loose, they'll remember that he laid up with you for a while and that you was doin' your best to take care of him when I happened along and got him, by luck, but not through no fault of yours. They'll remember that and they'll remember that it's your time to come in for a little reward. They can't keep friends through the mountains if they don't act handsome to them that stand by them when they're in trouble. I guess that's pretty good logic?"

"I'll never see no penny of theirs!" growled out Sam Dervitt. "Not even if I'd take it, which I wouldn't. Lemme tell you how he happened to be here before. He was . . ."

"I ain't hankerin' to hear none of your lies," the sheriff stated coldly. "I know why he was here. Because you're one of them rats that ain't got the courage to step out and raise the devil yourself, but you make a wind brake for them that *have* got the nerve. You get twenty dollars or so every time you put up one of the longriders. And when you're in a bad pinch, you can always get a few dollars out of 'em to tide you through. That's the way of it. I don't have to read it in no book to understand that. And this time they'll bring you a present, too. Well, Dervitt, what I want ain't you. What I want is the gent that comes along here to bring you the coin. And until he comes, the three of us is gonna sit right quiet in this here room, and not one of us is gonna stir except for when I tell 'em to. Y'understand?"

"Sheriff Marvin," cried the woman, "are you plumb batty? What have honest folks like . . . ?"

"Shut up!" growled out her spouse. "You talk like a fool. And he knows it. We been friends to Lew, and he knows that, too. He ain't blind."

72

"If you're gonna start one kind of a lie, why don't you stick to it?" screamed the woman. "You . . ."

He raised his hand and turned an ugly glance toward her; instantly she was still. And Sam Dervitt said, still with a fixed and grim eye holding her: "All right, Sheriff. I guess I see the game. You wait here until the gent comes, like you say, to bring me money. And when he comes, you grab him and try to make him show you where Lew Corrigan is cached away."

"Guessin' games," the sheriff said, "is sort of amusin'. I dunno that I'm here to give answers, though. I ain't no riddle editor."

So, with his gun beside his plate, and his eyes covertly upon them all, he finished the breakfast that they placed before him. After that, he went to the corner of the room and threw down two blankets that were hanging from the wall. On these he settled himself.

"Now gimme another cup of coffee," he said. "I got a long time to keep awake, maybe."

"Sure," Mrs. Sam Dervitt said busily, as she caught up his cup and took it to the big, black coffee pot on the stove. "Sure you can have some more coffee. And that ain't all. Sheriff, you been pretty white to us in this here house. You might've jailed Sam . . . on suspicion of something maybe . . . not that he ever done nothin'. But you might've jailed him . . . but you didn't. Why, man, you don't have to look for no trouble here. You go to sleep free and easy whenever you like. They ain't no kind of harm gonna come to you here. We're your friends, Sheriff. That's what we are, and . . ."

So she rattled on as she passed the great tin cup to Chick Marvin, until her husband cut in upon her a second time.

"Will you chop off that fool talk?"

"What sort of fool talk?" she asked, fierce with anger. "Ain't you friends to the sheriff? Ain't it only yesterday that you says to me ... 'If they's one white sheriff in ...'"

"Aw, shut up!" said the husband. "I'm tired of these here lies, and so is the sheriff. He knows that we hate his guts. And he hates ours. I'd put a chunk of lead into him if I had the chance, and he knows that, too. And now he happens to have the drop on us ag'in, and that's all they is to it. You carryin' on like that. Think he's forgot how you tried to poison him like a rat?"

There was a shriek of protest from Mrs. Sam Dervitt — then silence.

"Sam," Chick Marvin said after a moment, "I sort of like the way you talk ... right out in the open. If you wasn't a crook, Sam, you'd be a darned honest man."

Sam grunted, and went on with the careful business of tamping some tobacco into his pipe and then lighting it.

After that there was very little conversation. They sat in that little room until it grew hot as an oven at midday. They still sat there, nervous, bored, weary, through the thicker heat of the afternoon, and until the first evening breeze came like a blessing from the west.

A dozen times Chick Marvin had to grind his teeth together to fight back waves of sleep. He smoked one cigarette after another. And then the evening came, and the night. The three lay down in corners of the room — the sheriff sitting where he was. But still he dared not close his eyes.

Midnight came, an old clock struck it with a tin-like jangling, dimly, from the front room. Then the quiet lay heavily over the place again, and the eyelids of the sheriff began to grow weak — weak! He felt them drooping, and he fought them wide open again, with a start. Again and again he rescued himself from sleep. The cigarettes had no more effect. The wind had died. The night was dull with drowsiness.

Suddenly a little thrill went through him, and he opened his eyes with a jerk. Between him and the dim square of the doorway, speckled with stars, was a looming bulk, and something glistened in its hand.

"Set down ag'in, Mister Dervitt," said the sheriff. "You'd best, I guess."

An oath came with an indrawn breath of viciousness from the admirable Sam Dervitt.

"You *was* asleep!" he snarled out.

"I was," said the sheriff. "If you hadn't been so careful and scary, you might've blowed me to the devil and back, by this time. But you won't get no second chance. You ..." He stopped short. For, from the distance, he heard the *clicking* hoofs of a galloping horse.

CHAPTER
ELEVEN

It was no horse running in the pasture. When a horse is loose, it runs with a long, loose, flaunting stride; when a man is on its back — unless it be, indeed, a thoroughbred — the stride is shortened and stiffened and becomes a pound. Neither does a horse galloping in a pasture run with a measured stride. It frolics here and there, rejoicing in the speed that God has given to it above all of his creatures upon the earth. But this animal that the sheriff listened to went with a steady, joyless, rhythmic pace, beating out the weariness of the miles at the impulse of another will than its own.

And it came nearer and nearer. Someone was approaching the house, and approaching it between midnight and dawn. The belated do not arrive at such hours on the great Western mountain desert.

The sheriff stood up and stretched his tired body and felt the blood creep tingling into nooks and corners long unvisited. He blessed that moment, for he felt that the time had come.

"Throw the key to the door to me," he commanded.

The key *jingled* on the boards at his feet. Mrs. Dervitt wakened with a groan.

"Stop your noise!" commanded her husband. And she was stilled.

"Stand yonder ag'in' the wall, Dervitt."

Dervitt obeyed.

"I don't want to hear nothin' from you," the sheriff said grimly. "I don't want to see nothin' of you. I'm gonna be outside watchin' this here house right smart. And when I see anything come out of it, I'm gonna begin shootin', and I ain't gonna waste no bullets. You hear me talk?"

"I hear you," grunted Sam Dervitt.

"You hear me, Missus Dervitt?"

"Would you fire on a woman?" moaned Mrs. Dervitt.

"Quicker'n a wink," lied the sheriff. "You hear me, kid?"

"I hear you," muttered the boy.

So Chick Marvin backed through the door, closed and locked it, and jumped down to the ground. He could see the rider at once, leaving the cattle trail and coming straight toward the house, the head of the horse bobbing up and down. By the swiftness of that approach, even at the end of what had probably been a long trail, Marvin could tell that the man was well mounted, and that in the mind of the horse there was the hope of a barn and fodder. He went hastily toward the rider. Then he paused and called.

The man drew rein at once. When his horse had paused, the wind from behind blew a billow of unseen, but throat-stinging dust about Marvin.

"Hello, Dervitt?" called the stranger.

It was not altogether an unfamiliar voice to the sheriff.

"Yep," he said. "That's me."

"Light a match and let me see your face."

Recollection became more vivid in the mind of the sheriff. He remembered that crisp-speaking, crisp-walking stranger who had tempted him with the temptation that was too great for his honesty.

"Ain't you comin' into the house?" asked the sheriff.

"What?" cried the other, suddenly startled. "Speak again, man!"

Something, it seemed, was not right in what he heard.

"What's wrong?" asked Marvin, coming nearer.

"Stand where you are. You're not Dervitt!" He swung his horse half around.

"Steady," said the sheriff, swinging up his Colt. "I got you lined up pretty neat ag'in' a flock of them white stars, stranger. I guess you and me is gonna have a little talk before the night is over."

"By the heavens," breathed the other. "It's not possible! It's not Marvin?"

"It's him," said the sheriff. "It's that yaller-hearted, calf-livered skunk . . . Marvin."

"Why, man," exclaimed the stranger, "is there anything wrong? You're not satisfied with the bargain I made with you?"

"Me? Sure, that was a fine bargain. But I told you that I'd start to get Corrigan, and now I almost got him. And when I land him, I'm gonna land him dead!"

"I don't understand."

"Get off your hoss."

"Marvin, are you intending to double-cross me after we have paid you . . . ?"

"Get off your hoss . . . *pronto!*"

The other dismounted in haste. "I'm not a fighting man with a gun," he said in explanation and with some dignity.

"Sure you ain't," replied the sheriff. "Crooked money that you've swiped from them that stole it . . . that's all that you fight with. Now git on ahead of me to the stable yonder. We're gonna need a span of fresh hosses, and old man Dervitt, he's got a couple of good ones . . . always kept handy for you and your kind, I reckon. Well, we'll be borrowin' them tonight."

He made the stranger, who had now turned silent, march before him into the barn. There he saddled a gray and a tall brown mare. The first, he made his companion mount. The second, he selected for himself.

When they were in the saddle, he looked back to the house of Sam Dervitt, but nothing stirred near it. His last threat had, apparently, been taken well to heart.

"Now," said the bribe giver, "I hope you'll explain what's in your mind, man."

"Tell me where they been huntin' for me?"

"For you? Who would be hunting for you?"

"You ain't follerin' the news, I s'pose," Marvin said dryly. "I mean the deputy sheriff and the rest of the boys from town. Where they been lookin' for me today?"

"A party went out to get on the trail of Lew Corrigan, if that's what you mean. They know that you're off on the same trail."

"They figger that him and me beat it together?"

"What do you mean?"

"What I say."

"Why, man, no one dreams that you set Lew free, if that's what bothers you."

The sheriff blinked. Yet he could not doubt the truth of what the man said. Truth has a metal ring to it like the finest steel struck on steel. It was bewildering. Young Joe, perhaps, had been advised by his father to spread the news no further. And Joe Peters, Sr., having rounded the news into the ears of some of his friends, had taken the trail after the delinquent sheriff. Joe himself, no doubt, would be glad to have that job, and had ridden forth to seize the traitor. There was a possible explanation in that.

"They found the steel bars filed through, of course," the other was saying. "What was left for them to suspect? Now, man, what on earth are you doing here, and what do you want with me?"

"All I want, friend," said Marvin, "is to be showed the way to your meal ticket. All I want is for you to lead me to Corrigan."

"Ah," chuckled the other. "There's so much prosperity behind Corrigan that you figure on changing your trade. Is that it? From being a hunter, you prefer to be one of the hunted?"

"I want to see Corrigan face to face. I got business with him," said Chick.

80

"Ah," murmured the other. "I begin to understand. You want to put yourself right by sending a bullet through Corrigan's head? Well, my friend, let me tell you that you'll not put eyes upon him again. As for me, I haven't the slightest idea where he may be."

"Ain't you?" the sheriff asked softly. "Well, old son, you're gonna have a chance to sit tight and think about it for a while. I've seen wheat grow. I've seen ideas grow, too, mighty sudden, when they's a gun near to encourage 'em to get ripe."

"In the name of heaven, man, do you mean to murder me because I am ignorant of where . . . ?"

"Easy!" said the sheriff. "You come here to see Sam Dervitt. Why?"

"Private business affairs . . . concerning cattle."

"Concernin' money," the sheriff said. "That's the only kind of cattle that you understand the herdin' of. You come here bringin' him money."

"If it's money you want," said the stranger, "I admit that I have a little with me, and I'd be glad to let you have . . ."

"Damn you and your money," groaned Chick Marvin out of the bitterness of his heart. "I'd rather take pizen quick than touch it or look at it. I've seen too much of it already. I say, what I want out of you is to be took where I'll find Corrigan."

"Perhaps. But, man, if I don't know . . ."

"You lie!"

"Marvin, you're mad!"

"Maybe I am. I feel sort of crazy, between you and me. Crazy enough to ride along with you until the

81

mornin' comes, and, if the sun gets up and you ain't brought me to Corrigan, I'm crazy enough to shoot you, partner, deader'n a stone."

"By the eternal heavens, I believe you mean it."

"I sure do."

"Marvin, we could never reach him by sunrise."

"Well," said Chick Marvin, "it wasn't hard to pry that out of you. You do know where that rat is?"

The other groaned. "I know," he admitted gloomily. "I've talked like a fool. Marvin, what do you want with him?"

"My throat is dry from too much talk," Chick said. "Ride along, stranger. I'll be here, three yards behind you, all the time, with my gun handy. I ain't gonna warn you more'n once for no funny moves. Keep straight and ride hard. You got a good hoss under you. Take me to Lew Corrigan as fast as that hoss'll carry you!"

CHAPTER
TWELVE

Red Mars swung low from the zenith and, dropping toward the west, began to lose the strength of his fire — the sun was rolling closer to the eastern horizon.

They had crossed the Río Piño; their legs were still wet from that rough fording, but Chick Marvin had not chosen to take the longer and the easier way around. He went straight for his mark, and he found it. He saved a full eight miles, in this fashion, eight miles of rough mountain work, but when they reached the farther side of the Río Piño, his guide turned to the west again. The sheriff stopped his horse at once.

"Are you takin' me in a circle?" he asked. "Or maybe we're playin' a game of merry-go-'round."

The other shook his head and yawned with a great weariness. "I only know," he said, "that I have taken the road just as it was described to me."

"I'll tell you what I know," declared the sheriff grimly. "We been runnin' around here, losin' miles and miles. We been wastin' so much time that the birds might be gone before we meet up with the place where they been. And if that happened" — and here he turned a gloomy face upon his companion — "if that happened, damn my hide if I wouldn't pity you, stranger."

"I believe," said the other slowly, "that you would actually shoot me down in cold blood."

"That," said the sheriff, "shows sense."

"I intend to do my best," said the other. "I only hope that they are not keeping a sharp look-out, for, if they are, we'll both be dead men as we come up, you because you're known, and I because they see me bringing you in."

"I'm mighty sorry for you," said the sheriff. He turned his glance with a new interest upon his companion. "I'd sort of like to know," he said, as the horses worked their way up a slope sown thickly with young lodgepole pines, "how you ever come to take up with this here sort of a life?"

"I don't look it, eh?" said the stranger with a touch of pride.

"No," said the sheriff, smiling to himself as he saw that he had touched the pride of his companion. "I'd take you for a businessman, and a damned successful one."

"I was," said the other, "until I became interested in a mine . . . a fool's mine, and I was fleeced. So I came West to make up what I'd lost, and," he added with satisfaction, "I've made it up."

"Suppose," said the sheriff, "that I were to arrest you, now, and take you in?"

"You'd have nothing against me, except that I had bribed you. And I don't think you'd be very free with that testimony."

The sheriff was silent. He looked at the smug and smiling face of his companion with a growing dislike, but there was nothing worth saying at such a time.

Meanwhile, they worked up the valley of the Río Piño until they came to a branching cañon that, in the spring, brought down a noisy flood of snow water to join the main stream, but that now showed a naked and dry bed of gravel and sand. Over this loose-surfaced natural road they passed still deeper into the mountans. It was the first glory of the morning, and the little man at the side of the sheriff waxed in self-satisfied good humor with every moment. He was a restless fellow, continually whistling to the squirrels in the branches above them, and making enough noise to have represented the advance of an army. And Chick Marvin was more and more deeply offended. To him the trail was a place for a discreet silence, always. He neither understood nor wanted to understand such unseemly racket. For only with the most sensitive senses could one be in tune with the things that lived in the mountain world. Such an uproar swallowed all. He said nothing, however, out of natural reticence and because we do not waste words, willingly, on those who we dislike.

Then the little man broke out suddenly: "They call you The Undertaker, Marvin, do they not?"

"Most like some do. I've heard that name."

"My friend, you're such a simple soul that I can't help telling you the truth. If you keep on this trail, you are riding to your own grave."

"I'm to die, am I?" said the sheriff without emotion. "Somehow I been figgerin' that this was my last trail. It's got a ghost-like feelin' about it. There's a sort of strain' look about the mountains. All right, partner. I'm to die."

"You don't understand me, Marvin. I understand that as a fighting man you are quite capable of handling even Lew Corrigan. But I am going to go so far as to tell you that Corrigan is not alone in the place to which I am bringing you."

"Hush," whispered the sheriff, and raised his hand to enforce silence, while he turned halfway around in the saddle.

"Well?" asked the little man impatiently.

"I thought I seen something behind us."

"Can you look behind you without turning around?" asked his companion sharply.

"There was a sort of a hint of something stirrin' . . . a sort of a wink . . . a red flash of somethin', like sunlight along the sides of a hoss . . ."

"Tush, Marvin, you were riding with your head straight forward."

"Maybe I'm wrong. Besides, if they're on my trail now, what difference does it make?"

"Who on your trail?"

"There ain't no use explaining. Well, partner, I'm mighty obliged for you tellin' me that Corrigan ain't alone. It'll be all the better. The more folks I meet up with at the end of this here trail, the better it'll please me."

"You think I am talking about ordinary people. No, no, Marvin. I've heard of some of your exploits. I understand that you real fighting men think nothing of smashing through a whole crowd of ordinary range riders. But the men I am talking about are extraordinary people. Every man of them is marked with a certain distinction. Resolute and grim as Lew Corrigan is, I give you my word that I felt he was almost the least of the lot."

"As a fightin' man he ain't the best in the world. Who might some of the others be?"

"If I knew their names, I'd tell them to you freely, simply for the sake of taking you off this insane trail. There is reason in everything, but there is no sense in this. Marvin, I've taken too much of a liking to you and your simple ways to let you go on in this fashion. On my honor I have."

"That's mighty kind," said the sheriff. "But nothin' you was to say would make me turn back. Howsomever, I'd sort of like to know what some of these here gents looks like."

"I'll tell you, willingly. The youngest fellow is a mere boy. I don't presume that he's more than twenty-one years old. A very handsome youngster, particularly at a distance, but when you come a little closer to him, there is something very peculiarly and very really ugly and formidable about him. His eyes . . ."

"Are wrinkled a bit at the corners," said the sheriff.

"Exactly."

"It's Tom Wilkie."

"I think they *did* speak to him as Tom. But tell me, isn't he actually a very formidable gunman?"

"There is only one or two that's worse. He done a murder when he was twelve. They sent him to the reform school. He come out ready for hell and fire when he was eighteen. The last three years he's been doin' postgraduate work in all kinds of deviltry. Ordinary things don't interest him none. There's got to be blood in it before he's happy. Y'understand?"

"Perfectly. It was his very look . . . a nightmare expression in the eyes of that young boy! There was a second man, in early middle age, a broad man with an ambling way of walking . . . his sleeves always rolled up and hairy arms . . ."

"Sam Tucker, I s'pose."

"I don't know. Does he fit that picture?"

"Mighty snug. I'm surprised at Sam being around these parts. I figgered that Sam was about fifteen hundred miles away . . . didn't know he'd aim ever to slide back here, so long as he had folks so dead set ag'in' him. "For what? He took a vacation from the longriders. He went out prospectin' with an old gent, found things was pretty dull, stabbed the old bird in the back, and went off to leave him to die. He ain't popular none, right around here, your friend Sam Tucker ain't. Not a mite," said the sheriff.

"Such a brute? Well, he was not such a devil to look at. Not half so bad as a left-handed man with a fleshy low forehead . . ."

"Lefty Walt Grinsby!" cried the sheriff, and struck his hands together in a sort of ecstasy of joy and surprise.

"Grinsby? Is that his name?"

"That's him. They ain't no doubt about it. They ain't no doubt at all. He's mostly around where Sam Tucker is. Him and Tucker is old friends. Tucker supplies the brains, and Grinsby does a double share of the hell-fire work. Who else, partner? Who else might be up there with the other boys?"

"You act," said the little man, "as if you'd be very glad to walk into the same room with them."

"Wouldn't I, though? Why, friend, I been hearin' about Tucker and Grinsby for a dozen years . . . since I was a kid. They've done more devilishness, they've lasted longer than anybody else except the daddy of 'em all . . . old Calamity Ben. Is there anybody else in with Lew Corrigan?"

"There's only one more. He's not at all like the rest. As a matter of fact, he seems rather a kindly, simple person, and the only thing about him that made me believe that he was probably a formidable person was the deference with which the others treated him."

"Deference . . . the devil!" exclaimed the sheriff. "Lefty Grinsby wouldn't take a back seat if the devil was to come prancin' in all smokin' with brimstone and wearin' his hoofs and his horns. Grinsby would still want to be in the first row."

The little man shook his head with much decision. "I tell you, Marvin, I am not mistaken . . . that oldish fellow . . ."

"Ah," murmured the sheriff. "Of course, for an old man they might talk down a mite, but . . ."

"He isn't more than forty-five, I suppose."

"No? Let's hear what this gent looks like. 'Most like they was gettin' ready to trim him."

"I tell you, man, every time he spoke, they stopped talking to listen."

"Well, what was the look of him?"

"A very thin, very tall man, with a most extraordinary long, thin face."

The sheriff drew his horse to an abrupt halt. "Say that over ag'in," he said hurriedly.

"I said he was long and thin, with a queer, long face with a great mass of a forehead to top it off . . ."

"A sad look?"

"I meant to say that. Of course, that's the most striking thing about him."

The sheriff moistened his white lips and stared at his companion. "He's got a low bass voice."

"That's it . . . a very low voice, and he uses it very softly. But what is there to get so excited about? He's really a very gentle fellow. I was quite attracted to him."

"Murder ain't gentle," said the sheriff with much emotion. "Partner, lemme tell you the truth of this here. That sad-faced gent wasn't nobody else but Calamity Ben himself!"

"You speak as if he were the very prophet of evil. I've never heard the name."

"You got something to learn, then. Nope, he ain't one of them newspaper badmen. Not him! He works secret, he works dark. But where we get down to the bedrock of real hellishness, there we're pretty likely to get down to Calamity Ben."

"Now, Sheriff, I've given you a description of the four. Besides them, there is Lew Corrigan. Certainly that is enough to persuade you to turn back."

But the sheriff seemed not to hear. "Calamity Ben himself," he murmured. "After all these years to get a crack at Calamity Ben himself."

"Do you hear me, Sheriff?"

"I hear you, I hear you, man!" exclaimed the sheriff. "Get me to that house and get me there quick!"

The other shook his head. "Don't you understand, man? I've taken you the most roundabout way that I could. By this time, easily, Sam Dervitt has had a chance to cut straight across the hills and get to them with a warning that you're probably on the way."

The sheriff drew a great breath.

"Are you convinced, Marvin?"

Chick Marvin lifted his weary, drawn face to the morning. "I got nothin' to wish for," he said, "except a good finish to a bad life. And this here finish is all that I need. What more could I ask for? If I can get one shot at Calamity Ben . . . then it's no matter what they manage to do to me."

The other stopped persuading with a frown of weariness. "I've done my best," he said.

"You have. Tell me where the trail goes from here and you're a free man, stranger."

"Do you mean that?"

"Yes."

"Cut straight up the hill to your left, then. You'll find the house straight below you. And heaven help you, Marvin."

CHAPTER
THIRTEEN

It was a hill beneath a hill, like a face beneath a hat. The enormous height of Thunder Mountain struck up into the heart of the sky, and under it sloped this hill, with an immense ravine running between them. No doubt hill and mountain had been joined at one time, but a twist of the earth's hot, working bowels had split open the crevice. The sides of it still remained raw and rough, only faintly smoothed over by the erosion of ages, and in the bottom of the chasm flowed a stream. The sheriff, working his way up to the head of the hill, rode close beside the lip of this monstrosity and where the way wound a little, from time to time, he caught dizzy glimpses of the heart of the pit, still dark with shadow, ever dark with shadow, until the erect sun of noon dropped a brief shower of golden warmth even to the bottom of the abyss. A stream flowed through the midst of the chasm; it was a roaring mass of white water, a dim streak far beneath him. But not a sound came up to him except, now and again, an echo flinging wildly from cliff to cliff and so up to the outer air with a voice-like murmur.

He told himself that there was little time remaining between him and eternity. Therefore, he filled his eyes and filled his heart with the view and so he came gravely to the top of the hill. All that he wished to see was before him like so many pebbles held in the palm of his hand. The slope beneath him dropped away for 100 yards covered with lodgepole pine, like the spears of eager soldiery, disordered by haste as they climbed. Below this small forest, the ground shelved out in a little plateau, below which the ground dropped away again. There was hardly more than five or six acres cupped in the side of the hill with a little house, a barn, a few sheds, and fenced pasture land. It was an ideal resort for people like Lew Corrigan and his ilk.

Even while he looked, six men hurried out from the house, and one of them was none other than Sam Dervitt himself. Truly the dapper little stranger had done well in taking the sheriff by the roundabout route. For now Sam had warned the lot of them. He could pick them out one by one. He might even be able to drop a few of them with long-distance shots of his rifle. But that was not what he wanted. If he opened fire and killed one or two, the others would soon have their fresh horses saddled and take up the slope toward him. He could neither escape nor fight back effectively in the open. Better, far better, to come to a close range, where his revolver would tell when they began to bark forth their song of battle.

He shortened rein, prepared to hurry straight down upon the house itself, but as he did so, he turned his head and looked back over the country through which he had just come, and there he saw five horsemen moving slowly up the rolling lands in the distant river bottom — five riders sending their horses along at a leisurely pace. They were, no doubt, some lesser members of this heroic band of criminal kings who had gathered in the loneliness of the mountains to let the noise of their last deeds be forgotten and to prepare in common some Herculean stroke of mischief.

For their coming, he did not care. His work would be done long before their arrival. They would have the pleasure of looking down into his dead face; he only trusted that some few of the renegades below him would lie in death also before his own fall.

Yet, as he gathered the rein and prepared his horse for the work by tickling his flanks with the spur, it seemed all very strange to the sheriff. He looked back by swift stages through his life. He had always been a quiet man. He had always loved peace. Chance, and chance alone, had foisted him into this continual struggle and taught him, at last, to love it — merely because he was accustomed to it. He had fought safely for so many years merely because he had never fought with the headlong rashness of one who loves battle for its own sake. Now, however, he was about to step into a different rôle. He was to be the single-handed assailant of six resolute men. He was to make a rear attack upon their base of supplies, so to speak, and then he was to attempt to hold that base while they swarmed back toward it. How long would he hold it? How many would fall before his own death? Or would one of their first bullets strike him down?

He considered these things quietly. And he was content. For he felt that, having betrayed society that had trusted him blindly, he was now about to repay her for the harm that he had done. They might have odd versions of it. When the news became known, they might tell one another that, having fallen from grace, he had gone to join the very outlaws who had drawn him to his fall. Then, quarreling with them, he had fallen in a murderous brawl. That would be their opinion of it. But their opinion did not count; what mattered was the judgment to be pronounced by that mysterious power that dwelt, men said, beyond the blue of the heavens. He who rewards good and strikes evil through with the final, eternal pang, would soon have Chick Marvin before Him. What would He have to say?

God was no clear conception in the brain of the mild sheriff. Indeed, he thought of the Creator as of a bright-eyed and frowning old man with a long beard in which a chance cloud, now and again, might become entangled. A gigantic figure, seated on a throne, supported by nothingness, his lance like treble-bolted lightning, flashing through the universe from end to end.

Chick Marvin raised his head to the sun-whitened sky, and then turned his glance down again, dazzled. Whatever might be above, here was his last work below. He touched the horse with the spurs again, gave it a bit looser rein, and began the descent rapidly. He had no hope to make that passage silently. All he could pray for was that he would make it so swiftly that the man slayers who were busy saddling their horses in the paddock beneath —

saddling, no doubt, for the very purpose of riding out to ambush him — would be unable to get back to their house before he was there.

He let the strong animal he bestrode go cannonading down the slope, casting before it a rattling shower of gravel, small rocks, dead sticks, and clouds of dust and wind-dried needles.

So he burst out into the clearing beneath in time to see a slender youth settling into the saddle near the opposite shed, turning the head of his horse toward the point at which the strange avalanche was rushing down among the pines. At the sight of the sheriff, he uttered a yell and jerked out a gun — jerked it out just as the bullet of Chick Marvin clove his heart. His head fell upon his shoulder. Then with a lurch of his horse, he swayed drunkenly and pitched from the saddle, holding his arms out as though in life to break the force of his fall. But on the ground he lay, oddly sprawling and oddly awkward.

The sheriff saw this as he swung down along the side of his horse and shot that animal toward the door of the house. He heard a yell; one gun began to chatter at him; there was the sickening sound of a bullet striking flesh, and the mare wavered in her stride. She shortened her pace, her front legs sagging, and the sheriff swung himself to the ground as she fell.

From the corner of his eye he caught sight of a tall man with a long, thin face under a great lump of a forehead standing at the corner of the shed with revolver raised. This was all he saw as he leaped through the kitchen door with a hot, searing pain through his left shoulder. He gave that wound a single look. It was no more than a stinging surface scratch, but the blood was flowing freely. A small price to pay, indeed, for he had killed terrible young Tom Wilkie, and even Calamity Ben was not sure death — he had run the gauntlet of that desperado's fire with only this small token to show for it.

They were sure to follow him up quickly. He had entered on the kitchen side. They were unlikely to charge him from that direction. So, ripping away the sleeve that was beginning to chafe his wound, he ran through the house to the opposite side in time to see, through an open window, Walt Grinsby running through the trees. He tried a snap shot — and Grinsby dropped on his face in the pine needles.

Two were gone! No matter what happened now, it was a glorious victory. All the work of his life up to this point could not compare with the destruction of those two master fighters and criminals.

Outside there was a clamor of noise. He distinguished the voice of Sam Dervitt screaming in a wild excitement: "He's killed Walt! Walt's dead!"

Then low, reverberating bass tones dominated the others, and they all became quiet. Calamity Ben had taken charge of the scene, as was to be expected.

For that, the sheriff cared not at all. Let the end come when it would. He had only the vague but burning hope that, in some manner, the truth could be told to Sally Deacon alone, that she might know he had fallen in a lone-handed attack on this crew of villains, not as a result of a brawl.

The bleeding from the cut in his shoulder was stopping, but it had become very painful. Moreover, it was stiffening the muscles of his left arm. It gave him only a single hand to shoot with, and for that he was very sorry. However, his right hand was his best hand with a gun; he could be thankful it had not been the right that was so partially incapacitated.

Making a swift round of the two rooms of which the house consisted, he could he sure, by glimpses through the window, that no one was attempting to approach the house. Only, as he hurried past a window, someone from the outside tried a quick shot, and the bullet hummed just a fraction of an inch from his head.

He went on, smiling. Now that they had decided not to rush the house suddenly, he felt that he had a moment at his disposal. He began to look over the interior of the house. It was a litter of saddles, bridles, guns, food supplies. There were some cards on the center table in the living-sleeping room. A jug of moonshine stood on the floor. There were five cups — tin and half-cracked crockery — and two of them had a bit of liquor remaining. A third had been tipped, and its contents spilled across the surface of the table, gathering a hand of cards in a sticky pool of filth.

Plainly the arrival of Sam Dervitt and his news had made a dramatic moment. And the sheriff sighed with pleasure to think that even these giants of their kind had feared him and made haste to go out to surprise him.

He pulled out a drawer of the table. There were three or four letters, one in a girl's hand to Tom Wilkie. His handsome face had always broken hearts. He read:

Dearest, Best, and Bravest Tom: When you left me last night so sudden, I went back home and . . .

He crumpled the letter and dropped it back into the drawer. For there was something in it that made his brain whirl and put a weight of sorrow in his heart. Tom Wilkie was dead, but still this letter gave him a strange life, and so long as the girl who wrote it lived, perhaps she would make Wilkie live, also, and transform him into a spotless hero in the purifying process of time.

He picked up another letter. It read:

Dear Corrigan: The best thing is to come right back at him. Old Holcombe is convinced that because his bank was robbed once it will never be robbed again. There are big deposits now. The safe is bulging with hard cash. And the new safe is no stronger than the old one. Holcombe found a chance to get a second-hand safe at a bargain and the temptation was too much for him. I think you could get this with a can opener, almost.

Take a try at it. Let me hear from you and I'll fix things. The same split as we made before will suit me fine.

Yours as ever,
J.C.

That was John Crawford, the cashier. The sheriff shook his head. Certainly crookedness lived where it was least expected.

CHAPTER
FOURTEEN

Someone was calling for him from the outside, a deep, strong, thick voice — the voice of Calamity Ben. "Marvin! Sheriff Marvin!"

He went near to the kitchen door and answered: "Hello, Ben?"

"Old-timer," said the other in a more moderate voice, and, indeed, every sound carried with wonderful clearness through the stillness of the mountain air, "we got a proposition to make to you. We got to get you, Marvin, you see that. And we got to get you quick. Otherwise, you'll be pryin' into our affairs in the house, yonder. Now, old son, I got a deal to make with you that'll give you a fighting chance."

"Come out, Ben, and talk it over."

"This here is a truce, eh?"

"Yep."

"Keep back, boys, and don't try no funny moves. I'm gonna have a chat with him."

With this, Calamity Ben appeared from behind the corner of the shed and started across the clearing toward the house. He seemed twice a man in height, half a man in width. When he reached the fallen body of young Tom Wilkie, he paused, turned the youngster

102

on his back, and examined him for an instant, and then, straightening, he remarked in the most casual tone: "Right dead centered through the heart. He didn't feel no sufferin', most like. When I pass out, I'd like to have it the same way."

He sauntered on across the clearing to the kitchen door. There he paused a moment and surveyed the sheriff, and the sheriff surveyed him. There was nothing formidable in his appearance — only a certain brightness and restlessness about the eyes that would hardly have been remarked.

"Why, Sheriff," said the outlaw, "you're only a little man!"

"I ain't none too big," admitted the sheriff mildly.

"That's an advantage," declared Calamity Ben. "If I'd been four inches shorter, I wouldn't've got this here." And he pointed to a long white scar across his forehead. "Are you makin' yourself at home?" he went on, running his eyes hurriedly over the kitchen.

"I'm pretty easy," the sheriff said.

"I hope the wound in your shoulder, there, ain't too painful."

"It's nothing."

"It'll be stiffenin' you up," said Calamity Ben calmly. "Stiffen a gent up something terrible, a cut like that in the shoulder. Seems like it takes all the life out of your arm. When I busted out of Fremont Prison, I got a cut from an edge of iron in my right shoulder. Had me just about done for. Well, old son, we'll get down to business?"

"Sure."

"This here house we put a value on," said the other. "We use it pretty frequent. Folks don't know about it. Even you, Sheriff, never come up here before till that smooth-faced fool Tompkins give it away to you."

That look of his boded ill for poor Tompkins when they should meet again.

"He does better with the money end of things," the sheriff admitted bitterly.

"Ah," said Calamity Ben. "That there is ranklin' in you, ain't it? Take an honest man and one slip makes him feel like he's damned himself. Why, man . . . you didn't do nothin' except to help out your brother. Tompkins says that he wouldn't't've had a chance except it was for that. I give him twenty-five thousand dollars and told him to give it all to you if it would do any good. But a gent like you, he don't bargain none with his virtue."

"All right," the sheriff said a little suspiciously, "and now about this business that you got with me?"

"We can burn you out. The wind is westering a bit. If we start a fire in the needles to the west of the shack, it'll burn right down on you. The old shack'll catch fire quick, and then you'll be toasted until you make a break to get away. That's one way that we could do it. But we don't want to lose this here house. We'll give you a chance, Sheriff. I b'lieve in givin' every man a square chance. I hate to kill a gent like a rat. We'll up and bring a hoss to the trees there in the west. It ain't ten steps from the house. We'll guarantee not to be in the woods on that side of the house after we leave the hoss there. You're to make a break from the window of the house to the hoss, and then ride for it. Y'understand?"

The sheriff smiled. "It's no good, Calamity," he said quietly. "That wouldn't be no chance at all. I know you and I know Tucker. Seein' is killin', with both of you. Dashin' ten steps don't seem much. But you two would kill me ten times while I was runnin' them ten steps. It ain't no go, old son."

Calamity sighed. "It means burnin' you out, then?"

"It sure does."

"Well, I'm a sorry man for that. You'll have less'n *no* chance if you're burned out, old man."

"I know that pretty clear. But it'll do you a harm, Calamity. Who knows how many valuable things out of the pockets of you boys might be right here in this house now? And how many of them will have to go up in smoke before I'm finished? Besides, the lightin' of those needles to the west might prove sort of hot work, mightn't it?"

"Nothin' at all, old son. Well, I wish to heaven that I had that rat Tompkins here. So long, Sheriff." He extended his right hand.

"We shake when we meet in hell," said the sheriff coldly. "I'm hopin' to take you along with me today, Calamity."

Calamity produced a plug of chewing tobacco and worked off a liberal quid between his teeth. "You swift and bitter gents," he said, "make even dyin' a sort of a hard day's work. But me, it's a pile different with. Dyin' with me ain't no more'n spittin'." With that, he spat through the doorway. He stood there a moment with

105

his back turned to the sheriff. "This here is a powerful clear day, Sheriff," he said. "I can see old Baldy off yonder."

"Mighty clear," said the sheriff.

"So long, old-timer. That was a neat trick that you turned on old Walt. You sure fooled him." So he sauntered across the opening. As he neared the barn, he turned around. "Hello, Sheriff, I forgot one thing that . . ."

"Well?"

He stepped into the doorway as he answered — stepped into it and then reeled back, for his eye had caught the flash of the gun barely in time. The bullet clipped a lock of hair from his forehead. Before he could recover and fire in turn, Calamity Ben had leaped to cover, and his strong, bass laughter floated heavily across the clearing.

"I pretty near carved my initials on you that time, Sheriff!"

The sheriff hastened to the front of the house, but the work had already been accomplished. Just within the edge of the trees there was a growing column of smoke, spreading rapidly in all directions at its base. It reached a little dead bush. Instantly the bush became a tiny tree of flame, and a reaching head of that flame leaped up into a lower branch of a tree — a half dead branch where the resinous pine needles were only waiting for the shake of the first rude blast of wind before they fell. They exploded into flame at once, and the fire ran rapidly through the neighboring branches.

"You blockheads!" thundered Calamity from the distance. "Are you makin' this here into a forest fire?"

It had all the indications of the beginning of one. For, as the flame leaped to one side and then to the other, two adjoining trees were quickly on fire. In the meantime, the thick carpet of needles between the house and the forest had gradually caught fire. It made a long red line, crowded with thickening smoke, and speckled here and there with little points of red flame and yellow. It ate a widening passage toward the house, and the sheriff glimpsed it coming and knew that he could not put it out — the surface which it would attack was too broad already for that. Besides, even at one's leisure, it is no easy task to put out a fire in thick, dead vegetation.

He heard a voice yelling out of the wood, behind the smoke: "Come out, old sawbones! Come out, old hoss! I got the sort of poison that you can't feed to dogs! Come on, Sheriff. Stand up like a man, will you?"

Such was the courage of Sam Dervitt. But the sheriff heeded him not. He had a last plan — one in which he had no confidence, but one which might give him a ghost of a fighting chance, if not for life, at least to fight as he died.

On three sides the house was very near to the woods. On the fourth side, toward the shed and the pasture, it was fifty times as far. A man fleeing from a burning house would, naturally, take to the nearest cover, and it would be strange if at least the great majority of the men were not close among the trees keeping look-out for him there. But the kitchen door opened fairly

107

toward the shed, and from it he could get a running start. He sat down calmly in a kitchen chair and waited.

First he heard a *crackle*, and then a flare of heat went through the house. As fast as that, the flimsy dried boards that made up the side of the house had taken fire! This was enough. They were calling to one another and to him — they were calling jovially among the trees as he stripped off his boots to lighten his feet. Then he leaped from the door of the kitchen and plunged across the clearing on wings.

He sped past the center of the clearing. Still they had not seen him. A mad thrill of hope rushed through him and doubled his speed. He had run in desperation; now he ran to conquer. Before him was the shed on the side — a green smear of trees straight before him. He passed the spot where Tom Wilkie lay, grinning with open mouth and horrible dull eyes as his slayer fled past him.

And, just at that moment, the fugitive heard a sharp cry like the bark of an angry dog behind him, then a bullet sang past him.

"He's breaking for the shed. For heaven's sake . . . if he gets to it . . . Calamity!"

But the distance before him had dwindled like magic. He veered and dodged their bullets as he ran. How strange, how strange that they did not strike him down a dozen times. But the god of excitement was striking for him and saving him in his time of need. Now not three swift strides away — a least part of a second — a blow struck him on the left side, high, behind the shoulder, and twisted him half around as he

108

fell. He spun over, using the very force of that fall to swing himself closer to safety, and, as he struggled into the trees, he was struck down again.

He hardly knew where that last bullet struck him. Or was it more than one? His entire body was filled with wriggling, snake-like pains that shot through and through him. And here, there, and again, the warm blood was streaming over him. He lay on his face for a moment, setting his teeth, swearing that he would endure, that he would rally his strength and strike at least one last blow before the end.

He could hear them shouting. It was the great voice of Calamity Ben.

"He's either dead or else runnin' for a hoss. Faster, boys. For heaven's sake, stop him . . . I ain't no runner!"

The sheriff dragged himself to his knees, and he struggled until he could slide down with a tree trunk at his back.

CHAPTER
FIFTEEN

It had cost him terribly in strength, but at last he was in a position to face their charge. And the surety that he could die fighting was sweet in his heart of hearts. Darkness, like flying clouds in a storm wind, was flicking across his brain and whirls of confusion came over his brain. Or did he, indeed, hear voices and horses coming through the more distant trees?

He drew out his second revolver. With a gun balanced over each knee, he waited. Would even his right hand be steady when the time came? If only the agony in his back — in his shoulder — if only it would abate for a single instant.

He saw three men in the same instant — Tucker, Corrigan, and Sam Dervitt, running side-by-side, sprinting like mad. Behind them, above the tops of the trees, the flames from the house were throwing out great yellow hands high into the air, and still behind these the smoke from the trees was rising. He fired with the left-hand gun at Dervitt, but Dervitt ran on, untouched. With his right hand he blazed at Sam Tucker, and the big man screamed and fell on his knees, with both hands clutching at his breast. But

110

there was Corrigan, his face distorted with fury, standing still and firing with careful aim.

A bullet glanced from the side of his head and knocked him flat. When he looked up out of an instant of swoon, he saw the faces of Calamity Ben and Corrigan looming above him. He fired blindly. And a great weight fell upon him and crushed him to senselessness once more.

Once he wakened.

"It's the sheriff!" he heard a voice say.

He wakened again; there was a cool wind in his face; there was a green pine above his head.

This, he said to his soul, *is heaven, not hell. And heaven ain't so different from the earth.*

He roused again, slowly, with a sense that vast æons of time had passed since last he knew himself upon the earth. He tried to stir his left hand. A stabbing pain prevented. He raised his right hand, and he touched a face on which the beard was long and thick.

"Look!" said a whisper. "He's goin' ag'in."

"Hush, Joe," said another whisper. "Maybe he ain't. Maybe . . . pray God he's comin' back to himself."

He opened his eyes. There, indeed, was the pine tree above him, and above the pine was the blue of the sky, and in his brain, suddenly, a thought like the flash of lightning — he was not dead!

He raised his head a little, and instantly a hand was slipped beneath it. He found himself staring up into the face of Sally Deacon.

111

"Lord, Lord," said the sheriff, "I never thought I'd be seein' this dear face of yours ag'in, Sally."

"Chick," whispered the girl. "You're comin' back to us. You're comin' back to us. You ain't gonna die in spite of the doctor."

"D'you want me, Sally?" he said, fighting against the dimming of the world and even her face.

"Oh, Chick, I'll die without you. I don't want to live no more without you!"

"Why, Sally," he said, "there ain't nothing can keep me away, then," he added. "Only, I got to sleep a minute . . . till my head . . ."

And, when he opened his eyes again, there was the white of canvas above him. He lay on a cot. But the girl was still there.

"Sally," he said.

She leaned above him, a drawn, thin face, with staring eyes of weariness. But what a smile for him.

"Sally, darlin', how come you could care for me, after . . . ?"

"How come anybody in the world could keep from lovin' a hero, Chick, like you!"

"Hush, honey. Ain't Joe Peters told you and everybody how . . . ?"

"Sheriff," said a trembling voice.

Amazement struck through the sheriff at the sight of young Joe Peters himself.

"He's been working with me every day over you," said the girl. "He wanted to come, and his father let him come. He's been a mighty fine trump, our Joe boy has."

112

"I got to tell him something," said Joe.

She rose and stepped back, smiling, but with wonder in her eyes. And Joe stooped above the wounded man.

"Turn and turn about is fair play," he whispered softly. "I seen you could've twisted my neck for me, if you'd wanted to. But you turned me loose. And so, I couldn't tell on you. Besides, I knowed that you'd make it up, some way . . . and you *did*." He added: "There ain't nobody that guesses nothin' . . . except you and me."

The sheriff closed his eyes.

"Joe, Joe, what have you done?" cried Sally. "He's fainted!"

"Steady," said the sheriff. "He's give me the best news that any man ever had. Now, Sally, set down and tell me things."

"Here's the governor's telegram. It was sent to town, and the boys brung it straight up. They got relays of hosses along the way. This telegram'll make you proud for life, honey. Here it . . ."

He brushed the paper aside. Excess of joy swelled in him. "I don't want to hear that. I want to hear you talk. I want your voice. Nothin' else means nothin'. Sally, what happened?"

"Don't you remember nothin'?"

"Wilkie, I remember, and then there was Grinsby. And I hope that Tucker flopped. I ain't sure of nothin' else."

"They found you lyin' under the tree with Calamity Ben dead above you, shot right through the heart."

"Calamity Ben?"

113

"That's what most of the talk is about, that you could've beat him when he had all the rest to help him."

"It was wild luck. Tucker?"

"He was found dying."

"And Sam Dervitt?"

"Was he the other one? One of 'em got to the hosses and got away. They chased him for two days."

"Who chased him?"

"Three of the five boys from town that come up in time to kill Corrigan while he was aimin' to kill you."

"What three?"

"Chet Stevens, he was the leader of 'em. When folks found that the jail was busted wide open, and that you was gone, Chick, they got pretty wild. They knew you'd get Corrigan ag'in. But they wanted to help you if they could. So Chet, he took the lead. He had an idea tucked away in his head all the time about this house up here in the mountains."

"That's enough. I'm gonna find a way to pay Chet back . . . God bless him. He seen me ridin' through the hills, I guess."

"Yep, and he trailed you to try to be in at the kill. And he was there."

"And Crawford?"

"You mean John Crawford? Did you know about that? He was the one in the bank who gave the information to Corrigan. Mister Holcombe was suspecting him all the time. He found out . . ."

"I don't want to hear no more about 'em. It's all finished. It's quite all done."

"What?"

"The fighting. I'll never wear a gun ag'in."

"Oh, Chick, God bless you if you mean it."

"Never. It's a game, honey, that nobody don't profit none by. After a while it sort of gets into your blood, you see?"

"I see. You're growin' pale, Chick. You ain't gonna talk no more. Not till I tell you that you can."

"Are you bossin' me, Sally?"

"Now and permanent, I guess."

"Ah," said the sheriff, closing his eyes in excess of happiness, "that sounds good to me."

WHEEL OF FORTUNE

"Wheel of Fortune" was published in the December 20, 1924 issue of Street & Smith's *Western Story Magazine*, under Faust's Max Brand pseudonym. It appeared under the title "Fortune's Christmas". It is a cautionary tale about the dangers of greed in which Anthony Hazzard, a miser whose love of money has blinded him to anything and everything outside the accumulation of wealth, must decide what to do about the reward offered for the capture of the escaped convict, Harry Fortune.

CHAPTER
ONE

There was no need for the noise or for the expense of an alarm clock in the house of Anthony Hazzard. For a full forty years, now, he had never failed to waken promptly at five in the morning. The bright summer season and the dark winter mornings made no difference to him. His eyes opened punctually at that hour.

Neither did he waken with a clouded brain like those of the riotous indulgers who fall asleep with heavily filled stomachs. But when his eyes opened, his brain opened, also, and all his senses were keen as the nose of a hungry wolf.

For an instant he remained in bed without stirring, feeling the house quiver and moan under the strength of that December wind. And on the windowpanes the sleet, blown into level streaks by the gale, kept up a continual small musketry. Anthony Hazzard listened, well content. That gale was icing the hills and the lower mountains; the upper peaks, of course, had been gathered in an Arctic whiteness for a month. But it was early for such weather as this on the lowlands. It was early, and being early it would be unexpected by fools who were not armed, as he was, against all calamities.

119

And every buffet the wind struck against his house was a blow struck at folly.

Moreover, it was a profitable storm — to him. For this sharp fall of the thermometer and this whipping storm meant hundreds or thousands of dead cattle on the range. He could see them now, head down, backs covered with ice, wandering helplessly before the wind until some fence line stopped them, where they would stand leaning against the fence, leaning against one another, while the snow piled on their backs, melted, froze again, and gradually sank the deadly chill deeper and deeper toward their vitals.

When those cows died, whose would be the profit? Those whose warm barns and provident supplies of hay afforded food and shelter for their herds. But most of all, the advantage was to the money-lender. Not so much to the banks, for their rates of interest were more or less fixed. But Anthony Hazzard had no fixed rates. He was a free adventurer in finance. He dealt with lost causes and with sinking ships. No paltry five or six percent for him! But when a man in vast need came to him and begged for money, he would always listen. Yes, there was money in his coffers for those in want. Even without security he had been known to advance it. But, at twenty percent interest the men he had "saved" slaved for him the rest of their days. Such a storm as this was sure to coin more desperadoes, men faced with ruin, men willing to sell their souls for a little ready cash. And that was why he smiled into the blanketing darkness of that December morning as he listened to the beat of the storm.

120

He saw himself as a grand figure, clothed with thunder, one who made calamity his very companion and table mate. Such was the inward picture of himself with which he filled his brain before he rose.

He fumbled first for his boots, which he always left near the head of his bed. And a thrill of warm satisfaction passed through him as he thumbed the leather. It was good, honest cowhide, strong as steel, and as uncomfortable. But how enduring. Eighteen months before he had bought them from a foolish store where they were unprized merely because a customer had worn them for a single day.

Pride ate the country down, he decided. Because of pride he had been able to buy those boots for less than a third of their nominal cost. And so he furnished himself with the first brand-new pair of shoes that he had had in ten years. Well oiled once a week, they might last as much as three years more, considering proper resoling.

All of this went through his mind as he touched the boots. He beat with them on the floor and shouted: "Anne! Hey, Anne!"

He did not hear a response at first. He beat again on the floor: "Anne! Anne! The devil, girl . . . ain't you got ears?"

It floated up to him faintly and sweetly from downstairs: "Yes, Uncle Anthony."

That staggered him. For it was very odd indeed that she should be up at this time in the morning. She must have been sick. That was it. She had got up sick. In fact, at dinner the day before she had complained that the beef they ate was not fresh. He shrugged his shoulders. If animals can eat and prefer to eat tainted flesh, why should not humans, also, except for certain foolish prejudices? Besides, it cost half as much as the ordinary red steaks.

Prejudice, prejudice ruled the world. Prejudice made men believe that they must have lights whatever they did. That was another folly. For instance, yonder on his table stood a lamp well filled with oil, with close-trimmed wick. He could, if he wished, scratch a match and light that lamp. But why waste a match and burn up the good oil when there was no need? He knew the place of every article in the room. He found his way about on this morning without a single mistake except that he miscalculated the position of the table, which he had moved the evening before. As a result, he stumbled and barked his shins, but that was a small catastrophe.

He went on with his dressing; since the weather was cold, he put on a pair of corduroy trousers, which he located readily enough in the dark of his closet by the stiffness of the grease-filled cloth. He put on for a coat the old Mackinaw that the tramp had left at his house five years before. Another would have burned the thing in disgust. But Anthony Hazzard, with his own hands, cleaned it, and here it had been serving him as good as new for five seasons, except where the elbows had been worn through.

At length he was dressed. He opened his door and started down for the first floor of the house. He rarely moved through it without being struck with the thought that it was much too large for a family so small as himself and his niece. There were as many as six rooms in it. Whereas three or four, or even merely two, would have been ample. He would have been glad to sleep in the kitchen. Anne could have a couch in the parlor. There was only one thing to do with such an ample house as this one, and that was to take in roomers. But whenever he suggested that sensible scheme to Anne, she evinced the most irresistible repugnance for the idea. This, he told himself, was because she had been with him only three years. Another season or two, and she would be reduced to a perfect obedience.

He had passed below the upper floor. There he paused, struck with dismay. From the lower floor there rolled up to him a rich warmth that penetrated through the chill that was congealing his flesh. It was almost as though the house were on fire.

He hurried down and cast open the door to the front room. A magnificent sight met his eyes. First of all, the great, old-fashioned hearth was heaped with logs aflame. Enough good fuel was at that moment embraced in the conflagration to have cooked 500 dinners — of a reasonable size! The chill that had made his body shake was replaced by another that struck him to the very heart. Nor was this, alas, all of the damage. Here in the corner stood a young fir tree that, in time, might have grown into a valuable tree. But, cut down in its early prime, it was now planted in a deep box, a poor, dead, useless thing. It would never know another day of growth. From its dark green branches hung glistening showers of tinsel things that sparkled and shone in the blaze of the firelight. And every ornament must have cost something. A penny here, a penny there, and soon the dollar is spent. He moistened his dry lips and looked wildly about him. There was more, much more. Woven wreaths of evergreen, made in time that might have been used with the darning needle to such profit, hung at the windows, and over the door there was a veritable triumphal arch of greenery. At the base of the tree lay three packages.

And fully in front of the fire stood Anne, the worker of all these misdeeds. She looked, at that moment, almost like the girl who had been thrust upon him three years before, with rosy cheeks and shining eyes, the very picture of over-eating and idleness. Since that gloomy day, a change had been worked in her. She had grown leaner, more sober, and she shocked his ears less often with laughter. In truth, he had often been proud of his work with Anne. He had looked upon her, at the first, as a thorough-going outlay of money with no return, but in due time he had actually made her an economy. He no longer had to employ a cook for the harvest hands or the haying or the plowing crews. And clothes, which with all his care might have fallen to pieces, were renewed as through magic by her deft needles. To be sure, it meant food for two, but there were few other expenses since he had told her that she must make her own clothes. So, by the time she was twenty, he had produced instead of a bundle of uselessness, a thrifty, neat, hard-working girl who almost satisfied him.

But now it seemed that all the good work was undone. The dam was broken; the dammed waters of spend-thrift recklessness had burst through with an overwhelming violence!

Here she was crying gaily, like a sinner unaware of her sin: "Uncle Anthony, merry Christmas! Merry Christmas!" And she danced up to him and threw her arms around his neck and kissed him upon each weather-beaten cheek.

He was so startled, so taken off his feet, so bitterly humiliated and shamed by this revelation that he could not answer at once. Before he could speak the proper stinging word to recall her to herself, she had run to the tree and brought him the three packages.

"Santa Claus must have been here!" she cried to him. "And he left these things for you, Uncle Anthony." She stood back, nodding, covered with smiles, and he opened the packages, one by one.

"Slippers?" he said. "Slippers? For what?"

"Why, when you sit by the fire on cold evenings, I suppose, Uncle Anthony. Santa Claus must have meant them for that."

"When do I sit by the fire?" he asked grimly, and, eager to know the full extent of the damage, he opened the next package. "A sweater! Good heavens, Anne . . . what's this for?"

"For biting cold mornings, like this one," she answered with some of the joy leaving her voice.

He threw it in the corner of the room, then, remembering that the garment had been pure wool to the touch, he hastily gathered it up again and folded it with anxious hands. There was such a thing as returning articles, in this day of reckless storekeepers.

There was such a thing as getting refunds of money. Heaven be praised!

He turned to the last of the three. It was smaller than the others. He had hopes, after all, that it might be less expensive. But when he opened it, he was staggered to find lying in his hand, in a neat leather case, a meerschaum pipe. Up to this point, he had managed to maintain a faint smile upon his lips, feeling that smiles, after all, are the proper order of the day for these festival occasions, such as Christmas. However, his spirit now quite failed him. He stared at the wretched pipe. He stared at the girl.

"My heavens," he broke out at last. "I have *two* pipes already!"

He saw her wince beneath the blow. All the color and the joy was struck from her face on the instant.

"But one of them had a cracked bowl, Uncle Anthony. And the stem of the other one is so short now that you have to keep holding the bowl in your hand."

He fumbled in his coat pocket and brought forth the second of these maligned pipes. In truth, it was an antique. He himself would never have been guilty of purchasing a brier. Cherry wood or even cheaper stuff was amply good enough for him. But this had been given to him by a rich rancher who, for a few months, had been a client of his to the tune of some thousands. That was many and many a year gone. Now that stout stem, having successively been tooth-worn and the new mouth pieces whittled in it, was so short that he could not venture to hold the pipe in his teeth without burning his nose. He had to keep the pipe in his hand.

126

However, he did not mind that so much. Or, if there were objections to the inconvenience, he told himself that men who smoked cigars, for instance, kept the tobacco in their hands most of the time. However, looking down at this wreck of a pipe, he decided that there was not much of an argument that could be advanced against his niece. He fell back upon the coward's chief reliance — sarcasm.

"Ah," he said, shaking his head, "it's not hard to find reasons for the spending of money, girl. That's something that most folks can find mighty easy . . . particularly fools!"

"It was my own money, Uncle Anthony," she said very faintly.

"Anne," groaned Anthony Hazzard, "d'you think I'm grievin' for the *money* these here cost? Lord, Lord, no! It ain't that. It's the turrible habit of waste that it shows settlin' on you. It's the terrible habit of extravagance. God forgive you for it. God forgive you for it. It ain't an encouragement to me to leave no great big legacy to you. It'd all be spent on fancy wool sweaters . . . not cotton, mind you, but real wool, fit for a millionaire or for a king."

She was too stricken to answer his spirit, but from her numb lips came some sort of reply as he glowered at her. "But, Uncle Anthony, aren't you *really* a millionaire?"

Suppose a blind old man beset with assailants young and strong; he shrinks into a corner; he fumbles about him and clutches a chance-found stick; he strikes out without aim — and fells the leader of the enemy

127

senseless at his feet and puts the others to flight. So it was with the girl. She had not even tried to strike, and yet she found that she had paralyzed all the faculties of Uncle Anthony. He could only gape at her for a time, looking immensely old and very cadaverously wan.

He muttered at last: "Who might've been fillin' your head full of nonsense like that? Or are you jokin' at me, Anne? A poor old miserable man like me? Millionaire? Why . . . why, Anne, it's mighty funny. I'd ought to laugh at it, but I can't. The beggarly poor savin's of my life of labor . . . the little mite that I've scraped up together . . ." Here his voice changed and grew almost to a scream: "Anne, Anne, if you go spreadin' talk like this around, you'll be bringin' robbers on us that'll kill me for the sake of my money! Yes, yes, you're bringin' murder and robbery into this house. I curse the day that ever brung you into it!"

CHAPTER
TWO

He stumbled off into the kitchen, noting that here, also, the fire had been kindled for some time and was burning hotly, so that the room was well warmed even to the farthest corner. Only between the foot-worn doorsill and the door the wind whirred through in a steady stream of ice. He held his hands above the rising heat. They trembled and wavered like hawks riding a storm wind. Sometimes he closed his eyes. When he did, faces peered in at him through the windows. Forms lurked in the hall. Out yonder the sea of darkness was a sea of danger.

A millionaire! Was that what men said of him? Was that really what had come to the ear of the girl?

He turned, shouting: "Anne! Anne! Come here!"

There was a little rush of footfalls; the door snapped open; there she stood, white-faced, before him.

"Uncle Anthony, what's happened? Are you sick?"

"You're talkin' like a fool," he told her sharply. "Now get your wits about you. Lemme know, Anne, who put that nonsense into your head. Who told you that I was a millionaire?"

"Why, Uncle Anthony, I guess most folks think that you must be pretty rich."

His smile was like the grin of a tortured beast. "Pretty rich, eh? Pretty rich? What might they think would be the reason for me livin' here in a poverty-stricken household, eh?"

"They think it's just your way, Uncle Anthony."

"They think that I got money *buried* on this here place, maybe? Is that it?"

"No, no! I never heard anything like that. But they say that you have a lot loaned out . . ."

"Not my money! Not *my* money! But friends of mine that got a trust in me. They gimme the money to loan out for 'em. D'you see, Anne?"

She nodded, but she looked down at the floor. Suddenly he ran to her and caught her, and drew her toward the light, and pushed her face with his hard, bony hand.

"D'you see, Anne?"

But all that looked back at him out of her eyes was abject fear.

"I see," she said.

She was lying. He knew that. She was deceiving him. Perhaps, at that moment, she was in league with cruel-handed robbers who would spill his blood for the sheer joy of slaughter — and afterward roll and revel in his money. She was lying, then. She did *not* believe. Perhaps everyday she was spreading abroad reports of his vast wealth. Everyday she was gathering danger upon his head. What was to be done about it? He had looked upon her as an encumbrance before. He began to see in her, now, a most terrible and staring danger.

130

He went to his corner chair and picked up his last bit of work — the mending of a leather tug that had broken the winter before when he was driving a team over the muddy road to town. He began to carry on that work, forcing the stout needle through with all his might and drawing the waxed twine after. But he did not see his work. He saw only the new face of his life as his niece had made him see it in the past few moments. And what he saw made him ill at ease indeed.

In the meantime, she began to make preparations for the cooking of breakfast. She cracked one egg into a saucer; she reached out for another. This enormity shocked him out of his old troubles.

"Have you took to eatin' two eggs for your breakfast, Anne?" he rasped out at her.

"One for each of us, that's all," she explained.

"One for each of us? One for each of us? Who is us? Not me, Anne. I ain't wastin' them good eggs that got a price in the market. Not while there's other food in the pantry just as good or better . . . maybe better . . . maybe more lastin' in the stomach!" He went to the cupboard and brought out an earthen dish with a few spoonfuls of baked beans in the bottom of it.

So he sat in the corner chair, with his work laid aside. And he began to eat the beans with a pewter spoon that he had taken out of the drawer of the kitchen table. His good spirits rose in him when he thought of what his economy was saving him. Reckless young men in the town, at this very moment, were doubtless rising sluggishly out of their beds and contemplating a breakfast for which they would pay almost anything — 25¢, 40¢, even 50¢ for the smallest meal of their day!

While he thought of this, the spoon sounded hollow against the bottom of the dish. He looked down and found that he had cleaned them up and still, in fact, he was hungry. He looked at the fresh bread on the table. A slice was newly cut, and exposed an inner flank as white as snow. How delicious would be the aroma when that slice was toasted. But the girl seemed in no haste to go on with the preparations for the breakfast. She idled over her work, and finally she sat, looking wistfully at the steam that whirred out of the muzzle of the kettle and rose until it curled like an opening lotus flower against the ceiling, then disappeared.

He felt that, if he remained too long within the kitchen, the pangs of his hunger would overcome him. He stood up, tightened his belt, and turned away. At the door he paused without looking back to her.

"Ain't you happy here, Anne?" he asked her.

There was no reply for a moment, and then a startled voice replied: "Happy? Me? Oh, I s'pose so. Of course, I s'pose I am."

He turned, now, and pointed a finger at her. "Rememberin' that if it hadn't been for me, girl, you might've been turned out to die in a snowdrift? Rememberin' that all the time, I hope?"

He had spoken in somewhat this fashion many times before, and always there had been some sort of shivering response, but now she merely sat in the chair with her head raised and her dulled eyes fixed upon him, silent, blank, immobile. It became impossible for him to look any longer into that weary young face. He hastily left the room and went into his office. It was hardly more than a great closet, but he sometimes felt that he would neither be able to live nor to think if he were separated from it.

Here he kept his office files. Here were his little cabinets filled with papers that were covered with notations in a cramped hand. But they did not contain the full record of his career. That record was in his brain only. These supplied only the notes, now and again, not to correct, but to verify his questions of himself. For he forgot nothing. All that had ever come into his life in the way of money remained in his thoughts.

In this closet he seated himself and folded his hands across his breast. It was still, for a half hour or so, too dark to start forth on the day's business. He devoted that time to meditating upon what lay before him. Not that he needed to refresh his memory, but because he loved to review his actions in the first place, like a general, overseeing the march of his men before battle. So it was with Anthony Hazzard.

When the picture of the day's work was completed, he got up, settled a battered felt hat on his head, and started out for the barn. There was already a streak of gray in the eastern sky, but in the barn all was so dark that he was forced to light the lantern that hung beside the sliding door. That illumination enabled him to see the old gray mare. She stood with hanging head, her lean withers and hips sticking up like three scalped mountains above her back. And Mr. Hazzard, regarding her, considered her not uninteresting history. She had been a wild mustang, in the beginning. Then some reckless cowpuncher had managed to tame her enough to sit in the saddle. She had become an expert cutting horse until she developed such a streak of vicious temper that her master sold her to a peddler who made the round of the mountain cow camps winter and summer. Lugging the heavy wagon behind her, she had lasted ten ghastly years at that work and, finally, even the peddler was ready to destroy her as one who has accomplished her share of work in life. At this moment, it was the good fortune of Anthony Hazzard to happen by.

He considered that she was only eighteen years old, that she was neither blind nor deaf, and that her hoofs were sound. He bought her for $2 and put her in his pasture. In two weeks she was able to move at a trot. At the end of the third week she even made a feeble attempt to buck the harness off her back. These things had happened five years before. Now, in her twenty-third year, her eyes were glazing, but she was still able to totter down the road at a shuffle that was fast enough to suit Anthony Hazzard. Speed, in fact, he did not like. Most of all, she performed her work on rations that would have starved a pony. In the summer, a slight chance to graze in the pasture was all that she needed. In the winter, however, he put her up in the barn and gave her a modicum of hay from time to time. Grain was a luxury she had quite forgotten.

He climbed into the mow, therefore, and worked loose a forkful of hay. This he weighed with care. He knew to an ounce how much nutriment she needed to keep body and soul together. When he had shaken off some of the fork load, he threw the rest into her manger, and at once she was greedily eating it. He looked down upon her, nodding his head with satisfaction. He felt a vague warmth of heart. Not because he was giving her happiness, but because the wrecked machine could still use fuel — which promised that it could still run. And, if she had to be destroyed in the next summer, he had a good chance of getting for her hide as much, at least, as he had originally paid for her.

This was a small thing. But out of such minutiae, in the beginning, he had built up his fortune. Still it was the little things that gave him his greatest pleasure in life, and not those bold business strokes by which he had made thousands and tens of thousands. Money, to Anthony Hazzard, was an abstract thing, like a philosophical concept, a power to be played with, loved, enjoyed in the distance. It was a mental speculation. But it was not a thing to be put to mundane use. As for life and the facts of life, they had no relation whatsoever to his fortune in hard cash.

He was climbing out of the haymow, when he stumbled against one of the stalls, and the noise he made received a strange echo from beneath the floor, a small, shrill noise, full of a whining complaint.

It came from the cellar, no doubt. A house had stood here, once, and the barn had been built over its foundations. So he opened the trap door and passed down into the damp, cold atmosphere beneath. There, almost instantly, the lantern light fell upon a pool of white in the corner, where, in a heap of yellow old straw made into a nest, a snowy pup was curled.

CHAPTER
THREE

Its head was raised; its mouth was open, protesting that it was hungry, very hungry. He brought the lantern closer. What the breed was, he did not know, but it was a short-haired sleek thing, with wide-open eyes filmed across with blue. It blinked at the lantern light, and still it howled with piercing, dreary voice, its weak head wobbling from side to side.

He was of two minds. It was barely possible that this creature, raised for a few weeks, might be sold for a dollar or two. But it was more probable that it would consume more food than its selling price. No, it was decidedly best to remove it from the world. He dropped it into his hat and carried it up the steps. From the corner hydrant he filled a bucket with water. Then he dropped it in and placed a quantity of compacted hay in the mouth of the bucket to be sure that the pup would be forced down under the surface. After a time he removed the hay and lifted the bucket with its dimly floating shape, and went outside. Water and the dead body he flung far out on the sleet-covered corral. The coyotes would find it the next night, no doubt.

He went back to the barn and took the currycomb and brush. Not that he cared to improve the appearance of the old gray, but he had been told — and he believed it — that a thorough grooming was as good for a horse as a heavy feed. So, if he diminished the rations, he increased the grooming, and, if the bones thrust out farther and farther through the hide of the old mare, he attributed it to old age, not to famine — just as he attributed his own physical feebleness and gaunt body to the same reason.

He had finished the grooming and the harnessing, when he heard again, from the cellar, a sharp, wailing, small voice. Sharp prickles of cold ran through the flesh of Anthony Hazzard. He bent his ear and made sure of the sound. The first premonition went thrillingly through him that the ghost of the murdered little creature had come back to its home to haunt him.

Superstition, however, had small place in the life of Hazzard. He picked up the lantern and went down dauntlessly to explore. When he reached the lower floor again, he saw one little puppy standing in the middle of the damp, hard-beaten ground, staggering with weakness, putting all its strength in the work of its lungs.

What had become of the mother, he wondered as he looked at the other pup. It had not been fed for a long time. That was obvious from the fallen sides of this youngster. But, after all, there were many reasons for a quick end to her life. Hardly a night passed without one or more of the timber wolves stealing down into the village to kill what they could. A champ of those bone-breaking jaws might have killed her. Or the hurricane itself was reason enough, if she had been caught out in it while she was hunting.

Here was one stroke remaining to be done to finish the history of this family. He picked up the small animal and carried it up to the barn floor. The moment it felt the warmth of his hand, it snuggled closer.

He put it down on the floor. It not only stood securely on its legs, but it even toddled awkwardly toward him, making little mewing noises, like a kitten. He did not like the idea of dropping that puppy into the water. For, thinking of drowning, it seemed a black and dismal death. The wind struck at the barn and made it shudder to the heel. That was the better way. Through every crevice in the wall of the barn the cold reached a hand at him. In a thrice, if it were exposed to the blast, the puppy would be cut to the heart by the cold, grow numb, and die. And must not death come, sooner or later, to all things? It must! He could not be called cruel, he decided, for sending this small life to follow its brothers and its sisters. So he stepped out into the brightening, bitter morning and dropped the puppy into a drift of snow. A quick extinction. It broke through the upper crust instantly. All that surprised him was that there had been no wail of complaint. Then, from the outer edge of the drift, the snow gave way and the puppy came waddling forth, staggering, gasping, but victorious. It came to him and climbed up until its forepaws rested upon the cuff of his trousers and so, shuddering with the bitterness of the cold, it looked up to him and wagged its ridiculous tail, as though, indeed, this had been merely a prank played

139

upon him, a sort of cruel game. The miracle that struck Anthony Hazzard was that it did not wail with the cold, the pain, the strangeness, the terror of this broad blank world that had been so suddenly revealed to it. Neither did Hazzard whine when fortune, at various times in his life, had struck him down. He had risen again without a murmur. He loved courage more than anything in the world.

He picked up the puppy, therefore, and went back with it into the barn. He was troubled, disgusted with himself. To change one's mind seemed to him the most shameful thing in the world. Here he needed only a pinch of his fingers, and this work would be done.

But suppose that this puppy grew, and the legs grew strong, and the jaws powerful, and the eyes keen and the heart great — that would be a different thing. Even he could not have killed such a mature dog without forethought — and afterthought. For the afterthought is what we dread. Moreover, since it had escaped death, even at his own hands, he could not help regarding the tiny creature with a renewed interest, a greater respect. It seemed that there must be something more than chance that had kept it safe — something more than chance that had kept it alive through the peril of the snowdrift and the cold. Even now it was so perfectly recovered that it was trying to crawl up his sleeve on the inside, wagging that tireless tail all the time and snuffling at his skin in search of food. Hazzard felt relieved. He had put the matter on such a plane that he could excuse himself, now, for changing that resolute mind of his. Moreover, a new use for the puppy had occurred to him.

There was little doubt, after this morning, that Anne was not as much altered as he had hoped she was after her three years with him. There were still girlish, foolish impulses in her. He would have banished her from his house at once, but when he thought what he would have to pay a cook to come for the working seasons on the farm, and when he thought how weary would be the work of cookery for himself which had been lifted from his hands during these three years, and of all the dollars she saved him in the course of time by her expert repairing of socks and clothes — those eternal perishables — he groaned. He must keep her if he could. He must make her contented. But what makes a girl contented? The gift of something that can be wholly hers to love, mother, guard, and to nourish.

That was why they hungered for children. Perhaps that hunger was working now in the breast of Anne. And might it not be appeased by the gift of the puppy?

Suddenly, as he appreciated how deep his intelligence had struck, he smote his hands together and chuckled aloud, a sound of mirth that had not passed through his throat for many a year, perhaps.

It was not the pretext for saving the puppy, of course, that warmed his heart. It was the immense satisfaction of overreaching the girl. So he carried the puppy to the kitchen door. He peered through the window, first, and there he saw Anne Hazzard sitting in exactly the same position in which he had left her, with her head a little raised, her eyes dead. It made him very serious. For, as

141

a rule, she was an active girl, as quick-handed as she was silent — since he had broken her to his wishes in all things. He opened the door.

"Well, Anne," he said, "turn and turn about is fair play. You give me some Christmas presents. Here's one for you." So he took the puppy out of his pocket and put it on the floor. It set up a loud wailing, at once. "That's its way of saying 'Merry Christmas,'" he said. And he waited, anxious.

There was only a moment during which the girl recovered from her absolute astonishment. Then the blank look left her and she ran to the tiny, wobbling creature with such a cry that the heart of Hazzard stopped. He had not dreamed that there was such emotional strength in her.

Now she had it in her lap, cuddling it, laughing over it, crying over it, and looking up to Hazzard with a face flushed and tear wet, and with eyes full of love for the whole world.

"Can it stand?" she asked him. And she put it on the floor.

Behold! It made straight for the legs of Anthony Hazzard with an uncanny speed.

"It loves you already, Uncle Anthony! Oh, a dog can tell its master. Isn't it a darling? Isn't it . . . ?"

He fled through the door and hurried back to the barn. The morning was bright now. But what disturbed him the most was not the lateness of his start, nor the finding of the puppy. It was the transfused, transfigured face of Anne Hazzard. For, in an instant, at a touch, she had left stiff, cold, angular girlhood behind her and become a woman full of loveliness. What would this lead to? What changes? And he hated change.

"I figgered on openin' the gate and letting out one cow, but the whole dog-gone' herd come busting through on me," said Anthony Hazzard to himself.

CHAPTER
FOUR

It had been a black, bleak world the night before, with all the trees naked except the night-dark evergreens herding thickly up the mountainsides; now all was white. From top to toe, where its mighty foot was planted in the heart of the valley, old Mount Matthew was purest, glistening white, pushing its head into the black storm clouds. Every bush and every twig of every tree was loaded with snow or shining with a thin coat of ice. Men went up and down the village street muffled to the eyes, and the frosted windowpanes shut out all inquiry of what went on within.

The gait of the gray was ideally suited for the icy surfaces of the road, for she moved at such a slow trot that her hoofs had time to take a firm grip before they were lifted, one by one. Ordinarily she traveled at the rate of four miles to the hour. Today, she made about three, an easy walking pace for a man. But not easy for Anthony Hazzard. All his strength was in his brain; his body had been long since wasted to a child's might. But his will was the will of a giant. Now as the cold struck him fully in the face on leaving the sheltered street of the town, he even scorned to turn up his collar. The flesh was no more to him than to some hermit of the woods. If it were mortified, he was only the better prepared for the hardships of the life that lay before him, and penury meant bitter days. These others, poor fools, lived each day for the joy they could get out of it. His course was how much wiser.

He looked back to the village. Every chimney gave forth great columns of smoke, and the storm tore them away from the mouths of stone and flung them heavily across the countryside. Each pouring funnel of smoke meant a fire raging through the day, beginning even so early, for the sake of cooking great feasts for those who were behind the walls. Anthony Hazzard regarded them with a sort of sad contempt. They were flinging away their substance for the sake of a filled stomach that would be empty a dozen hours later. They were pouring forth money from their pocket-books for the sake of bewildering and stupefying their brains. And, at the end of all of this, they were roused at the end of the week by the fat bills coming from the grocer, the butcher, even from the dressmaker.

Anthony Hazzard sighed. Nine tenths of the money in the world is spent by fools on their folly, he decided. But for every mistake they made, somewhere stood some grim-handed genius to make a profit of their errors. Such a one was he. All those feasters in the village, all those pouring chimneys in the ranch houses through that range of mountains, were laboring, in the end, for him. The money that went to the butcher should have gone to pay the interest. But the butcher's bill was new; the mortgage was an old affair. Surely, when they had made all of the other payments so promptly, they should be able to dodge the money-lender for a few days or perhaps even for weeks.

They knew him not! They knew him not! Better attempt to dodge fate than to try to avoid him. Mercy was not in his heart. Tenderness was not in his soul. When the tears rose in their eyes and the quiver came into their voices, he only scorned them the more bitterly. For this was the chief article of his creed — that a fool must digest the fruits of his folly.

These thoughts so warmed him that he did not notice that the snow was beginning to fall once more and the wind rise until a small handful dropped from the brim of his hat down his neck. He turned up his collar, after that, and still the increasing wind drove the sharp edge of the cold through his bones. He had an old sheepskin robe in the buckboard for such times as this. It was a yellow, worn, tattered thing, but it was thrice as warm as blankets. In this he wrapped himself to the neck and drove on in comfort. The snow blew thicker. It made a blinding sheet before him, ever falling, ever renewed, but he paid not the slightest heed to that. The gray mare would keep to the correct way. She had an extra sense that made it impossible for her to go astray. So he plodded on at a walking pace, although the mare was at her dog-trot, until half a dozen forms, clotted with snow, came up through the storm behind him.

It was the sheriff and five of the young men of the town at his side. They shook off the snow and beat their hands together to restore the circulation while the sheriff came closer to the buckboard and mumbled through frost-stiffened lips.

"Have you seen a rider go down this road, Hazzard?"

"Is there trouble up?" asked Hazzard. He reached under the seat to make sure that his double-barreled shotgun with the sawed-off barrels was with him. Time had been when a revolver would have been sure enough for him. But since gathering weakness had unsteadied his hands, he needed a weapon with a broader cast. The shotgun was made to order for his purposes. As well might a highwayman face a cannon as that blunderbuss. He kept it constantly in good condition and heavily loaded. Twice he had had cause to use it, and on both occasions it had served him well.

"Harry Fortune has busted out of prison and come back," said the sheriff.

Anthony Hazzard nodded. He remembered the Fortune boy well. First, he had been one of those freckle-faced mischiefs who are the cause of broken windows in houses. He had grown up with a saucy grin on his face and his hand doubled into a fist. All of this was very well in childhood. But when he reached manhood, he was still filled with the same spirit, and, as a result, he was brought to trial accused with the killing of Sam Marberry. The trial was a mere formality. People were ready and willing to believe that such a fellow as Harry Fortune, constantly hunting for trouble, had finally scared up trouble that was big enough to suit the ambitions of any man. The judge gave him fifteen years in prison. All that had happened some four years before. No, it was in the same year in which he had acquired the Mackinaw that at present helped protect him from the cold.

"Did he drop anybody while he was comin' out of prison?" asked Hazzard.

"He got out without bein' seen. But he was sighted a couple of times yesterday and this morning around these parts. I figgered that he might be makin' out for his chum's house . . . young Crawford, you know?"

"Was Crawford his chum?" murmured Hazzard.

"They were pretty thick. You've seen no trace of him out this way?"

"I ain't passed a soul."

"Well," said the sheriff, grinning, "an eagle might miss something, but I guess you ain't begun to overlook nothin', Hazzard. We're on the wrong trail, boys. Harry Fortune ain't out this way."

They turned back. In another moment the falling snow had curtained them away, and Anthony Hazzard drove on. He thought of young Harry Fortune blundering through the snow, frozen, starved, but still like a foolish moth fluttering back to the flame that had burned it. After all, Harry was not so young now. He must be close to thirty. Certainly, if he had brains, he had need to show them. Usually the careers of criminals impressed Hazzard in that way — he was amused, not horrified. Often he had said to himself that, if he had chosen the pathway of crime to high fortune, he would have given all the sheriffs and the marshals in the West something to think about before he was captured.

148

These lawbreakers were, almost all of them, totally unfitted for their work. They were passionate men; their crimes were the result of their passions let loose. Whereas it was obvious that the only successful criminal must be one who acts in the coldest blood. He who professes to be a gunfighter should never taste alcohol or any other stimulant. Tobacco and coffee and all other nerve poisons should be taboo. He should work with his guns every day, not for a few moments, but for hours. A pianist must have certain hours of practice every day. But only his living depends upon his skill, whereas the very life of the gunfighter hangs on a thread. He must always be perfect. Anthony Hazzard, if he had chosen, could have been a gunfighter whose deeds would have filled a great space. However, there were few or none like him. The others were of the nature of this poor Harry Fortune who, the moment he escaped from prison, headed straight back for the district where his face and form were sure to be instantly recognized.

Whereas he, Anthony Hazzard, loved nothing in the world so much that he would care to return to it. He could never have been betrayed by friends, because he had none. As he thought of the invincibility of his nature, a spirit of thankfulness rolled through his heart, thankfulness to God and admiration of the Creator who had, at the last, made one perfect man.

With these pleasant thoughts the miles had been drifting slowly behind him and now he found himself at the Crawford place, which was his destination. He drove into the shed where the gray mare would be sheltered from the wind. Instantly her head was buried in the hay with which the manger was filled on this Christmas Day. But for that matter, the Crawfords were always the same. Their foolish liberality every day of the year hung out a sign that made all men welcome. Well, there would soon be an end to their career. Before the morrow ended, they would be known through the world for what they were — fools.

When he attempted to get out of the buckboard, his legs failed him. The cold had eaten far deeper into his body than he had suspected. He had to remain there for a moment, kneading the stiff muscles before he could clamber out. Then he brushed the snow from the back of the gray and grinned as he pushed an extra feed of hay closer to her. She was making such good use of her time that he decided that this day and all of tomorrow he would not need to give her fodder at home.

Then he went to the house, reeling and staggering in the force of the wind. He was met at the door by young Sue Crawford, her sleeves rolled up to the elbows, her face crimson with Christmas cheer. She caught him in her strong young arms and drew him into the house. She closed the door behind him. She drew off the great sheepskin. She took off his hat and knocked the snow from it.

"Lord, Lord! Mister Hazzard!" she said. "Your age and comin' out in weather like this!" She cast open a

150

door into the great living room, where the fire roared loudly on the hearth.

"Ma! Dad!" she called. "Here's Mister Hazzard come out to wish us Merry Christmas. Think of that!"

Perhaps Mr. Crawford would think of something else, also. No, he came with his broad red face covered with smiles. He would have put his guest into a chair near the fire, but Hazzard asked him for a private word. So they went together out of the living room.

In the hall they encountered Sam Crawford, taller than his father, a lean fellow with a gloomy face. He started at the sight of them, and drew back against the wall to let them pass.

"I been hearin' news about your old chum," said Hazzard.

"Chum?" snapped out Sam. "What chum?"

"Why, who but Harry Fortune? Don't you know that he's loose?"

"Aye," said Sam. "I know about that. And I know that they's fifteen hundred dollars' reward offered for him. Who's gonna get the money? That's the next question." And he shouldered off down the hall.

"He seems sort of excited," said the money-lender.

"Him?" answered the father. "Oh, that's just Sam's way. There ain't much content in Sam. He don't see nothin' but trouble in this here world. He's been up in his room all day foolin' around with his guns like he was gettin' ready for a fight."

"Well," said Hazzard, "he's a fightin' man, they tell me."

151

"Tolerable." said John Crawford. "It ain't the sort of thing that I like. But here we are, Hazzard," he went on, opening the door of a smaller room. "Here we are. It's a mite chilly here, but we can talk private. I'm glad you come. Partly to see you, partly because I got good news for you."

"Good news?"

"Yes, I can pay."

CHAPTER
FIVE

It was a staggering blow to Anthony Hazzard. He had already seen the big Crawford place, with all of its acres, all of its buildings, all of its horses and cows and sheep, passing into his hands. Not that he wished to live in it. No, but as he had done before with other estates, he would have managed it carefully for a year or two, put all in good order, and then sold for a cracking price. Such was the picture that had just been blotted out by the words of John Crawford.

"You can pay, eh?" he muttered. "Maybe you've struck a gold mine on the place, Crawford?"

"Not that. But I was in to see the bank yesterday. It was a pretty long fight. Young Hallett is a bit sweet on Sue. Otherwise, maybe it wouldn't've gone through."

"And the bank," breathed Hazzard, "has give you enough to clear off the mortgage?"

The other turned a startled glance upon him. "Clear it off, man? Of course not! But they've advanced enough to pay off this year's interest."

Dancing lights of joy appeared before the brain of Anthony Hazzard. He was able to breathe deeply again.

"Interest is interest," he said dryly, "but principal is principal. This here was a five-year mortgage,

Crawford, and the time is up, and the grace is up. I just dropped out here today to sort of remind you that tomorrow is the day."

Mr. Crawford had been smoking a cigar, and a good one. Now he removed it from his mouth and began to turn it around between thumb and forefinger — that had turned to iron and ground the tobacco leaf to a shapeless pulp. He stared at his guest.

"Look here, Hazzard." he said faintly, "I don't hear you right. You don't mean that you're gonna come out here on Christmas Day and hold a gun to my head like this here?"

"There is three hundred and sixty-five days in the year," said Hazzard, falling back comfortably upon an old doctrine of his. "Some folks splits them days up and says that here is a day for rest, and here is a day for work. Well, sir, I don't see no reason at all in that. I never seen a Sunday come along when I wasn't as strong as I am on Saturday or on Monday. Sunday is a mighty long, mighty tiresome day. These here extras, like Christmas and Thanksgiving, don't bother me none. The earth is still turnin' around. Men and women are gettin' older, folks is dyin' and bein' born, just the same on Christmas as on any other day. So I've come out here mighty punctual to let you know that tomorrow is the last day. You can make your plans better, maybe, with that in your mind."

The glance of Crawford wandered vacantly around the room. The color was dying from his face, and the light from his eyes. The gray mare was eating the hay in the Crawford barn, and the heart of Anthony Hazzard was at peace with the world.

"Hazzard," said the rancher in a husky voice, "this here is death to me."

Anthony Hazzard, shrugging his shoulders, said not a word in reply, but he fixed his glance steadily upon the other. He was not averse from scenes like this. They were his comfort. For, every time he saw a man stricken down, it was a surety to him that his own way of living was the right way. Here was big Crawford, for example. If anyone had been asked, that day, who was the happiest man, whose lot he would prefer, that of Crawford with his big ranch, his big happy family, or the money-lender in his starved household, would they have hesitated to choose Crawford and his destiny? But they were wrong, wrong. Here, in a word, he had crushed the rancher utterly.

"I mean," said Crawford, "that you ain't looked into this here, or you wouldn't talk this way. I've put out a lot of money into the ranch this year. It ain't payin' me back right away. But next spring I'll get the harvest of it. I've got hay in the barns. I got extra sheds built. Hazzard, maybe you don't know it, but, with this here hard winter comin' on, I got enough to hand feed every one of my steers right through to the time of the thaw. I can keep 'em all in good shape, while there's thousands that are dyin' out on the range. What's the result? Next spring, when beef is short and prices is high, I can sell early and sell fat beef that'll bring the luxury prices in Chicago. Well, Hazzard, I'll make enough in May to clear off this whole dog-gone' mortgage. Y'understand? Meantime, I got enough to pay this year's interest. The bank seen that I was really in good shape, or it would never have loaned me the money. I'll tell you what I'll do. Take the interest . . . I got it ready for you now. Then let the mortgage ride till May. I'll pay off the mortgage then and pay you a whole year's interest for the five months. Ain't that fair to you?"

It was all Anthony Hazzard could do to keep from smiling. Here, indeed, was the very king of fools. Here was a man who showed him beforehand how much he could gain by seizing the property at that moment. The idiot expected him to hold off. However, he managed to maintain a decently grave expression.

"I hear what you say, and I believe you, Crawford," he answered. "The only trouble is that it's a gamble. I ain't a young man. I've been in this here business for quite a while. I've watched cattle and I've watched the cattle market. It'll take a wiser man than Solomon ever was to know in December what the price of beef is gonna be in May. A mighty sight wiser man. They got millions of tons of beef on ice, the packers have. Because we got some blizzards down here in this little corner of the country, d'you think that it's gonna make much difference to them? No, sir, I don't.

"They're preparin' for May, right now. But that ain't the main thing. If it was my own money that I loaned to you, it would be different. But it ain't my own. How could a beggar like me go around lendin' money in

156

lumps of twenty thousand at a time? I couldn't do it. That stands to be reasonable. No, sir, what I told you when I give you the money is true. This here coin come from friends of mine that trust in my business judgment. They give me a mighty small commission to work on for 'em. Hardly enough to think about. Well, sir, can I gamble on price with their money? Suppose that a fire was to come hoppin' along and burn up some of your sheds? Where would you be then? Suppose that you've made a mistake on how much hay you need to carry them cows through? I got to think of all those things, Crawford. It ain't what *I* want to do. I'm a tender-hearted man, Crawford. I wouldn't spoil your happiness. It's the friends that have trusted me that I got to look out for."

A dark flush passed over the face of the rancher. His jaw set. "Is this final, Hazzard?" he snapped out.

"I'm mighty sorry. It's got to be final. You can pay that interest tomorrow. If the principal ain't ready, I got to foreclose, Crawford. But, if things is as good as you say, you'll get a buyer who'll pay you the full value of the place."

"At this here season of the year?" said the other bitterly. "With the blizzard blowin', with everybody pinched, with the ranchers runnin' to the banks for help? With all the money loaned out and none comin' in? Who's gonna buck this weather and these roads to even come out and *look* at what I got?"

"Weather," said Hazzard, "ain't made to order for no man."

"How much would you offer yourself?" asked the other sharply.

"I might talk to the friends that made that loan. I dunno that they'd be willin' to take the place at much more'n the mortgage they got ridin' on it now. They don't want it. They don't want to own land."

There was a groan from Crawford. "That," he said, "is ruin." He took a turn through the room, then came back and faced his companion. "Well, Hazzard," he said, "five years ago, when I went to you, I laughed at them that told me that I'd gone to a wolf that would eat me. But they were right. I'm down, and now you're putting your teeth in my throat the same as you've drunk the blood of a pile of folks before me."

Hazzard drew back a little, not from fear, but rather to view the other more carefully. Anger, to him, was only less ridiculous than cowardice itself. But it was an infinite enjoyment to see this big fellow shaken and crumbling with shame and rage and grief. It was a proof, again, of Hazzard's greater wisdom, his greater strength.

"That's savage talk," he said. "But it ain't me that you're aimin' at, Crawford. I'm only a poor man . . . the same as you'll be after tomorrow."

"Poor?" thundered the other. "Why, you infernal hypocrite, d'you suppose that you've pulled the wool over the eyes of anybody that wants to see what the truth is? Not a bit! Everybody in the range knows about you, Hazzard. They know that you're worth a cool million, at least. Or maybe more than that.

Maybe millions! Off the Steele place you cleaned up a hundred and fifty thousand flat. Off poor old Emmett you got a quarter of a million. And there's a pile of others too many to mention. Wherever there was bad luck, you've come like a buzzard and got fat!"

"You got a pile of language," said Hazzard without the slightest emotion. "But words don't mean much when you need dollars."

"Dollars? The devil, man . . . d'you think that dollars is the only thing in the world worth livin' for? Right now, would I trade the life that I got ahead of me for the life that you got? Here we are the same age to a month. You're half a step from dyin'. And I'm still young enough to make a new start. And when I make the new start, no matter how small it is, I'll be happier in a day than you are in a year."

"It ain't you that I pity," said the other coldly. "An old fool deserves what he gets. But your kids I'm sort of sorry for."

"Bah!" sneered Crawford. "We don't need your pity. They'll stick by me to the last of 'em. And they'll be happy, too, doin' their bit to help out."

"Sam," said Hazzard in his acid voice, "might be kind of missin' the money to pay his gamblin' debts, don't you think?"

He had touched the sore point, and Crawford winced. "Leave Sam be," he said. "You've stayed long enough here on Christmas Day. I'll be forgettin' myself if you hang around much longer." He followed his departing guest to the front door. "Mind you this!" he thundered as old Hazzard staggered out into the gale. "There'll be more happiness in this here house between now and night than there ever was with you in a whole life! Mind you that, Hazzard, and . . . Merry Christmas!"

CHAPTER
SIX

He could not help feeling that, on the whole, his Christmas morning visit had been a failure. However, although the courage of John Crawford had sustained him under the first blow, it might be a different tale on the morrow. Still, the heart of Hazzard was a little warmed by the courage with which the veteran had faced his fortune. Even of young men, few could have withstood the shock so well. He went out to the gray mare and found her still gorging herself, so he made his preparations for departure slowly, spending a full fifteen minutes wrapping himself in the sheepskins and gathering up the reins before, reluctantly, he drew her from the manger and backed her out into the storm once more.

It cut him from the side now, instead of straight before his face, and the mare, warmed and strong with food, set off at her best gait. It was a storm that came in gusts, like a spring wind. One moment it howled and tore at him and sent an Arctic chill to the very marrow of his bones. The next moment it eased away until he could hear the *crunching* of the wheels through the snow and the rattle of the thousand loose boards and bolts in the wagon. However, no matter for the weather.

161

Tomorrow, unless a miracle happened, he would be the master of the Crawford ranch. Yes, and more than that, he would make the very brains of John Crawford work for him. A masterful rancher John Crawford had ever been. His frailty had been in the spending of money, not the making of it. And all of his ideas about fattening his cows through the winter and selling them in the spring seemed perfectly sound to the money-lender.

When May came, two things would be chiefly needed — hard cash and fat cattle. And Anthony Hazzard would have both. Before all was done, what with the cattle sales, and then the sale of the Crawford place itself in the summer, together with what he would be able to make as premiums on short loans, he would clear a clean half million at the very least.

It was a shock to find, for the second time that day, that the world was not quite so blind as he had given it the credit of being. They could at least see the length of their own noses. Which meant, in the figures of Crawford, that they suspected him of being worth a million. Even then, how vastly their imaginings lagged behind the truth. Stored away here and there in small sums, but on the whole, working steadily for him at immense rates of interest, he had between $8,000,000 and $9,000,000. Every morning when he rose, it was that beautiful thought that warmed him. Three times a day when he sat down to his naked board, it was the knowledge of his working millions that fed him fat. $9,000,000 in

162

round figures before the spring was over. Another year, and the sum might be $10,000,000!

At this, he forgot even the storm itself, and smiled at the ears of the mare pressed flat back along her neck as she forged down the road. She hated him, but he compelled her to his will. She was a symbol of the world in which he lived. All hated him, but all were compelled to do his will. As for applause, approbation, whose did he wish for except his own? Shall a wise man ask for the praise of fools?

He crossed a bridge that, in a lull of the wind, sounded hollow beneath the hoofs of the mare. On the farther side of the bridge the mare shied and snorted. There, barely perceptible through a drift of snow, he made out the outlines of a downed horse. Anthony Hazzard drove on with a melancholy mind. This thing alone, in all the world, had the power to make him sad. For, when his own life came to an end, who would be able to carry on his work? Aye, or who would be able to enjoy the benefits of it? Who, in all the world?

They reached a hill and went up it at a walk. From the top, he looked over the crystal-white countryside, all closely powdered. For as fast as the wind shook the snow from the trees, fresh showers of the flakes piled every branch full. A small whirlpool of snow was going down the farther slope, not on the road, but cross country. No, it was not a whirlpool in the storm, for it was traveling against the wind. He strained his eyes. It was a man on foot, struggling against the cyclone.

Anthony Hazzard watched with a dull interest. Another fool, challenging the elements as John Crawford had just challenged him. Retribution was not far away. He saw the man pause, then fall. Was he to die there? No, he was up again and struggling ahead. Perhaps that horse by the roadside had been his. Once more he went down.

They would not find him until the spring of the year. Some people, perhaps, would have ventured forth through the snows to save the man. But why should he, hated by all things in the world, lift a hand to save another? Indeed, among all living things, what was there that did not dread and shun him? Only one, a feeble, dim-eyed, foolish puppy a few weeks old.

The traveler came to his feet for yet a third time. It was very strange. Anthony Hazzard, in his excitement, actually stood up in the seat to watch, for when men went down in the cold and the snow from exhaustion, they rarely stood up again. And, if they did, the second fall was the end of them. But yonder was an indomitable will that struggled forward still. Such a man, indeed, might be worth saving; it appealed to the one weakness in the invincible heart of Anthony Hazzard — his admiration for courage and for physical endurance.

He made sure that the brandy flask was in his pocket. Then he jumped from the wagon and started across the field. It was bad going, but he was too interested to mind that. Just as he reached the man, the latter went down again and lay in a heap as Hazzard came to him and lifted his head to pour the brandy between his lips. Anthony Hazzard saw that it was the hunted man, Harry Fortune himself — and very changed from the joyous and mischievous youth who had been sent to prison for murder. Here was a strong-faced man, pale with the prison pallor, strong-jawed, deep-browed, a handsome and arresting face.

The money-lender stared down at him bewildered, and then a picture in his own mind crossed the face before him. There was a reward — a $1,500 reward for the body of Harry Fortune, alive or dead.

$1,500, at ten percent — and he never made loans for a smaller interest — meant a $150 a year. Why, when he was a young man he had worked for less money than that. $1,500!

He fumbled through the pockets of the senseless man. There were two revolvers, new, well kept. He transferred them to his own pockets. Now he was master of the situation. How fate and fortune favor the strong-minded, the keen of eye. But to the soft, maudlin heart, whatever comes, except calamity, in the end? Wherein was Achilles merciful? Wherein was Alexander kind? Wherein except in nothing. And so with Anthony Hazzard. The same great spirit breathed in him, he felt.

He had two alternatives, or three. He could wait for the cold to kill this man, which it would do in a very few moments, or he could put a bullet through his head, which would be the simplest way. But there was a better thing, and that was to take the living prisoner to the town. The living prisoner, when the sheriff and the young warriors had been battling with the elements all the day in the search for this man. Exhaustion would make him helpless. If not, his guns were in the hands of Hazzard.

So he put the flask to the lips of his captive and poured down a generous dram. A small investment for the sake of $1,500, one would say, but Anthony Hazzard muttered as he saw the precious liquid flow. It was the only medicine he would keep in his house. For he who uses medicines, in the end uses doctors, and doctors cost money.

The effect of the stimulant was almost instant. The fugitive staggered, and with the aid of Hazzard was drawn to his feet.

"A friend, young man, a friend," Hazzard kept saying as though he were speaking to a drunkard.

And the other, staggering, sinking: "Do you know me?"

"I never seen you before," lied Hazzard with perfect calm.

"Thank heaven . . . that you've come. Get me to a house. I've got money to repay you for your trouble. Get me to a house and food. I haven't eaten for . . ."

His voice thickened and fell away to a mumble. But Hazzard was already supporting him toward the road. It was a fearful struggle, for the meager strength of the old man gave way under the burden. Only the thought of that reward sustained him. Even so, twice he had to pause and administer more brandy, but at last they reached the wagon and by a mighty effort, with Harry Fortune struggling to help, the fugitive was hoisted into the buckboard.

166

There, Hazzard wrapped the sheepskin around him. For himself he needed no extra covering. Over the sheepskin he heaped the snow with which the bed of the buckboard was filled. Then he drove on toward the town.

He needed to give no attention to the gray mare. She would find the way home with a flawless instinct. He could keep his eye on the exhausted man, for fear lest his senses and his strength returned under the influence of the brandy. But he hardly stirred. Only his voice raved of the wind, the cold, and of Sam Crawford.

Why was young Crawford so fixed in his mind? Perhaps, since they had been old friends, because he had been traveling to the house of Crawford in the hope of assistance. Yet, when Hazzard discovered him, he had been traveling in the opposite direction. This, however, was a question that did not matter. The $1,500 was all that counted, not what went on in the brain of the fugitive.

They reached the town. What if someone should see the bundle lying in the back of the wagon? No, not a soul looked forth. The houses were half buried in white heaps. The windows were curtained across with congealed steam and frost. He would go to the sheriff's house — and yet that might not be wise. When he left the wagon to get the sheriff, the fugitive, warmed and rested, might escape. It was better to take him home and guard him while he sent Anne Hazzard for the man of the law. So he let the gray mare amble down the street and turn in at the familiar entrance.

CHAPTER
SEVEN

In the back yard he restrained the gray mare from tugging on toward the barn and shouted: "Anne! Oh, Anne!" After a time her voice answered. The kitchen door dashed open and she stood above him. So very dark was that Christmas Day with all the army of black clouds massed across the sky, that Anthony Hazzard noticed how the lamplight from the kitchen followed Anne and clung about her like a soft yellow mist.

"Anne," he said. "Come quick."

She seemed to fly down the steps and was instantly beside him, holding one of his hands. "Uncle Anthony, dear Uncle Anthony!" she cried. "You've frozen yourself, driving out on this terrible day."

There was something caressing in her voice that he had never heard in it before and he analyzed it quickly. She had decided that he was very angered by her absurd purchase of Christmas gifts. Therefore, she was determined to make up all of her lost ground with him, in the desperate hope that, in the end, she would receive a legacy that would be worth her while. He felt that he saw this with a perfect clearness. And he said dryly: "I'm doing smart enough. But I got something in the rig, here, that I might need your help with. Look here." He raked away the snow and tugged off the sheepskin robe. The form of the fugitive was exposed.

She was full of excitement. Who was he? Why was he there? Had her uncle picked him up on the road?

He made no reply to any of these questions. It was rather a habit with him to overlook ordinary questions in a perfect silence. He and the girl now had their hands full. Harry Fortune was completely collapsed on the floor of the wagon. He lay on his back, with his head fallen to one side, incapable of stirring. Yet it seemed a deep sleep rather than a faint, because he mumbled and murmured an attempt at an answer when they spoke to him.

"Poor fellow." The girl sighed. "Oh, Uncle Anthony, you've saved one poor little life today. And now here is another. Where did you find him?"

Uncle Anthony was silent still. He waved the girl to the head of Harry Fortune. He himself took the sleeper's feet. So they worked him out of the buckboard and into a standing position in the snow. Whenever his feet were under him, Fortune seemed to recover some of his strength. So he did now, and bore most of his own weight going up the back steps into the kitchen, with one arm flung over the strong young shoulders of Anne.

They laid him down on the kitchen floor beside the stove, in which Anne built up a rousing fire. As the fire roared and the chimney began to turn red, a strong glow of heat rolled across the room. Harry Fortune was swathed in blankets after they had torn off his boots and his soaking coat. He was wrapped in thick blankets

169

and a pair of pillows placed under his head. Over him hung Anne Hazzard.

"Is he going to die? Is he going to die?" she kept moaning. "Will he die, Uncle Anthony?"

"You talk plumb foolish," Uncle Anthony said at last. "Of course he ain't going to die. He's more exhausted than anything else. Must've been going days and days without no sleep."

"What in the world could make him do that?"

"Girl," he said, "don't you know who that is?"

"No, no. Ah," she whispered, drawing back a little. "He who killed . . ."

"No matter who he killed," said her uncle, "there lies Harry Fortune. Or, take it another way," he said, grinning at her. "There lies fifteen hundred dollars ready to be gathered in by somebody. Fifteen hundred dollars . . . that's wages for a cowpuncher for two years and a half, easy. All for a part of a day's work."

"As if you would, dear Uncle Anthony," said the girl, looking at him with the same new, bright caress in her eyes that he had first noticed when she had run down to the wagon. Yes, an expression of actual fondness and tenderness. Could it, indeed, be hypocrisy, or had something brought to light in her a great well of real love for him?

He put aside that second surmise the instant it popped into his head, and still it returned again, persistent as a ferret. For there was a genuine ring to her voice. There was a real light in her eyes. He could not deny such things as these. But what had worked the change? Certainly his crisp treatment of her that

170

morning could not account for it. It was as though the spirit of this Christmas Day had possessed her with invincible good humor, invincible love for all the world.

A fear passed through Anthony Hazzard, the same fear that sweeps over a brave man at the very thought of a ghost.

"As if you *would* take a reward and turn over that poor man to the law. But I know you better."

"You do, eh?" he growled out at her. "You know me better? Since when did you start readin' me like a book?"

She merely laughed in his face, and all the while her eyes were swimming with tenderness. "Jerry and I know all about you, dear Uncle Anthony," she said.

On a chair by the stove stood a basket. Out of the cloth with which it was turned into a nest, she lifted a morsel of white puppyhood and placed it on the floor. It blinked and yawned. Then it made straight for Anthony Hazzard and planted its forepaws on his instep and looked up to his face, towering high above, and wagged its tail.

"You see?" cried the girl. "Jerry knows. You can't fool a dog, Uncle Anthony. But, oh, how you've fooled *me* until today."

He thrust the puppy away from his foot. Then he hurried outdoors, muttering. But the fear in his heart was colder than the wind and the snow that whirled up into his face. He had denied resolutely, forever, that there was any reality in these festivals, these holidays. They were mere names that men erected so that they might devote certain times to indolent folly.

171

Yet it seemed, indeed, that some inner spirit of this day had crept into the girl just as it had crept into the household and the heart of John Crawford. It was not the mere personal courage of John Crawford that had sent him singing back to his family after Hazzard dealt the blow, but it was the irresistible determination to keep this day merry. And there is a holiness in merriment. He had never thought of that before. What gives the sacred touch to childhood except that innocent joy in the world? What makes manhood a stained thing except the solemn gravity of the man's face and the man's mind? Gloom and sorrow, like hatred, are poisons. One stroke of laughter is the antidote.

The laughter of the girl haunted Uncle Anthony. He found the gray mare standing shivering in front of the barn door. So he unhitched her and led her in, and, while he was unharnessing her in front of her stall, he was truly delighted because she made a clumsy attempt to kick him. That was the world in which he believed, in which he had lived — a world in which the horse hated the man and the man hated the horse. Fear ruled the one and necessity ruled the other. Except for that, they would have destroyed one another. And so it was among men.

But if he were wrong — if there were truly such a thing as selfless love and devotion from one human heart to another — then how vast a desert was his life. And all that seeming pleasantness in the lives of other men, which he had ever looked upon as a mirage, was no illusion, but a truth, the greatest and the most beautiful truth in the world. If this day of Christmas were set apart not for indolence and self-gratification, but because of deep human kindness and a desire to make one another happy, then it meant that he had scaled the wrong mountain with his life's work.

It is not to be thought that Anthony Hazzard reasoned these things out so carefully as this. Brave as he was, he had not the courage to face such facts. But, growling, muttering, damning the hypocrisy of the world, he finished the unharnessing. He was so gratified by the viciousness of the gray mare that he reached for her another portion of hay in spite of all she had eaten in the Crawfords' shed.

Turning away, he reasoned further. There might be hypocrisy in everything and everyone. There might be sham in John Crawford, and folly and hypocrisy in Anne Hazzard, but little Jerry, as she called the dog, was not wise enough to attempt deceit. And little Jerry had crawled to his feet. If there were selfless love in the beast, why not in the human being? The gentle light that had been in the eyes of Anne Hazzard haunted him and drove him fiercely forward through the snow. He would, at least, deal her belief in him a death blow. When the sheriff came for Harry Fortune, that would be sufficient to waken her from her idle dream of his goodness.

He hurried on through the dull twilight of that stormy mid-afternoon. The wind, for the moment, was not touching the village. Although the storm clouds rolled in a vast procession, massed a mile deep across the sky, not a breath of the gale disturbed the little

173

town. A waiting silence hung around it through which there was nothing so loud as the *crunching* of his feet through the brittle snow. Behind the frosted white windows, the lights gleamed yellow and a happy stir of voices was everywhere. Children were beating drums and blowing new tin horns that would be broken and useless and scarred before the nightfall. And the fragrance of mint and of roasted turkey and of candied sweet potatoes escaped from chimney and window and floated around him. Children, for one day, ruled the world. And why?

A step approached. Around the corner came Tom Lawrence, a man who he did not care to meet on this or any day, since, three years before, he had broken Tom Lawrence and then gathered in the fragments of his broken fortune. Big Tom paused in going by, then turned and put out a hand. Hazzard met him with a scowl, but he found the other smiling.

"Well, Hazzard," he said, "after all, maybe I was a fool and deserved what I got. Besides, old-timer, I'm a pile happier right now than I ever was when I had coin."

This was as great a shock as any that had befallen Hazzard on that day of days. He gaped at his companion. "I dunno that I heard you right," he managed to say at length. "You mean that you are really happy?"

"I am. The farm that I got ain't much after the ranch that I was used to. But I get along on it. I do my own plowin'. I cut my own hay. I sow my own grain and watch her grow."

"Maybe them things make *you* happy," said Hazzard. "But how about Missus Tom?"

"You're a queer gent," said Tom Lawrence, shaking his head. "Man would think that you don't want us to be happy. Missus Tom is better'n you ever seen her. Them nerves of hers is plumb forgot. She's too busy milkin' the cows and runnin' her creamery to think about nerves. She does that all by herself and keeps house and does the cookin' on the side. She's a real cook, Hazzard. If you don't believe, drop in, someday, and try us."

"But your boy, Jack. I suppose it hit him pretty hard?"

"It was better for him than for any of the rest of us. All he'd learned was how to spend. Now he's startin' to learn how to make. He's got a plan for irrigatin' that southeast forty . . ."

"Even Jack?" murmured the money-lender. He stared at Tom Lawrence as at some hydra whose heads have been struck off, but that spring back redoubled in number.

"I've give up having rheumatism, lost thirty pounds, told the doctor to go to the devil, and I'm livin' a real life, oldtimer. I've got to hurry along. Merry Christmas, Hazzard!"

He strode on up the street and left Hazzard too dazed to make a last response. Truly, many deadly years had been stripped from the face and the shoulders of Tom Lawrence. But what stung Anthony Hazzard the most was a ringing note of cordiality in the voice that had bade him Merry Christmas.

Here, however, was the sheriff's house at hand.

CHAPTER
EIGHT

He stood on the porch for a moment, knocking the snow from his clothes, and, while he stood there, he heard the sheriff talking in the front room with some man with a piercing, disagreeable nasal voice.

"Why didn't you take him, then?" the sheriff was asking.

"I didn't have no gun on me," said the other.

"Well," said the sheriff, "I dunno that anybody would like to start about takin' Harry Fortune without a gun in his hand. I wouldn't, Sam."

It was Sam Crawford, then, who had ridden to town to give information about his former chum. Mr. Hazzard grew rigid with interest.

"Besides," said the sheriff, "I s'pose it wouldn't've looked very well, if you'd come in with your old partner . . ."

"Looks don't make a bit of difference," said Sam Crawford. "What I need is that money. Fifteen hundred is a stack of the long green."

"It's eighteen hundred now," said the sheriff. "It'll be two thousand, I suppose . . . before tomorrow. Folks are sort of wrought up about the way that he busted out of prison."

176

Anthony Hazzard started. What a fool he would have been to turn in his prisoner before the ultimate reward had been offered!

"He wanted food," said Sam Crawford. "He looked mighty spent, and said that he hadn't had a meal for a long time, and that he hadn't slept for a long time, neither. He wanted a place where he could sleep. I told him to go into one of the sheds and bed himself down in the hay . . . that I'd bring out the chuck to him that he wanted. I seen him get fixed in the hay in a warm place. Than I went to the house for a gun. When I come back, he was gone. He must've smelled a rat."

There was a little pause. "Maybe he did," said the sheriff coldly. "Would you've fought him, Sam?"

"A bullet through the head would've been the best way with him. I'm tired of havin' folks tie up my name with a murderer like him. Because we played around together when we was kids don't mean that him and me are the same sort."

"No, it doesn't mean you're that sort," said the sheriff in the same odd intonation.

"I want you to write that down in your memory so's you won't forget," declared the young man. "If it comes to hunting down this here Harry Fortune, I'm with you as much as any man. But the main thing is that, when I follered the back tracks of his hoss, I seen that they headed back toward the town."

"They did!" cried the sheriff.

"If he aimed back this way, where'd he go? I tell you, by the looks of him, he couldn't've lasted long. He's just about spent. Sheriff, some place in this here town is where he's hid. If I was you, I'd rouse the town and start a search for him."

"He was far gone?"

"Any kid could've handled him . . . except for his guns."

"Why, Crawford, it looks to me like you hate him."

"Why shouldn't I? They been calling me his friend these years since the murder. Folks have sort of shunned me on account of me knowin' him, once."

Mr. Hazzard waited to hear no more. There was a storm of perplexity in his mind. In the first place, to give up his man before the maximum reward had been offered, seemed the height of insanity to him. But, on the other hand, to have his house searched and to have the fugitive found in it, might be construed in a dangerous sense, as though he were giving shelter to an outlawed man and protecting him from the vengeance of the law. However, cowardice was not one of the faults of old Anthony Hazzard.

He shrugged his lean shoulders and walked briskly back toward his house. He went at once to the kitchen door, and looked through the little window beside it. There he found a strange spectacle, for the wanderer had recovered so tremendously by being thoroughly warmed that he was able to sit up, and now he was at the table, finishing the remnants of what had once been a vast platter of ham and eggs.

Yes, there was no doubt about it. From the traces on the platter, two, three, even four eggs must have been cooked for him by that wastrel niece of his. In addition, the last of a slab of ham was now poised on the end of his fork. The money-lender took acute interest in the thickness of that slice. It had the ample dimensions of a steak, rather than one of those papery slices of ham to which Anthony Hazzard was accustomed. Before Fortune stood a pitcher of milk, more than half emptied, while beside the plate there was a steaming cup that the mad spendthrift, Anne, was at this moment replenishing with coffee.

Hazzard felt a mist of rage cross his eyes. Here was a total of some 40¢ or even 50¢ in raw food products poured into the insatiable maw of this young man. Here was given to him fuel that he would convert, instantly, into tremendous strength for immediate action. A few minutes before, he had been a helpless hulk. Now he was again capable of acting the part of a fighting man.

Hazzard opened the door and looked in upon an ominous tableau. The fugitive, at the first sound of a hand upon the doorknob, had caught into his hand a revolver — one of the old guns that Hazzard kept in the house. Now he faced the door, not with the weapon aimed and leveled, but holding it negligently upon his knee, as one who could shoot accurately by the mere pointing of the gun — the carelessness of a sure and desperate man to whom the rest of life is a brief and uninteresting story, at the best.

"Don't shoot! Don't shoot!" cried the girl. "It's Uncle Anthony!"

Harry Fortune cast the pistol aside upon the table and stood up. He seemed much larger now than he had been when he was helpless in the hands of Hazzard. He stepped forward with a firm stride — no symptom of wobbling or uncertainty. He took the icy hands of Hazzard in a great warm grip. And what a smile he gave the old man.

"Mister Hazzard," he said, "what I feel about you ain't easy to put down into words. I'm not going to try. I owe you my life. That's all. If I live long enough, I'll make you know that I put some value on what you've saved for me."

"Ah," said Hazzard, and, turning his back, he shuffled across the room to hang his hat and his wet coat on the wall. But, chiefly, because he wanted to hide his face from young Harry Fortune, for he felt that if he met the eyes of the man, the fugitive would read grim things that he should not guess, as yet.

"When I'm cleared of this here mess," said Harry Fortune, "I'm going to let folks know what you've done for me. They call you a tolerable hard man, Mister Hazzard. I'll show 'em how you took me in when I was worth about fifteen hundred in cash."

"Nigher to two thousand," Hazzard said dryly, managing to turn to him again.

"Harry Fortune, Harry Fortune!" breathed the girl. "Have the brutes dared to put a price on your head?"

"They got no sense of humor," said Harry Fortune with a wan smile. "They put a pretty high value on what ain't worth so much. I ought to feel that they've done me a great honor, I s'pose."

"But it means," said Anne Hazzard, "that the first man who sees you can shoot you down . . . shoot you through the back, Harry Fortune, and no one can harm him for it."

180

Hazzard crossed to the stove and stood warming his hands over it, twisting them rapidly back and forth over one another.

"You've got a gun, Harry."

"It's a pure bluff, Mister Hazzard. I've never used a gun on any man. I'll never begin. It ain't worth the risk."

Hazzard's opinion of the intelligence of this young man waxed apace. Your cheap crook tries to bluster his way out of trouble by assuming a loud voice to proclaim his innocence, but Harry Fortune spoke quietly, as one sure of himself. He was certainly of the superior order of criminal.

"Then they're wrong when they lay Marberry's death to you?" asked Hazzard, still without turning his head.

"Uncle Anthony!" cried the girl in indignant protest.

"Of course they're wrong," said Fortune.

"You'll clear yourself?"

"Do you think that I'd've broke out of prison if I hadn't felt that I had a ghost of a show to clear myself?"

"Why not? Most men would bust out of prison if they could . . . I suppose."

"Not me! Why, man, I was in for fifteen years. Good behavior and that sort of thing would shorten the time to nine or ten. I've served four long years . . . the longest years of the lot. I was a trusty. They gave me a lot of liberty. I was managing to live. Five or six more years, and the thing would have been over with, and I'd still be not much more'n thirty. No, sir, if I hadn't felt

181

that I could clear myself up, I'd have stayed in the prison. I would have been a fool to do anything else."

Hazzard turned this time and looked the young man over. He felt, again, that there was decidedly stuff in this youth. Even if this were a sham. He could not help saying: "You've got sense, young man. But how'll you prove it?"

"By the help you'll give me."

"Me?"

Harry Fortune nodded. "All I want is some sort of a place to work from. As long as you'll let me stay in this house, I can get out secretly into the town."

"Suppose they trace you here? Sort of a mess for an old man, I'd say."

"I'd blow my head off, Mister Hazzard, before I'd let a harm come to you through me."

Hazzard yawned. These violent protestations were not to his liking. Nothing is so easy or so cheap in the world as words. He nodded amiably. But the essential thing, of course, was to make the youth feel that every word he spoke was believed. Put all his apprehensions to rest, and let him use this house as a hiding place. Hazzard, by a single word to the sheriff, could convert the house from a shelter to a trap.

"I'm gonna go up and lie down for a minute," he said. "I'm fagged." He passed through the door, but, the moment it had closed behind him, he dropped to his knees and pressed his ear to the keyhole.

CHAPTER
NINE

Such methods did not appear shameful to Anthony Hazzard. Wherever one can get at the inner mind of another man, he felt, there is a reward for the effort. Feeling that Harry Fortune was about to tell his story, Hazzard particularly wished to be apparently absent from the scene. When the coldly critical ear of another mature man is listening, a liar will tell his tale with more accurate care. But to the credulous ear of a woman, he is apt to let his fancy run more easily at large.

In fact, Mr. Hazzard had not been in his place of concealment for two minutes before the story began. And Anne was directly asking for it.

She said: "Ever since I came to town to Uncle Anthony, I've heard about you and what they accuse you of doing. Oh, Harry Fortune, I'd give a great deal to know the truth."

"There's no use talking," answered young Fortune. "It's a queer-sounding story, you see. No use telling it until I have some sort of a proof to back myself up. When I get the facts . . . and God help me to them . . . then I'll be ready to talk to a judge, and you can hear along with the rest."

"You don't understand," she answered. "It won't be hard for me to believe you."

After that, there followed a little pause, and Anthony Hazzard could feel the eyes of the youngsters fixed on one another.

"That's a kind thing to say," murmured Harry Fortune. "But although it is a queer-sounding yarn, I'll try to tell it exactly as things were. Four years in a prison," he went on gravely, "make a mighty lot of difference in the way a man looks at things. The first week in the penitentiary was seven years of hell boiled down small. I hated the world, because it had done me a wrong. I wanted to get out and make trouble. If all the people in the world had been living in one house, about that time, I think I'd have put a match to it, if I could. You know?"

"I know," said the girl. "Sometimes we don't understand things. That's the worst. Think what a truly kind, good man Uncle Anthony is. And yet I've gone for three years thinking that he was only a cruel old miser."

"Everybody thought that," said the youth. "But God knows what I think of him now. And there's the pup . . . look yonder. He's scratching at the door, trying to get out and follow Mister Hazzard. An animal like that can tell a good man. They've got an instinct for it, my mother used to say."

His heavy steps approached the door behind where Anthony Hazzard was crouched; there was a faint squeal from the puppy, then the steps retreated.

184

"Give him to me, Harry," said the girl's voice. "A man doesn't know how to handle such weak little things. See him kick and struggle now. Why, he's like a grown-up dog already. He wants to be on the floor hunting mice, I suppose."

There was laughter from Fortune. There was laughter from the girl.

"Please go on," she said. "Be quiet, silly Jerry."

"I was saying," went on the fugitive, "that I took it pretty hard at first. But after a while I had so much time to myself that I started to do a little thinking, and I figured out that maybe it was a pretty good thing for me, that trip to the prison."

"Oh!" cried the girl.

"You see, Anne," he went on, "I'd been one of these troublemakers all of my life, and I fought because I liked fighting. I used to like to get another boy against a wall and beat him till he yelled. I used to like to ride a horse with the spurs. There ain't much in the way of trouble that I didn't make. I was pretty big when I grew up. And strong by nature. I'm not boasting, Anne. But some men are big without being strong. And some men are strong in spite of the fact that they're little. Well, I was naturally strong. I could always do things that other fellows couldn't manage. I'm still pretty hard. Take this poker, for instance . . ."

There was a pause.

Then: "Harry, Uncle Anthony will be furious!"

"No, he won't. There . . . it is straight again."

A cry of admiration came from Anne.

185

Hazzard, behind the door, felt as though the hands that had bent that stout poker were buried in his own throat. He drew a breath.

"That looks like showing off," went on Harry Fortune. "But I don't mean it that way. Suppose a boy gets a lot of money for a gift. First thing he does is to go out and make a fool of himself trying to spend it for things that don't count a little bit later. That was the way with me. I found myself grown up, one day, and a lot stronger than other men. And I wanted to use that strength. I liked hard work . . . but mostly I liked hard fights. Well, people got to be afraid of me. I suppose there weren't many men in the town that wanted to stand up to me.

"Then Marberry came along. He was a fellow from Montana. He was about my age, I suppose, but he looked older and he acted older and he talked older. He'd been on the range since he was a little kid. He was hard as nails, quick as a flash, and he had a reputation for being a gunfighter. He was good-looking, mighty straight standing, had a good eye in his head, and knew how to get along with men and girls, too. Sort of a man you'd pick out from a crowd pretty quick. That was the face of him, you might say. Behind the face I guess that he wasn't much good. Not the sort of a thing you want to say about a dead man, but I had ways of knowing. He was a gambler, and he was a crooked gambler. He got what he wanted, and he didn't care how he managed it. But he had such a frank sort of hearty way of talking, that people didn't suspect him . . . at first.

The only trouble with him was that he couldn't stay very long in any one place.

"Well, Marberry and I had our hatchets out for each other's scalps right away. You might say that I was the town bully, and that he was the new boy in the school and mighty sure of himself. Sooner or later we was sure to have trouble. It come at last over the cards. Playing at the same table in back of the old Carson saloon, I thought I saw him make a queer pass with a pack of cards, and I grabbed for his wrist and turned his hand up. It happened that I was wrong. But, of course, it couldn't go at that. He hit me, and I hit back, and he went down. When he got up, I mopped the place with him. He tried to get out his gun, but I got it away from him, and pretty near broke him in two. When I finished, he was willing to admit that I was the better man of the two, but he swore that he'd put a bullet through my head the next time we two met up.

"Well, I was pretty handy with a Colt, but I supposed that I wasn't in the same class with him. I left town quick and went out on the range. I decided that I'd spend about a week practicing and getting my hand in. Then I'd come back to town and have it out with him."

"Harry!"

"That's it. I deserved all the prison that I got. Nothing but luck kept me from doing a killing . . . or getting killed. I went out on the range, all right, but, after I'd fired about a couple of hundred cartridges, I'd used up my supply, pretty near, and I figgered, besides, that I was good enough to beat any man to the draw and then shoot him dead. I sat down and cleaned my

187

guns, shoved 'em into the holsters, hopped on my horse, and came back to town. It was night, and pretty late when I came. I went to the house of Marberry and asked for him. They said that he was away at a dance. He was that sort. I'd given him some pretty bad bruises in that fight, but he'd go to the dance, anyway, and, if anyone dared to laugh at him, he'd've made them wish that they never knew how to laugh.

"I waited around the house for a while for him. Then I went home, had a nap, and started back. It was about one in the morning, and I was afraid that I'd miss Marberry on his way back from the dance. But when I was about three hundred yards from the Keene house, I seen a girl . . . I suppose it was Nora . . . standing in front of the house, and a couple of men along with her. She went into the house . . . or, rather, she went up on the porch. One of the men started away, and the one who was behind him must have pulled a gun, for there was a shot, and one of the two dropped. The other ran away behind the line of the house. I got there as fast as I could, and found Marberry lying on his face, dead. While I was calling to him, a couple of folks that had heard the shot came up to me.

"Well, I forgot to say that on my way in from the range, after my practice with the guns, I'd seen a rabbit jump across the trail, and had taken a flyer at it . . . and dropped it, too. That gave me an empty chamber in my gun.

"That made the case perfect against me. Everybody knew that I'd had a fight with Marberry, that he'd promised to shoot me on sight, and someone had seen me off in the hills practicing. Then they find Marberry dead, me leaning over his body, and an empty chamber in a revolver, the same caliber as mine. What could be clearer than that? All I could do was to talk about a shadowy-lookin' gent who had run away after the shooting. That wouldn't wash. The jury, when the time came, just smiled."

"But what did the girl say? What did Nora Keene say? She could've told them that another man had been with Marberry and with her."

"Aye," muttered Harry Fortune, "and that's just what she didn't say. When she was called upon the witness stand, she said that she'd come home from the dance alone with Marberry. She said that nobody had joined them. And there it rested. What could I do?"

"She would have let you hang?"

"No, it was sort of queer. She came to see me in jail. She whispered to me, after I'd been found guilty . . . 'Harry, I won't let you hang. But if it's anything less than hanging . . . ' And then she left me. Of course, I didn't have no defense. I went to prison. And I think that I've stayed there long enough to get some sort of sense in my head."

"But how can you prove that you're innocent? Unless she'll talk?"

"I have some ideas. I'm going to see how they pan out."

"And if you . . . ?"

Here a heavy knock sounded at the back door of the house. The voices in the kitchen ceased.

CHAPTER
TEN

Anthony Hazzard went up the stairs as fast as his lean old legs could carry him, and in his own room he sat down with a beating heart. He had not felt such excitement since, some years before, a stealthy creaking on the stairs had apprised him that someone was in the house. He had blown a double charge of heavy shot into the head of that would-be thief and housebreaker. He had gone out dauntlessly through the darkness and stood in front of the door of his room until he made out the shadow of the interloper against a distant window. He had been wonderfully excited, but he had not been afraid. Now it was otherwise. He was both excited and afraid. For in the other case he had had the stalwart bulwark of the law behind him, and in the present time the law was the weapon that was raised against him, but now he had no resort. He could not take a gun to the invaders of his house. They came with authority behind them. What would they do?

He had long known that he was hated with a consummate hatred. But it had been his care through his life to give no enemy a possible loophole through which he could be shot at. Whatever they cursed him for, they could find no illegal action as the merest finger hold through which to seize him. He had gone safe, he would never have gone safe, if it had not been for his encounter with young Harry Fortune. He told himself that it was because, in this instance, he had attempted to get something for nothing. $1,500 for nothing.

True, he had made a hundred times that amount at a single stroke, but always that had been some investment of sums of money. He felt that he had been guilty of the sin of illogic; no, it had been the sin of blind greed. For, had he simply walked on into the sheriff's house when he heard the man talking with Sam Crawford, he would by this time have lodged the criminal in jail, and Anthony Hazzard would have almost $2,000 to add to his hoard.

He wandered gloomily to the chest of drawers in the corner of the room. In the biggest drawer, in the very center of the chest, secured in a little wooden box with a tiny lock that a child could have broken, was his store of ready cash. He never looked at it without smiling to himself. Ten times, in his absences, his house had been searched by curious thieves keen to get on the trail of some store of hidden treasure. But they never yet had suspected that the treasure of the money-lender would be secured in so easily found and frail a hiding place. They could not imagine that. They had combed the attic and dug up the cellar. But they had never looked under their noses. Once he found nearly all the floors in the house torn up when he returned home. But the money had not been secured. And if he had acted otherwise than as a fool, the reward money for the capture of the murderer should have gone into that box, also.

It was his standing joy, his standing agony. His joy because sometimes it seemed to him that the few thousands he had here to look at, to touch, to examine as though reading a book, meant more to him than the large millions that he had invested in greater concerns across the countryside; his terror because every hour of the day and in his dreams at night he beheld an eager hand snatching up the box and dashing it to pieces against the floor while the heaps of greenbacks, neatly and closely compressed, spilled forth. This thought was a poison-pointed dagger ever striking him to the heart. Yet he could not give up that habit of keeping a little hard cash near him at all times — the greenbacks above — sometimes as many as $20,000 worth when he was feeling recklessly self-confident. Sometimes the sum shrank to a few hundred when terror had gained the upper hand. It was a sum ever in fluctuation. But in the little tray at the bottom of the box was a sum that never changed. There, bedded in softest cotton that permitted no jostling or jarring, he had fifty double eagles, fifty $20 gold pieces, fresh, bright-faced as when they came from the mint thirty years before. If he looked at the greenbacks until with an inward qualm he said to himself — "This is mere paper." — then he could take out the tray and unfold, with delicate touches, the deep cotton, and look in on the broad, smiling face of gold itself. It was the point of the story that the paper money told.

But now, if they seized him and threw him into prison for sheltering an outlawed man, what would become of this long-hidden treasure? Could he take it with him? No. Could he leave it behind? No, he would perish of anxiety within twenty-four hours if the money had to be left to the security of chance.

Aye, he might die in prison. There was no end to the malignity with which the world at large regarded him. There was no end at all. They would hound him to the death. If the maximum penalty in the law were fifteen years, the judge would be sure to give it to him, and the decision would be received with applause. So, in a prison cell, he would end his days, and the priceless joy of all his fortune would be lost to him.

Such were the thoughts in the bitter mind of the money-lender as he sat crouched on his bed and cursed the folly that had not made him put a bullet through the head of the fugitive, or, at the least, leave him to die of the cold before he brought him in for the reward money.

The sound of loud voices from the kitchen interrupted these thoughts. Then a quick, light step on the stairs, and his door was thrown open. He started up with the shotgun in his hand. It was Harry Fortune who stood before him.

"I've tried the windows. They're frozen solid. I can't budge 'em," said Harry Fortune. "Is this the way to the attic? Through your room?"

A wild impulse formed in the mind of the money-lender and swept across it like a wave. A touch upon those double triggers and Mr. Fortune would be

193

sent into the other world. Then he could simply declare that he encountered the fellow in his house, perhaps in the act of robbery. Aye, at a stroke, he would free himself from his difficulties and regain the reward money that was slipping through his fingers.

How beautiful, how simple in its beauty, was that thought. But hard common sense prevented. As well attempt to outspeed the snaky head of a weasel. As well strive to trick the watching eye of the lynx as to attempt to baffle this man, calm, grim, alert. His hand would be the lightning flash, unavoidable, and sure. So Anthony Hazzard banished the cat look from his eyes.

"Don't go to the attic," he said. "Nobody but a fool hides in corners. Corners are the first place they'll search. Get out of sight in that closet, yonder."

"You said corners . . ."

"They'll never search *my* room," said the money-lender grimly.

A boom of voices coming up the stairs decided the fugitive. He cast one wistful glance at the window — then he stepped into the closet. And the fall of the foot, as Hazzard noted with admiration, made no sound on the floor — no sound, although it creaked dolefully even under the light tread of the old man. To be sure, if such a devil as Harry Fortune came to search his house that money would never be safe. He must get rid of it at once — on the morrow. He must put it in a safe in the bank, much as he hated all banks with their six-percent loans that encroached upon his business.

Fortune had hardly disappeared when a heavy hand knocked at the door. He had barely time to lie down on

194

the bed and call to them to enter when the sheriff stepped inside with three men shouldering close behind him. Each had a drawn Colt in his hand.

Danger brought to the money-lender a vague sense of humor.

"Have you turned into a robber, Sheriff?" he asked.

"Harry Fortune is loose in town, we think," said the sheriff, his eyes flicking about the room restlessly. "We're searching every house. This was your turn."

"I've heard about him," said Hazzard. "That there door leads up to the attic. Go ahead."

They went up the stairs with a rush, the sheriff giving directions. For a time they stamped about, pulling discarded furniture here and there, dragging trunks away from corners. A thin shower of dust fell from the shaken ceiling.

Then they came trooping back. "We ain't had a look through this room," suggested someone.

"Take a look now, then," said the sheriff dryly. "You can see for yourself, I guess. It's as clear as the palm of your hand, unless you think that he's in one of them drawers, yonder."

For once, Mr. Hazzard loved stupidity. His heart warmed to the sheriff.

"That door . . . where does it go?" asked the sheriff's man.

"A closet," said Anthony Hazzard.

"Can I have a look?"

The heart of Anthony Hazzard stopped in his breast. "Sure," he said lightly.

The other stepped forward. His hand fell on the door.

"Wait a minute!" shouted Anthony Hazzard. "Sheriff, ain't you got any wits about you?"

They all faced him, startled.

"Ain't there a price on the head of the murderer?" asked Hazzard.

"Nigh to two thousand."

"Two thousand? Well, there you are," said Hazzard. "Does it stand to reason that I'd keep this here gent secret when I could scoop in two thousand by sayin' one word?"

The sheriff smiled at his men.

"You're right, Mister Hazzard," he said. And his glance wandered rather insolently over the threadbare clothes of the old man. "You're right. Not if he was your own blood, I s'pose. Boys, come along. It was just a matter of makin' a clean search," he explained to the owner of the house. "We're makin' a sweep through everything."

"Bah!" sneered Hazzard, and then closed his eyes as though to sleep. But, really, because he feared lest the immense relief he felt might show in them like two signals.

The sheriff and the three disappeared. Their heavy steps, their heavy voices went down the stairs. Then Harry Fortune came out and looked at his preserver. His face was a little pale, but his eyes were shining.

"By the heavens, Mister Hazzard," he said, "you're true blue. When I get cleared of this mess, I'll do something that'll make you know what I think of you."

"I'll wait till that times comes," Hazzard said a little feebly. "Hold back till they're out of the house before you go down."

Fortune began to pace up and down the room. Still his step made not a sound more than the fall of a cat's paw, padded with velvet.

"I thought she'd crumple when they talked to her," he said more to himself than to the money-lender. "But she didn't. She's like you. All steel inside, no fear. Calm as oak, she was, Mister Hazzard. I wish you could've heard her talkin' to them. She offered them coffee and said that she was sorry they had to work in such cold weather."

"And coffee twenty-eight cents a pound," groaned Hazzard.

"What's that?"

"Nothing."

"They came near not going ahead with the search. But the sheriff made 'em go ahead. Then I slid upstairs. Mister Hazzard, it was a lucky thing for young Cochrane that he didn't open the door. Better for him to have turned loose a wildcat." He said it through his teeth, but quietly.

There was a snarl of determination in his voice that made Hazzard look at him again. Yes, this was the stuff of which murderers must be made, and, remembering the story that he had overheard the fugitive telling to Anne, he could not help smiling to himself. There was wit in this fellow, also. Wit enough to pull the wool over the eyes of a girl, at least. But he, Anthony Hazzard, was not made to think like a fool.

"They're gone," said the younger man suddenly, although the ear of Hazzard had not caught a sound of a closing door. "I'm going down to Anne to see how she's bucked up through it all. Ah, she's an ace of trumps."

CHAPTER
ELEVEN

Anthony Hazzard roused himself, at that, and followed down in the wake of Harry Fortune. He was in time through the door to see what Harry Fortune saw — that is to say — a picture of the girl lying collapsed in the chair with her head fallen back against the wall and her face white, her eyes half closed in exhaustion. Harry Fortune sprang to her.

"Anne! Anne!" he cried softly to her. "Are you ill?"

She smiled up to him with a sort of contentment, like a child in a sick bed. "They're gone at last," she said. "While they were upstairs, I more than died every five minutes. It was a fearful thing, Harry."

Hazzard went gloomily to the stove and stretched his hands over the warmth. Even if this man Fortune escaped and cleared himself of guilt, as he hoped to do, he would still be a burden in the mind of the money-lender, for he could undo great hopes by marrying the girl. Already there was love between them. Anthony Hazzard was too experienced a man not to understand the meaning of the foolish smiles that they gave to one another, the changing color, the trembling hands when they were near. It was love, and love portends mischief. What greater mischief could happen to Hazzard than the loss of his cook who worked for nothing?

He began to listen to their talk again.

"I am going out to do my best now," said Fortune. "Will you give me good luck, Anne?"

"The best there is in the world. The very best, Harry. But you must wait until they've ended the hunt."

"I'll go now. They've gone on with their hunt. Good bye, Anne."

She could not speak. She could only wring his hand. So he waved to the money-lender and was gone, clapping his hat on his head, huddling the coat around his shoulders. When he opened the kitchen door, the gale stopped and staggered him, but he leaned into it at once and strode away, like a man strong in body and in mind.

When he reached the woodshed, he paused to survey his position. He was behind the line of houses on that side of the village. From the kitchen windows, hazy lamplight showed behind the whitened glass, like so many glazed, blind eyes. He need fear no outlook from these. In fact, even if they caught a glimpse of him with his wide-brimmed hat pulled down over his face and with the snow spotting him, how could they know him? He might even be taken for one of the hunters who searched for him at this time.

So he held down behind the houses until he came to an old, low-shouldered house surrounded by naked poplars whose stems and pointing branches were strongly outlined in white. Here he turned in. At the kitchen door he bowed his head to listen. What he heard first was the familiar, deep voice of Mrs. Keene, and then the clattering of pans at the sink and the rush of water from a groaning hot-water faucet. But presently:

"I'm goin' upstairs," said Mrs. Keene. "You watch the oven. You'd better baste the turkey in about ten minutes."

He heard the cheerful voice of Nora Keene answer, and then the heavy step of the mother of the household departing. After that, he risked what chance there was that still another person might be there and tapped at the kitchen door. He heard Nora come singing to answer that knock. When she opened it, it was as though a midday ghost stood before her. He had to take her under the elbows and hold her firmly to keep her from falling, saying all the time, softly and rapidly: "I've not come to do you harm, Nora. There's nothing to be afraid about."

Her strength came back to her as suddenly as it had gone. She backed away from him toward the door, step by faltering step, watching him with hunted eyes.

"I won't keep you from goin'," he told her. "And I can't make you stay, unless you stay of your own free will."

So, with her hand on the knob of the door that led to the next room, she paused, with the question fighting in her eyes. Fear made her clutch the knob, but curiosity and the imp of the perverse would not let her turn it. Then, suddenly, she came back to him and stood squarely in front of him.

201

"I'm *not* afraid," she said, more as though she wished to convince herself than to assure him.

He smiled a little at that. "You see, Nora, I'm not the same man you sent away to prison. I'm not so wild, eh?"

"I think you're not, Harry," she said. "You look a lot different. You look sadder . . . heaven forgive me. And . . . and wiser, Harry."

"I hope I am, a mite."

"Oh, Harry, how you must have been hating me all of these years."

He was able to shake his head and smile again. "Only at first."

"Really?" she asked.

"When I first got inside the walls, every time I seen stone instead of sky over me, I used to hate you pretty hot, Nora. Afterwards, when I got some sense, I began to understand."

"Understand what?"

"That second man . . . whoever he was . . . was a gent you was pretty fond of at that time. You couldn't tell the truth without hangin' him. That was it, wasn't it?"

She did not answer. She merely grew a little whiter, staring at him. "Maybe it was, Harry," she said at last. "I'm . . . I'm not talking before a judge, now."

"What you say to me would never be believed by anybody else. Not if I was to tell it. Well, Nora, if that gent had really cared a pile for you, he'd've married you, wouldn't he? He wouldn't've waited all of these here years?"

She flushed, at that, and bit her lip.

"He *does* love me, Harry Fortune. But he's had a lot of bad luck. And just when he was about to set the day, lately, his father had bad luck . . ."

"Does his father keep him?"

"Why . . ."

He went on readily, to make the way easier for her: "I understand. He's one of these educated gents. A doctor, or something like that. Their work starts late. They don't make money at first. Is that it?"

She shook her head.

"I can't talk about him, Harry. If I was to put you on his trail . . ."

"No, no," he protested. "Do you think that I'm out to do a murder? Not a bit. I'm not out for revenge, either. I've got no bitterness inside of me. All that I want is to have a chance to live my life. You see?"

She nodded. Still she watched him with fascinated eyes, as though she were seeing more than she could understand easily at a glance, as though her eyes were reading in a strange and fascinating book.

"Now," he said, "I've got a proposition to make to you, and to him, through you. Let him go right down to the sheriff and say . . . 'I'm the gent that done the killing. It wasn't Harry Fortune at all.' Let him do that. What d'you think will happen? Well, that killing took place a long time ago. The folks that were worked up about it then have near forgot it now. If the man steps out and takes the blame because he says that he doesn't want an innocent man to be hunted for a crime that he did, why, it'll stand pretty much in his favor. If he went to prison, it would only be for a short time."

"Two or three years . . . in prison . . . to come out as a . . . a convict!" cried Nora Keene. "How can you say *only* a short time in prison? I'd rather die than be in a penitentiary."

"That's what I thought," he admitted to her. "But right now I'm glad that I went. It was better than school. You have to learn there or else you got to go mad or die. But, Nora, there won't be trouble for him if he'd confess."

"Oh, Harry," she said, "I have no influence over him. I could never get him to do such a thing. He might except for . . ." She paused.

"Except for what?" he urged.

"Except that . . . the shooting was done from behind. He'd be ashamed to stand up and say that he shot from behind."

A faint flush spread over the face of Harry Fortune. "I'd been around this here town all of my life," he said heavily. "Folks knew that I didn't turn my back on a gent that was makin' trouble for me. I mostly went up and knocked at their front door and asked 'em out to a finish fight. But when the time come, there was twelve men and a judge to say nothing of the rest, that believed that I was a sneakin' murderer that shot a man in the back. But if I was out of prison, I wouldn't keep no malice. It ain't worthwhile to hate a man. Just to know him is enough. Well, I know a few folks better because I was tried for 'em or in front of 'em. Nora, I tell you that a man good enough for you to love is good

204

enough to have sweated because I was servin' his time in jail for him. And that man, when you put it up to him, will be mighty glad to do that much for you and for himself and for me. He'll be willing to risk a few years behind the bars for the sake of being able to call himself a white man the rest of his life. After it's over, you'll thank heaven that you got him to do it."

She would only shake her head.

"You're not going to even try it, Nora?"

"Oh, I'm going to try," she said almost wearily. "I'm going to try, but it won't be no good. He won't listen to me. He goes his own way . . . he goes his own way and runs things to suit himself."

"By the heavens!" he cried with a little start of anger. "What sort of a gent are you aimin' to marry, Nora? A spunk that would shoot another man in the back and that would let another man hang for it?"

She bit her lip.

"I'm sorry, Nora," he said at last. He even was able to smile, finally, as he went to her and took her hand. "Oh, it's all right," he said cheerfully. "I trusted a lot to this last throw of the dice. But now I've lost, I'll forget it."

She clung to his hand with both of hers. "But what'll you do? Will you go on south? Will you go into Mexico, Harry?"

He shook his head, saying: "There's something that means more than my life. I've got to stay near this town."

"But that . . . oh, Harry, my heart it breaking for you . . . I hate myself . . . I'm a bad woman. But I love him, Harry. Will you try to forgive me?"

"I've forgiven you already," he said gently. "I've learned to face the music. If I have to go back to it . . . I'm going to manage to stand it."

A step came down the back stair, and, waving a hasty farewell to her, he slipped through the door and closed it after him, in time to hear the strong voice of Mrs. Keene crying: "Nora, Nora! Ain't I been smelling something burning? It *can't* be that turkey!" Then: "Why, child, what are you crying about?"

Harry Fortune waited to hear no more. He blundered from the door through a thick drift of snow, waded into better going, and turned the corner of the house in time to meet a whirl of snow dust borne on the arms of a hurricane of wind. So thick was that driving cloud that he did not see a man who, struggling down the street toward the Keene house, marked Fortune at the back of the building. Neither did he know that, as he went on, the other was following stealthily, from covert to covert, until the trailer saw Harry Fortune come, at last, to the back door of the money-lender's house, saw it opened instantly in answer to his knock, and saw him disappear in the lamplit interior of the kitchen.

CHAPTER
TWELVE

When the outlaw had left the house of the money-lender, his late host drew a breath of the most profound relief.

"Oh, Uncle Anthony," he heard his niece say, "how I pray that Harry Fortune will get what he wants."

Uncle Anthony merely grinned.

"When they saw him . . . when they looked into his honest, brave eyes," said Anne Hazzard, "how could the judge and the jury ever dream that he had shot a man in the back?"

"Judges and juries have a fair amount of sense," her uncle said without emotion.

"But you think Harry will win?"

"I think nothin'," said the money-lender, "about what don't concern me, and, if you got a head on your shoulders, you'll do the same thing. All I know is that he's gone . . . and that, if he'd been found here, they'd've sent me to prison for protecting an outlawed man. That's what I know. And if he . . ."

She broke in upon him. "If you knew how he felt about you, Uncle Anthony," she declared. "He says that he'd die for you . . . and he means it. He says that in the whole world there was only one man who has been kind to him . . . not any of his old friends or the people he knew well . . . but a stern man saved his life from the snow, and brought him home, and gave him . . ."

"Bah!" exclaimed Hazzard.

He expected to see her cringe under this explosion of bitter scorn and contempt. To his vast astonishment, she lifted her head and laughed in his face.

The money-lender recoiled a little. It was as though a lamb had put forth the claw of a tiger. His head fairly swam with bewilderment, and then rage began to grow hot in his heart. To be held lightly by a chit of a girl.

She went on: "Oh, Uncle Anthony, I've thought you were a grim man and a cruel man . . . really. But I don't think so any more. I know you, and poor Harry Fortune knows you."

Here there sounded a shrill, by no means uncertain voice from a basket in the corner of the room nearest to the stove. She ran to it and lifted out the white puppy — new washed, sparkling like snow — and straightway Jerry ambled across the room and strove vainly to crawl up the leg of Anthony Hazzard.

"You see? You see?" said the girl. "Jerry knows best of all. It was Jerry who showed us the truth about you. Jerry wasn't afraid. God bless him, he knew how much kindness there was in you and . . ."

"Damnation!" growled out Anthony Hazzard. "D'you expect me to stand here and listen to such tommyrot, while . . . ?"

Behold, she laughed again, happily. "It doesn't make a bit of difference what you say," she declared. "The proofs are all against you, Uncle Anthony. They're all

208

against you. Oh, you may pretend that you don't care a whit for Christmas, and such things, but I've seen today that your heart is full of Christmas every day of the year, and full of kindness and trueness and tenderness . . . and . . . and . . . it makes my whole soul ache to think that other people don't understand as Harry and Jerry and I do."

He reeled before this flood of bewildering nonsense. But there was still more. She ran to him and threw her soft arms around his neck. Her kiss touched each of his hard, weather-drawn cheeks.

"Dear Uncle Anthony," she said.

Dear Uncle Anthony was speechless. He felt that his dignity had fled. He felt that the armor of his grimness had been pierced in many mortal places. He turned on his heel, shook her off, and fairly fled from the room. And upstairs he went and began to pace back and forth.

After all, perhaps it was better this way; anything that might lull the suspicions of the outlaw so that, when he returned, he would be sure to stay while Hazzard hurried to the sheriff and brought that worthy. Truly there would be no delay after Harry Fortune came again. Straight to the sheriff with the tidings — afterward the reward money would pass into his treasure trove. It would be a happy day, after all. This Christmas he would remember. But, in the meantime, he had better go back to the kitchen so as to know the instant that Fortune came.

He acted on the thought and hastened back — hastened back to arrive at the very instant that Harry

Fortune opened the back door and stood there in a flurry of snow, looking like a giant spirit of the storm. Then the outlaw strode in, took off his hat, and shook the snow from it on the floor.

"Oh, Harry . . . ," began the girl hopefully.

But there needed only a single glance at his face to understand that he had failed. Her voice died away. She made a hopeless gesture while she stared at him. Yes, it was very apparent that she loved this man, very apparent that, if Uncle Anthony wished to keep his free cook, he had better remove Fortune to the safety of steel bars and a world of stone cells.

"I missed," said Fortune calmly. "I've come to say good bye."

"Harry, Harry!" cried the girl in a broken voice. "You can't have tried everything in these few minutes. There must be some other hope."

"There's no other hope," he said. "When I . . . ah, what's that?"

The wind had been shrieking and raging and beating at the window with great soft white-moth wings of snow; now it fell away, leaving the window heavily clotted. Through the momentary lull in the noise they heard a voice outside saying: "This way! He went in here! I saw him!"

Other voices murmured an answer — many voices of men.

"Ten thousand damnations!" gasped out the money-lender. "They've come again. If they search this time . . . Fortune, get out of the room . . . hide . . . hide . . . for heaven's sake . . ."

210

A heavy hand fell on the door. Fortune vanished into the front of the house.

"Who's there?" asked Hazzard.

"In the name of the law," called the voice of the sheriff, "open this door, Hazzard!"

He cast a glance at the girl. She was white and stricken in the corner.

"Get that fool look off your face!" snarled out Hazzard to her. "They're not going to get in. Not till I've given Harry Fortune time to get out of the house." He set the door ajar, and, stepping back, he placed himself near the double-barreled shotgun that leaned against the wall.

The sheriff pressed in. Half a dozen keen-eyed men followed him.

"Hazzard," said the sheriff, "you have Harry Fortune in this house. The door was opened to him . . . he was seen to come in."

When lies and reason fail us, we fall back upon passion.

"By the heavens!" cried Hazzard. "I've had enough of this fooling. Do you think that I'll have my house searched a dozen times a day for a gent that I never seen in my life?" He caught the shotgun from the wall. His lean right hand gripped the trigger guard and the triggers. The barrel rested in the hollow of his left arm. So he swung the muzzles and controlled them. "Keep back and get out of the house!" he thundered at them. "I been bothered enough. Ain't a man got a right to a little privacy . . . on Christmas Day?"

The others shrank a little. But the sheriff was too accustomed to looking death in the face even on sterner occasions than this. He merely shook his head and smiled. "That's a good bluff, Hazzard," he said. "Lemme tell you that, if you give up the man now, maybe it won't go so hard with you, but if . . ."

"Man? What man?" shouted Hazzard. "I'll give you till I count ten before . . ."

"You old hard-faced rat!" snarled out the sheriff, his fighting blood getting the better of his calm. "Put down that gun or I'll sink a chunk of lead into you. Put it down! If the man ain't here, why is the girl sittin' in a corner lookin' as white as a sheet?"

"Keep your hand away from your gun!" answered Hazzard. "I give you warning, Sheriff, keep your hand away from your gun, or I'll . . ."

A door yanked behind him. A draft of wind played coldly on his back.

"It's no use, Mister Hazzard," said Harry Fortune. "I'm not worth it. Sheriff, I surrender freely. This is no fault of Hazzard's. I forced him at the point of a gun to give me shelter."

"You forced him to take a shotgun and stand us off, eh?" growled out the sheriff. "What the devil has got into the old man? I'll have both of you along with me. You can think this here over in the jail, Hazzard. Grab them, boys!"

They tore the shotgun from the numbed fingers of Hazzard. He could only groan to his unwelcome guest: "You coward, Fortune."

212

But Fortune merely smiled at him. "Do you think that I'd turn man killer for the sake of getting free, Mister Hazzard?"

"Harry!" cried a wailing voice from the corner of the room. "Harry!"

"Steady, Anne," answered the fugitive quietly. "It's all in the day's work. I took my chance and lost it. It had to be this way, in the end. Maybe the sooner the better."

"Busy with the womenfolks, Fortune?" asked the sheriff sneeringly. "Watch old Hazzard, boys. He's got the devil in his eyes."

"We'll mind him," they said.

Another voice rose in the room — the voice of Jerry, high and piping with wrath and grief, for a careless hand had overturned his basket and spilled him out on the floor. The last that Anthony Hazzard saw as he was pushed through the doorway was the picture of Anne lifting the little dog and cradling it in her arms, weeping over it, still striving to comfort it out of the excess of her own grief. Until, at the last, it thrust its cold nose under her chin and against the warmth of her throat and hushed its crying.

Then Hazzard was in the outer cold of the storm. He went as one in a daze. Ah, what fools were all the men of the world that they should presume that he, Anthony Hazzard, would defend an outlawed man with a price on his head against the arms of justice. Yet they believed it. How could he explain to them that what they considered a defense had been merely a trap to catch the very man they wanted?

Ah, he said to himself, *they do not wish to understand. All they know is that, at last, they have caught me.*

CHAPTER
THIRTEEN

For what could have been more logical than that, since he despised all other men, all other men should hate him? Hate him they did, as he had often received the proofs. Only one thing kept most of them from showing their utter detestation, and that was the fear that, someday, they might have a need of him — or rather, of his money. On account of this fear, they were forced to keep their anger within bounds. But now that he was helpless in a prison, they would show their rage.

He prepared for it with mingled rage and scorn — rage because it seemed that here in the end, for a mere nothing, the work of his life had been balked and brought to a small conclusion. Not that the millions of his fortune were really nothing, but they were as nothing compared to the giant thoughts that had been brooding in him, growing from year to year as his fortune grew. For every mile that he walked, he dreamed of a vaster journey stretching ahead. Now he had millions, indeed. His hand was everywhere along the range. His mortgages extended through some of the finest properties in the mountains. Lumber lands, cattle lands, mining properties were included in the varied extent of his interests. And here and there, when the proper times came, he was striking home, crushing the weak, drawing in their lands. Every $1,000 that he made made him greedy of $10,000. If God spared his life for a few more years, might not his millions stretch to tens and even hundreds of millions? Far cities might feel the force of his energy. The thought born in the barren little room in the wretched little house in this Western village might cause Wall Street on a day to quake to its nethermost foundations.

Such were the dreams of the good Anthony Hazzard as he sat bowed on his cot in the damp cell where he was confined. It was not a modern jail — one main cell room, with the cells partitioned off, merely, with tool-proofed steel. But each cell was a separate room, walled, floored, and ceilinged of massive rock. A little window, six inches square, pierced his outer wall and gave him a dull shaft of light that made the dank dreariness of his chamber visible — and no more.

After he had been there for a time, Tom Curtin, the jailkeeper and cook, combined, brought him food — a plate of stew, half cold, covered with congealed grease, a few thick slices of stale bread, and a big tin cup of coffee.

He was not hungry. But it occurred to him that if he did not eat, they of the outer world would attribute his loss of appetite to the effects of terror. He disdained such a thought. They were no more to him than so many terriers barking at his heels. The majestic striding of his thoughts they were incapable of following.

Here there was a sharp, small voice — it brought him out of his ponderings with a start. But it reminded him of the voice of Jerry, squeaking a sleepy protest. This, however, was only a rat. He began to eat his clammy dinner; after all, it would have been a shame to allow good food to go to waste. He might need strength. With proper care of himself he would outlast the prison term they imposed upon him. With proper care, men lived on to advanced ages. Yes, if he were now sixty-five, he might go on to an age of ninety. Then, suppose that he spent five years in prison — there still remained before him a glorious stretch of twenty years remaining. His fortune would have grown slowly while he was confined. When he issued forth, he would be equipped like a giant to multiply his millions. He would have evolved many great schemes in the five years of solitude and thought.

Another rat squeak came from the wall. But what would become of Anne? While her uncle and while Harry Fortune went to prison, the girl would be turned loose in the world with only a dog for her sole possession. She need expect no support from him. It would be good for her to find how the world treats single women with no fortune, saving their wits. But Jerry, in the meantime, would grow up and be a companion to her.

Very odd, though, how the little tike had from the first instant preferred his master to his mistress. Mr. Hazzard looked down to his boots up which the puppy had mainly striven to crawl. After all, beasts have wise instincts. They know strength where they see it — even strength of mind.

Tom Curtin came back for the dishes and found them eaten empty and cleaned with the bread. Not a scrap remained. "You ain't had much Christmas dinner at home," he commented. "Well, there's gonna be trouble on account of you this here day. I don't mind tellin' you that the boys are up, and the sheriff is mighty worried."

"About what?"

"Havin' a jail mobbed . . . is that good for a sheriff? Havin' a jail mobbed to get at you?"

He went on out, leaving Anthony Hazzard to reflect over this wonder. What had he done so evil that men should wish to take him out by mob force and lynch him? He began to reflect seriously.

After all, people took very much to heart certain things that he had accomplished. When widows and helpless children are beggared — yes, they take these things very much to heart. Now, in a passion, who could tell what they would not do? For a mob is a headless beast. It does not use reason.

He heard them gathering, after a time. Then voices came through the falling storm. The sheriff had gone out in front of the jail.

"I tell you, boys," Hazzard heard him saying, "you'll be trying a fool thing. And some of you will get hurt bad if you start it. Hurt mighty bad. I mean business pure and simple. I tell you to keep out and let the law take its course."

"I'll tell you, Sheriff," said a thunderous voice in reply, "that we want him and we're gonna have him. You can't keep him in there. Not on this day!"

218

"I *will* keep him," said the sheriff, "until he answers . . ."

"Bah!" exclaimed the other. "Boys, do you want old Hazzard?"

"We do!" they shouted.

That shout made even the stern soul of Anthony Hazzard quake, for it seemed to come from scores of voices, as though every man in the village had turned out for this occasion. How bitterly they hated him, then, to brave the rigors of the winter storm and leave their warm Christmas fires for the sake of their vengeance. No doubt, since his capture, they had been rehearsing all that they considered his crimes, his legal crimes, his cold acts of extortion, as they would call them.

He smiled to himself. After all, when the time came, they should find that he was not wanting in courage to meet whatever they should do to him. But, alas, that all his giant schemes should be stifled with his life by a crowd of ignorant yokels.

"Hal Stewart!" shouted the sheriff. "Keep back, or . . ."

"Damn keeping back! Boys, here's where we start!"

There was a wild yell of joy, the sound of rushing men, the curses of the sheriff, and then a storm of noise broke into the interior of the jail itself. Not a shot had been fired by the sheriff — by mere weight of human poundage Anthony Hazzard was to be lost. Not a blow in his behalf. *Ah,* he thought, *to be young and free and armed again . . . then I would have taught them what it*

219

was to corner a lion. He would have made them run like whipped dogs.

Now the flood of the noise beat around an inner door. They had caught up something for a battering-ram. They dashed the door down — they crashed into his cell.

Big men loomed before him.

"Hey, Hazzard!" they shouted through the semidark. "Is this here you?"

"I am Anthony Hazzard," he said with the dignity befitting one who was about to die.

Large, mighty hands were laid upon him. The force of those cruel fingers crushed through his thin, soft muscles and ground his nerves against the bones. He was caught up, dragged forth, and brought to the outer light. There had not been room in the jail for all of the units of that crowd. Out yonder were all the men of the village. All the men, yes, and it seemed that most of the women were here, also, covered with coats, shawls wrapped around their heads. He had never dreamed that there was such fierceness in the feminine heart. Yet, after all, were they not secret tigers, selfish, relentless?

Those who had captured him forced him through the doorway.

"We've got him!" they called.

The enormous throat of Lew Saylor opened wide and his vast voice thundered across the crowd above all their clamoring. "Gents and ladies," he said, "we been sittin' at home talkin' about Christmas, and thinkin' about Christmas, and givin' each other popguns and handkerchiefs, and, while we was gettin' ready to fill

220

our stomachs, here was a gent that was ready to lay down his life for the sake of another man. While we was talkin' about gifts and kindness, we was tryin' to hunt down that other man for the sake of the price on his head. But Anthony Hazzard, he took him in out of the cold and brung back his life, and then he stood up for him with a gun in his hand. We got Christmas in our talk . . . Anthony Hazzard, he had it in his heart!"

They shouted again. They swarmed closer to Hazzard. They reached out their hands to him. And he saw, suddenly, through a golden haze of wonder, that there was no fierceness in those faces, but joy and kindness. This was no lynching party, but a Christmas frolic!

A voice of authority shouted: "We'll take him home! We'll take him back to his house! If the law would put a man like Hazzard in prison, we'll bust the law to pieces!"

Who was that who dared to speak thus? It was none other than that cold-faced man who had never given him so much as a kindly glance in his life. It was none other than the great Van Zant himself. So, shouting, waving their hats, regardless of the snow that whirled into their faces, they bore him down the street in high triumph.

"Here's the sheriff!" someone called.

He came hastily through their ranks.

"I'm with you, boys!" he cried to them. "This here is Christmas. I'll leave him in your custody for today, but tomorrow he must answer to the law."

Thereby, 10,000 votes were won for the sheriff on his next election day.

On they went. Women darted into their homes as they passed and came out again, bearing covered things in their hands. They poured on down the street, slowly, for everyone was jumping and dancing and shouting at once. They reached Hazzard's house. They surged around to the back door. They crashed the door open and there stood Anne Hazzard, white and frightened before them, with a whining little white dog in her arms that straightway stiffened and began to bark defiance.

To Anne Hazzard they gave her uncle. And they poured in behind him. Suddenly upon the tables and even on the window sills appeared great slabs of roast turkey, mince pies, dishes of fruit, and a score of dainties and scarlet cranberries in transparent molds.

What hands were these that reached to him, that wrung his cold, nerveless fingers, that beat upon his back? What beaming, happy faces were these? What voices that thundered good wishes to his ears?

The very end of the world had come to Anthony Hazzard. All his old opinions were falling dead and in ruins around him. For it seemed, after all, that these men of the outer world were more kind than stupid, more warm of heart than slow of brain.

CHAPTER
FOURTEEN

Through that crowded doorway another face and another voice came and made itself heard.

"I want the sheriff. Where is the sheriff?"

He struggled through the mass and came to her. It was Nora Keene, trembling with excitement, with anger, and with grief.

"What's wrong, Nora?" he asked her. "What's happened?"

"I don't know, yet," she answered. "I don't know. I hope to heaven that it ain't as bad as I suspect. But I want to know from you. Where's Sam Crawford? Is he here, too?"

"I'm here," Sam Crawford said from a far corner where he stood, taking no part in the festivities around him.

"Come here, Sam," said the girl. "Come here! I want you to stand in front of the sheriff. I want to have you hear me ask him some questions."

Sam came, reluctant, down-faced.

A sudden silence began to pass through the room, like a palpable wave. All faces turned to this new scene.

"Sheriff, you found Harry Fortune here."

"I sure did. No thanks to Hazzard, though, that I got him in the bag."

"But somebody came to you and told you that Harry was here?"

"That's right, of course. I can't be everywhere and see everything for myself."

"But I only want to know . . . was the man that told you this Sam Crawford?"

The sheriff looked down at her with a puzzled frown, and Sam Crawford suddenly changed color and slipped away through the crowd — unnoticed, so keen was the interest of the girl, so intense was her excitement, as she faced the sheriff.

"I dunno," said the man of the law, "what difference it makes *who* told me, because the main thing is that we got Mister Harry Fortune again. And we got him safe behind bars."

"You don't understand," she said. "Oh, it makes all the difference in the world . . . all the difference in the world. Sheriff, tell me quickly . . . who told you where you could find Harry Fortune?"

"Why," said the sheriff, bewildered, "I dunno that there's a fault in telling you that. The point is that we got Harry Fortune, so you might as well know who gave him to us. The gent that gets half of the reward is Sam Crawford, since you want to know."

She closed her eyes and, fumbling behind her, found the wall and leaned against it. "I knew it," she said, still with her eyes closed. "I guessed it. I guessed it. Oh, there was never such a sneak . . . such a traitor . . . such a coward in the world. And I'm done with him. I've cut

224

my care for him out of my heart. I'll . . . I'll never look into his face again."

"Sam Crawford?" repeated the sheriff mildly. "Why, Nora, what makes such a difference to you because Sam told me?"

"I'll tell you, then!" she exclaimed. "Sam should have hung for the thing that sent poor Harry to prison. Sam should have hung for it. Oh, heaven forgive me for keeping back what I always knew. But when a man like Anthony Hazzard would risk his life for the sake of Harry, why should I care for the shame when people know that I've lied . . . and lied . . . and sent Harry to prison with my lie?"

Only two people moved in the room. One was the sheriff who started back a little, and the other was Anne Hazzard, who drew slowly forward, fascinated, toward the narrator.

"Nora," said the sheriff, and his voice was a mere gasp of breath, "don't you see what you're sayin'?"

"Tell me what, then?"

"You're practically sayin' that Sam Crawford killed young Marberry five years back when . . ."

"And I mean just that!"

The sheriff gaped at her.

"You all laughed . . . laughed like fools . . . when Harry Fortune told about another man that had run away after the shooting. Why, if you'd had brains, if you'd had sense, you'd have known that a man like Harry Fortune wouldn't've shot even a dog through the back. He'd face a lion . . . he would have faced a lion then. But there was another man that didn't have the heart. It was Sam. I'll tell you everything. I want everybody to see the shame in me. Oh, I want folks to know that I got the courage to do with my pride what Anthony Hazzard done with his life . . . throw it away willingly to keep poor Harry from harm. I sent him to prison. I'll take him out of it."

"Wait, Nora," said the sheriff. "This'll have to be wrote down . . . and we want Sam . . . where's Sam?"

He was gone. Some keen foresight had given him an intimation of what was coming. And he had fled. Half a dozen willing volunteers rushed in pursuit of him, but the sheriff was not among them. His duty kept him there to hear word by word the first of that strange confession of the girl.

"I was engaged to Sam," said Nora Keene, facing them with doubled hands as she strove to key up her courage to *the sticking point*. "And we kept it secret . . . then, and all these years. First, because we weren't ready for marrying. Afterward, because he didn't love me any more, I suppose, but he was afraid to break off the promise in case I'd afterward tell what I knew. But I'm telling it now, and I hope to heaven that justice comes on him." She paused for a moment, closing her eyes. Then: "That night there had been a dance and poor young Marberry had paid me a lot of attention. Sam sulked and told me I was cutting him. But I kept right on, and finally I told Marberry that he could take me home. He did, and, at my gate, Sam joined us. He had words with Marberry and me. I told him in a huff that I didn't care what he thought about me. Marberry would have hit him, but Sam backed down and showed yellow. But after I'd gone up to the porch, I looked back and saw Sam pull out a gun behind Marberry and shoot him through the head. Then Harry Fortune came running up . . . and . . . and afterward I couldn't tell the truth. That's all I have to say. But, oh, the coward, the cur, to have turned on Harry Fortune again today, and send him back for the thing he did himself. And heaven bless Anthony Hazzard for teaching us how to do something for other folks."

She turned back toward the door. They made way for her in silence. Then two older women came to her side and threw a cloak around her and so led her away toward her home. She left behind her a dull silence that was finally broken by the sheriff, saying: "Boys, it looks like this here mess was gonna turn out better than we thought. Looks like we owe a lot to poor Harry Fortune. And the first thing that we can do is to turn him free. I'm going back to the jail now. Does anybody go with me?"

They came instantly, in a swarm. The house was emptied from top to bottom. In the waves went Anthony Hazzard, drawn along against his will. But he could not be left out of the ceremony. He had become the most necessary man in it, for the nonce. The sheriff himself walked beside him.

"A good thing for Harry Fortune that you live in this here town, Mister Hazzard. That was a fine thing, as I'm here to state, when you stood off the bunch of us. I'll say, free and easy, that I wouldn't've chanced walkin' into the mouth of that shotgun . . . what's that?"

Someone crowding through the door had jarred against the kitchen stove, and there was a great rattling. But they came on through and out of the house and flooded in great excitement through the street.

"Mister Hazzard, now that I have the first chance to speak to you I want to . . ."

It was the Congressman, Mr. Alexander Elkin, a famous rancher, a famous fighter, a clean-lived, strong-minded politician. He had come up on the other side of Anthony Hazzard and was pouring forth what lay in his heart.

"I want to tell you what it has meant to me. The whole story that Harry Fortune told after he got to the jail . . . of how you found him in the snow . . . brought him home . . . fed and revived him . . . and what we know of how you would have fought for him . . . why, sir, one story such as that is enough to turn all of our young men into generous-minded heroes. Really. For my own part, I want to thank you, Mister Hazzard, for the way in which this thing has filled my heart. I hope that the lesson you have taught me and all of us on this Christmas Day will never leave me. I hope it brings some good action out of my life. And . . ."

But here a universal clamoring drowned his voice as the crowd's foremost ranks reached the jail. He could only take the already bruised hand of the money-lender and wring it.

Anthony Hazzard, looking down at his hand, looked down on his heart, also. And what he saw was stranger than all else that had happened. For he felt that all his money, multiplied 10,000 times, could never have

228

bought for him a thing so precious as this overflowing of kindness and love from all about him. It had been strange food for his soul at first, and he had been moved to scorn and almost to laughter by it. But now that emotion changed. He felt, instead, that for the first time in many, many years — perhaps the first time in his life — his very soul had been awakened. Now that it was roused, now that it looked about through his eyes, like a new-created god in man, what did he desire most of all? Not that his millions should be increased, but only that he had a just claim upon the outpouring of affection that surrounded him.

The jail doors were opened again; arrangements would be made to secure Fortune's pardon. Here was Harry Fortune coming out with a radiant face. There was Anne Hazzard meeting her lover with unshamed joy in the face of all the crowd — ah, how merry a Christmas Day for all saving only Anthony Hazzard himself, who was looked upon by all the rest as the very mainspring of all the happiness. No time for meetings and congratulations now, but he felt one thrilling touch of joy. At least, out of the sham of this day's accomplishment, there would be one concrete termination — and that would be the marriage of Anne and Harry Fortune. God be praised for that one thing.

Then a rumor — then a loud, clear shouting rushed upon the crowd. "Fire! Fire! Fire!"

Whose house? It was Anthony Hazzard's house. He, and perhaps one other man, might have remembered the rattling noise of the jarred kitchen stove. From that accident, perhaps — but who could tell? The sweet

229

nothings that had filled his brain suddenly vanished. The keen, cold wind of reality rushed over his soul. Yonder was the mounting cloud of smoke, every instant swelling, and within the grip of the flames lay $20,000 in hard cash! He began to run like a youthful athlete.

CHAPTER
FIFTEEN

When they reached the house it was plain that it was utterly doomed. No bucket line could ever feed water into the place fast enough to extinguish even a corner of the fire. Fanned by a thousand little drafts, the flames had already run over the lower floor of the building and every window was black with smoke or brilliant with leaping red tongues. Harry Fortune tried to run forward. Half a dozen strong men threw themselves upon him and nailed him to the snow.

"It's no use, Harry. We know what you'd like to do for Hazzard, so does he, but, whatever you do, don't throw yourself into the fire for nothing. Look there!"

The house was very old, built of dry wood, and the flames had scoured quickly along the rotten moldings. Now a stroke of the heavy wind, pressing against the door, tore it from the jamb that the fire had half rotted away. It fell in with a noise drowned in the yelling of the gale, and exposed a dark interior of the hallway, quivering with flames.

"Look what would have happened to you, Fortune."

"It's Anne's dog," said Harry Fortune, still struggling against those strong hands. "It'll break her heart if it's not gotten out."

"If there's a dog in there, it's dead already."

Dogs, dogs — they could talk of dogs when in his own room neatly stowed in the little case, $20,000! He broke into a run, skirted swiftly through the crowd, and, before his intention could be discerned and himself stopped, he had crossed the intervening space and was lost in the darkness of the hallway.

Not darkness, either, for the gloom was half deepened with smoke and half relieved with flickering lights from the flames. But the fire itself was not half so dreadful as he had expected. Outside, he heard the wild yell of the crowd.

"Come back, Hazzard! Come back!"

Cowards and fools — while a small fortune, worth the price of all their heads, consumed to ashes in his own room? He sped up the stairs. To his horror, the fire was already there. All the way up the red hands reached for him, seared his face, clutched at his body. If he had only had the foresight to dash water over himself.

But it was too late to pause for that. He reached his door and cast it open. A great cloud of smoke rolled sullenly forth into his face, like a great spirit beating him back. He sank, gasping to the floor, more than half throttled. But the air near the floor was fresher. He crawled ahead. He reached for the chest of drawers in which his treasure was secreted — and his hand encountered smooth, soft fur.

Jerry was there!

A stroke of awe and of terror fell upon Anthony Hazzard. For although he could understand that the flames and the smoke might have driven the little dog up the stairs, it was strange that it should have managed to get into his room. Suppose that, having reached the room, the wind had blown the door to behind him, still, what made Jerry crouch just before the treasure of Hazzard?

The puppy came crawling to him, gasping, but wagging its tail, and tried, again, to crawl up his leg. He sent it, head over heels, the length of the room away from him. His business was with $20,000, not with a morsel of dog flesh. He tore open the drawer and brought out the little box, but as he turned to flee with it, a staggering little white thing limped toward him across the floor.

Anthony Hazzard cast a hand before his eyes to shut out the sight of it and cried out in a wild voice. Then he dropped the box, he caught up Jerry, and ran to the window. A blow of his fist beat out the pane. He leaned above the crowd and what a shout rose and rang in his ears. He had a glimpse of a sky in fierce tumult, and one low-winging cloud that seemed to be driven straight toward his face. This he saw as he held the puppy straight out before him by the scruff of his neck. Half a dozen men instantly stripped off their coats and held them out like baskets to catch the prize. Yonder was Anne Hazzard, running swiftly toward the spot.

He dropped Jerry and saw it safely caught. Then he turned to find the box. But a great red arm of fire was flung out before him. He recoiled. A dozen teeth of flame sank into his flesh. He started again, and again the fire rose like a spirit before him. Still a third time he lunged forward and this time he managed to catch up the box and, whirling, started for the door. But as he turned, a part of the fire-crumbled ceiling sagged and fell.

He sprang away. He could see clearly by the flame lights; he could think clearly. He could hear the roar of the flames and the overtones of the winds that screamed, rejoicing, around the house. He seemed to know that it was the hand of God that was striking him down, after three warnings to leave the money behind him.

This was death; this was the end. Some men said that, in dying, they saw all their lives before them like pictures brightly painted. But his life had been money, and he saw nothing of that now. He saw only the face of Anne Hazzard and of Harry Fortune as they had been raised to him in the crowd, and the fall of Jerry to safety.

I am getting old and weak-minded, said Anthony Hazzard to himself. *This is certainly no time for such nonsense.* But in spite of himself, he smiled, and his heart was content. *Jerry*, he said to himself, *will miss his first master.* That was the last thought of Hazzard.

A groan from Hazzard, as he struggled back toward consciousness, was the guide for the sheriff and Harry Fortune. For, when the money-lender did not appear at once after Jerry had been dropped, they had made for the flamechoked door of the house together. Now they heaved the solid beams and the litter of slats and plaster aside. They reached Hazzard, and Harry Fortune lifted him like a child, then down the stairs and out into the

234

sacred coldness of that day while the whole roof crashed in and cast out a huge circle of smoke, streaked through with flying sparks.

A flying timber knocked down Harry Fortune with his burden. It was the Congressman and the sheriff who picked it up. They carried Anthony Hazzard into the nearest house; they leaned above him like mothers over a sick child until he opened his eyes.

"How's Jerry?" asked the money-lender.

"I told you," whispered Anne Hazzard, and placed the dog in the hollow of his arm.

SPEEDY'S BARGAIN

Frederick Faust's saga of the youthful hero Speedy began with "Tramp Magic", a six-part serial in *Western Story Magazine*, which appeared in the issues dated November 21, 1931 through December 26, 1932. As most of Faust's continuing characters, Speedy is a loner, little more than a youngster, able to outwit and outmaneuver even the deadliest of men without the use of a gun. He appeared in a total of nine stories. The serial has been reprinted by Leisure Books under the title *Speedy*. The first short story, "Speedy — Deputy", can be found in *Jokers Extra Wild* (Five Star Westerns, 2002); "Seven-Day Lawman" can be found in *Flaming Fortune* (Five Star Westerns, 2003); "Speedy's Mare" appears in *Peter Blue* (Five Star Westerns, 2003); "The Crystal Game" in *The Crystal Game* (Five Star Westerns, 2005); "Red Rock's Secret" in *Red Rock's Secret* (Five Star Westerns, 2006). "Speedy's Bargain" was originally published in *Western Story Magazine* in the issue dated May 14, 1932.

CHAPTER
ONE

Cort swept in his winnings and collected the cards to deal again, when his companion shook his head, pushed back his chair, and stood up with a *jingle* of spurs.

"I'm busted," he said.

The concern that William Cort showed was entirely professional in its smoothness, but, like many experienced gamblers in the West, although he had not the slightest scruple in palming cards or running up a pack, he made it a practice to return some of the feathers whenever he had stripped a victim bare.

"Flat broke?" asked Cort. "Well then, take a twenty for luck," said Cort, pushing the money across the table.

His victim picked up the money, hesitated, and then put it down again. "My luck's out at cards," he explained, "and twenty dollars' worth of whiskey won't be good for my liver. Keep the coin, brother. I don't mind losing it, but the game was kind of short. That's the only trouble."

Cort picked up the money again with a graceful gesture of regret and glanced over the faces of those who were lingering in the corner of the saloon to watch the game.

"Anybody take a hand?" he asked. "Plenty of you to make up a game of poker," he added.

But Cort's manner was too calm and his hands were too long-fingered and well kept; the air of the professional gambler was clearly stamped upon him, and the men of San Lorenzo, Mexican and white, hesitated and then held back, although most people west of the Mississippi seem to regard an invitation to a card game like an invitation to a fight, something that must necessarily be accepted out of sheer manhood.

However, there was one fellow who accepted now. He was a slender youngster with dark, almost femininely expressive eyes, and he said: "I'll take a hand with you, stranger."

Cort looked up at him with a welcoming smile that turned almost at once into a look that was almost fear. Then he pushed back his own chair. "Matter of fact," he said, "I forgot that I haven't time to tackle a new game. But I'll buy you a drink, stranger, and play with you some other time."

The other went with him to the bar and asked for beer, a small one.

"Still the same old Speedy, eh?" said Cort. "Nothing strong enough to make the head dizzy, eh?"

Speedy did not start. He merely said: "You remember me, Cort, do you?"

"Remember you?" said Cort. "I'd be a fool to forget the hand you dealt yourself and a few more of us in Denver, that time. Oh, I know. You were wearing a

240

slightly different face, Speedy, that evening, but enough of you was showing through. After that night, I don't play with you, Speedy. I make my living out of cards. I don't aim to lose it."

Speedy raised his glass of beer and gravely regarded his companion over its foam. "Happy days," he said.

"And plenty of 'em," replied Cort.

They drank, and Cort went on: "How does it come that everybody in town doesn't follow you around, Speedy, on a day like this, when your man is going to be sentenced to death right here in San Lorenzo? They ought to be making a hero out of you."

"I'm not a hero," said Speedy calmly. "Besides, they've never seen me wearing a white skin, in San Lorenzo. I've always been a peon, when I was here before."

"I remember," remarked Cort. "I remember the whole yarn. You went up disguised with a scar on your face and got into the camp of Dupray and kidnapped that murdering scoundrel. I remember it all. It was a cool play, Speedy. A mighty cool play." From his own superior height, he looked over the smaller man with an air partly of pleasure and partly of admiration. "The judge will be sentencing Dupray in an hour or so, Speedy," he added. "Is that why you came to town?"

"That's one reason," said Speedy. "Not that I want to hear Dupray sentenced to be hanged by the neck until he's dead, dead, dead, but I want to see what happens afterward."

"What will happen?"

241

"I don't know. I'm just here to look on. It's not my show, now." He shrugged his shoulders. "How have things been using you, Bill?" he asked.

"I've been getting along fairly well," said Cort. "I haven't run into any young Speedy lately. That's one reason why I've had some success." He smiled a wry smile and squinted as he tried to probe the dim, calm shadows in the eyes of the other. "You never play cards except when you find an expert, Speedy. Even then, you never play until you're broke. But how does it happen that you're broke now?"

"Why shouldn't I be broke?" asked Speedy mildly.

"How could you be?" asked Cort. "You collected nearly two hundred thousand dollars' worth of loot out of Dupray, people say. And you let the same chunk of money go to the fellow who was with you. Wilson was his name, wasn't it? You don't mean to say that you've run through that much coin in a month?"

Speedy sighed and shook his head. "Every penny, Bill," he said. "And that's bad luck, isn't it?"

"Bad luck? It's the wildest luck that I've ever heard of, except at a gambling table. And you can't lose at cards and dice. You know how to make them talk French for you."

"Well," Speedy said, sighing again, "I must say, I thought that I'd never have to work again, when I collected that stake. But I was wrong. The luck was against me."

"What happened? Break into the stock market?" asked the gambler, his eyes twinkling with surprise and with an eager curiosity.

242

"No, not that. But I dropped half of it through a scheme a fellow had to buy up the dumps of some of the old mines and work them with a new process. It had to be done fast . . . buying up the old dumps, I mean to say. There was somebody else in the field, I was told, and we had to grab the best dumps quickly. So there was a lot of money to be advanced before the new process was put to work. After I'd put in a hundred thousand dollars . . . well, my man with the great ideas simply disappeared."

"The devil he did!" exclaimed Bill Cort. "And you on his trail, eh?"

"I didn't trail him," Speedy answered with a troubled frown. "After all, it was only money that I lost," he added.

"Only one hundred thousand dollars!" gasped Bill Cort. He hastily refilled his glass with whiskey and tossed off the stiff dram. Still he was blinking as he considered what had just been told him. There were other tales in the air, to be sure, and he had heard them many times — tales of how Speedy had been cheated over and over again by cunning charlatans with all sorts of schemes. But it did not seem credible that the man would let the cheats go free — this youngster who could follow a trail across the face of the world as easily as a hawk in the sky can follow the small birds far down closer to the ground.

"Well," said Bill Cort, "that accounts for half your money, but what became of the last half of it? Another get-rich-quick scheme?"

"Oh, no, not at all. Just a straight business proposition that would pay five or six percent only," Speedy replied. "It would have done some good, too. It was to put up a good hotel in the mountains, back there, where the air is the purest in the whole world, I guess. Then we'd put in a skilled physician and take only consumptives who were too poor to pay big rates. We'd just charge 'em actual expenses and five or six percent over to keep us running. It sounded like a good idea. There are plenty of sick people in towns who'd like to go to a place like that. And we had a good site in mind. My friend was to put in half, and I put in half, but I made my payment first." He paused and shook his head, adding: "You see, we had gone into partnership and either of us could sign checks. So after I'd made my deposit, he signed a check, drew out the whole shooting match, and disappeared. That was only the day before yesterday."

"The day before yesterday, eh?" murmured the gambler. "And you're not burning up the trail behind that hound?"

"Well," said Speedy, "I don't know. It would be a hard job to locate him, the yellow hound. Somehow, I didn't feel like starting out to rush all over the world after him. I might catch him some time."

"Otherwise, he gets off scotfree?"

"I suppose so."

"You beat me, Speedy," said the larger man, pushing his hat back on his head and then wiping his brow. "You beat me complete and entire. Here you are, a fellow who'll ride a thousand miles to get into a brawl of some sort or fight for somebody else, and yet you won't lift a finger to take care of your own affairs?"

"Well, there's a law in the country, isn't there?" asked Speedy. "It's supposed to take care of a man's private affairs, isn't it, Bill?"

There was something plaintive in his voice and the other grunted as though struck by the idea for the first time.

"You have me stopped, Speedy," he said. "I don't understand at all. I should think that you'd be on those slimy cheats like a hawk. You hound other fellows who get on the shady side of the law, now and then. A fellow like me who makes his living out of the cards . . . we have to watch you, Speedy. It cost me personally ten thousand dollars and more. Yes, more than ten grand for the privilege of sitting in at a game with you for one evening." He groaned. "But where your own business comes in, you let the first fly-by-night little crook get away with it, bag and baggage."

Speedy looked puzzled in turn. "I don't know, Bill," he said. "I simply didn't seem to have any spirit about it . . . about following the thugs, I mean. I'm going out into the street opposite the courthouse. Coming that way?"

"Sure," said Bill Cort. He paid and went at once down the street with his companion, adding as they went along: "Here you are in San Lorenzo, and everybody in the town would turn out and give you a cheer if they only knew that you're the man who . . ."

245

"Listen to me," said Speedy.

"Well?"

"Forget it, will you?" pleaded Speedy.

CHAPTER
TWO

If Cort found it hard to forget what he had just been talking about, he was at least able to keep silent on the point, although only at the cost of continually shaking his head. To him, it was as though he had just heard of a lion being struck by a lamb, and submitting to the blow!

When they came near the courthouse, Cort said: "Why don't you go inside, Speedy? Why not step in there and see Dupray take it?"

"And hear the judge sentence him to hang?" Speedy asked with a shudder. "I couldn't do that, Bill. I haven't the nerve to stand it."

"You haven't the nerve?" exclaimed his companion. "But, great Scott, Speedy, there isn't anything in you but nerve . . . tons of it!"

"I couldn't stand it," repeated Speedy firmly. "To hear one man, in a black cap, say to another . . . 'I condemn you to be hanged by the neck till you are dead, dead.' No, no, Bill, I couldn't stand that."

"But there was never anybody in the history of the world that needed killing as badly as Dupray does," urged the other. "Why, that devil and his gang have killed scores and scores. You know that, Speedy. You must know all about it."

"I know a good deal about what Dupray and his people have done," said Speedy. "But it makes me sick when I think of one man standing up in cold blood and sentencing another man to be killed. It seems to me like murder, like vicious murder. Let's stand over here and see if anything happens after the sentence is pronounced."

Cort took his place beside Speedy, across the street from the little courthouse of the town. "D'you think that some of Dupray's gang may come down here and try to shoot up the crowd to get their boss away?"

"I don't know," Speedy said, his eyes absently wandering over the steady stream of men and women who were hurrying up the steps of the building.

"I don't think," said the other, "that the gang of Dupray will ever lift a finger for him. Most of 'em are probably glad to be rid of that Gila monster, that frog-faced devil."

"You've seen him, eh?" asked Speedy with interest.

"No, but I've heard how he looks. Like a nightmare, eh?"

"He looks like something not human," Speedy said dreamily. "He looks like something wrong in the brain, something wrong in the soul . . . or with no soul at all, perhaps, would be the best way to say it."

He shook his head because of the ugly thought, and again William Cort was amazed, for he felt that he was being privileged, on this day, to see a side of Speedy that was rarely, if ever, shown to the world. If he tried

248

to repeat what Speedy had said to him, other men would not believe the tale. It did not fit into the usual conception of that nerveless, keen hawk of a man, who hovered over this world looking for trouble and loving adventure for the sake of the peril that was in it, and for no other reason.

It would appear from his conversation today that he was peculiarly gullible, in fact, easy prey for the first green goods salesman, the first clumsy confidence man. It would appear that his nerves were so finely attuned that he could not endure a brutal speech.

The whole town of San Lorenzo seemed to have emptied itself up the steps of the courthouse and through its double doors. No one appeared in the street except a twelve-mule team that now entered the foot of the street and came slowly onwards, hauling a wagon with wheels as high as the head of a man. A real old-time freighter was that.

In the meantime, a hush settled over that little white town, and the quiet became so intense that finally Cort could hear out of the distance the wavering, shrill sound of a baby, crying. As the silence grew, so did the volume of that complaining sound appear to grow.

The long wait lengthened. They could hear the distant creak and rattle of the big freighter as it drew nearer. They could watch the tall man who walked beside the near wheeler, with a blacksnake draped over his neck and one hand on the jerk-line. He was becoming an important item in the landscape, and William Cort watched with an eye fascinated, like that of a small child on a drowsy, weary afternoon. Then he was aware that Speedy had started suddenly, and, looking down, he saw that the smaller man had actually put his hands over his ears. His head was bowed; there was a wrinkle of pain across his forehead, and it was plain that he was suffering.

What troubled him? Only now did Cort hear, from across the street and through the wide-open double doors of the courthouse, a droning voice that came faintly to his ears, smaller than the humming of a bee, so was it shrunk by distance. He understood suddenly that it was the voice of the judge, pronouncing sentence.

Speedy had drawn back a little, so that he was resting his shoulders against the wall behind him. Still his head was bowed and his shoulders raised. He was for all the world just like a man facing a bitterly cold wind.

"It's over," said Cort, looking curiously at his companion with a little touch of contempt in his eyes. "And right now Dupray can start getting ready to die. He'll have a lot more time to prepare for death than he's given some of his victims. What's the story about what he tried to do to you, Speedy? You and Wilson? Making you hit a half-inch line with a knife at twenty feet, eh? Otherwise, he'd cut your throats? Wasn't that the story?"

Speedy lifted his head with an impatient light in his eyes. "Bill," he said, "do you hold it against a mountain lion when it slaughters a calf?"

"That's the nature of the beast," said Cort. "Of course, that's different."

250

"Well," said Speedy, "Dupray's a beast, and that's his nature."

"Then he surely ought to die," said Cort.

"I suppose so. But I'd never lift my hand if somebody tried his rescue right here in the open street. I'd rather help him get away, I think," muttered Speedy.

"And let him go gunning for you again, afterward?" suggested the other.

"Perhaps," Speedy said, muttering. "But here they come."

Out through the double doors of the courthouse came the throng. They were talking rapidly, earnestly with one another, nodding their heads without exception, as though they all had heard things with which they were in perfect agreement.

But the sound of their voices could not be heard, for the twelve-mule team was close at hand now, the hoofs stamping into the dust with a deep, muffled sound, the bells ringing above the iron-bound haws, while the great wagon lurched and rattled along behind.

In the doorway of the courthouse, when the throng had passed out, there now appeared a rather small man with a brooding, round, pale face, ugly and featureless even from a distance.

"That's Dupray!" exclaimed big William Cort. "That's the frog-faced devil! I'll know him from today on, if they don't hang him as they ought to."

About the condemned man moved no fewer than six guards, two with rifles in the rear, the others with revolvers. One pair had linked arms with Dupray, while

251

the third pair of guards marched in front with naked guns, as though ready to charge through any attempt at rescue.

"They've got him tight enough," said Cort, pleased at the spectacle. "They'll keep him in spite of the devil and high water. Won't they, Speedy?"

"I don't know," Speedy said, shaking his head. "There are too many of them to please me."

"What's wrong with having six guards?"

"This is wrong with it," said Speedy. "Every one of the six is trusting something to the other fellow. They're sure of their numbers. They won't have their ears and their eyes open as if one guard had him in tow. You never can tell what will happen to a crowd, and six makes up a crowd, I'd say. I'd rather trust one proved guard than six. One guard, or maybe two, seeing that it's Dupray."

"A couple of 'em might be carrying sawed-off shotguns, just to make sure, but otherwise everything looks hunky-dory to me," commented William Cort.

He had hardly finished speaking when there came a yell from some people who were crowding the street. It seemed that the near mule in the lead had become caught by a snarl in the jerk-line that controlled it. At any rate, it was throwing up its head and swerving rapidly to the right, as though obeying the harsh command: "Gee!"

Swiftly it swung over, crowding the off mule of the span, with a great jingling of bells. The driver, a tall man with buckteeth and, therefore, a fixed and mirthless smile on his face, rushed forward and shouted loudly.

"That's Bones, I think," Cort remembered afterward hearing his companion murmur. "Bones. A nervy devil to come down here in broad daylight."

In spite of the shouting of the driver, the near mule in the lead veered more and more uncontrollably, then, as though dreading punishment from the long-legged driver, bolted to the rear.

Six spans of mules, in an instant, were curling back, scattering the crowd as if with a cavalry charge. Straight back toward the armed escort of the prisoner they rushed, and the guards, with yells to one another, started hauling Dupray back from the danger.

But the speeding line of mules came too fast. They dropped their charge and ran for their lives, while Dupray sprinted straight inside that danger and made for the wagon.

Out of it, at the same instant, there came four armed men, who closed around the escaped man and, doubling around behind the wagon, dashed across the street.

Not twenty yards from the place where Speedy and Cort were standing, they headed into the mouth of an alley that led down toward the San Lorenzo River.

Cort had pulled his own revolver instinctively, but Speedy knocked up the muzzle of it.

"He deserves to win today," said Speedy. "Anyone who can induce that many men to risk their lives for him certainly deserves to get away."

253

Into the mouth of the alley, in pursuit, poured the guards now, screeching with rage, shouting orders to one another, with the whole town behind them.

"A mob," Speedy said calmly, "and a mob will never catch Dupray."

CHAPTER
THREE

"Lend me a hundred dollars, Bill, will you?" asked Speedy. "I have to line out as fast as I can pelt. I have a long ride ahead of me now."

"Sure," said Cort. "Two, if you want it."

"Two is better," said Speedy, "because I have to buy a mustang and a saddle and bridle. Listen to them yelping like a hunting pack down there in the distance."

For the hunt already had reached the edge of the river, and they could tell by the peculiar quality of the echoes that floated back through the troubled air of San Lorenzo.

"He'll get off clear," Cort said, shaking his head. "He'll get clear away. If they've planned everything as carefully as all this, they're sure to have a fast boat waiting for him down on the water."

"Of course they have," said Speedy. "Now they're shooting from the shore, and they wish that they had cannon instead of rifles, I suppose. But they'll never get at Dupray that way. He's beaten them. That fox has beaten 'em fair and square."

"He's beat 'em," said Cort, counting out $200, and adding $100 for luck. Then he continued anxiously: "Speedy, when I pulled this gun, I was about to take a snap shot at Dupray as he ran, and he turned his ugly frog-face and marked me with his eyes. I saw him, and I've an idea that I'll hear from him later on."

"He won't forget," agreed Speedy. "You can be sure of that. I'm sorry, Bill. But I couldn't let you shoot him down when he was one step from freedom. Besides, you might have missed. You probably would, at that distance and shooting at a running man."

"I might have missed," muttered Bill Cort, "but he won't miss when he takes his crack at me."

"He doesn't miss," agreed Speedy. "He's one of the people who can't afford to."

"By thunder, Speedy!" exclaimed Cort, sweat standing on his forehead. "I begin to feel a little nervous. What about you?"

"About me? Oh, I've got to catch him if I can. Anyway, I must try to warn some friends of mine. I've got to get the news to them as fast as I can."

"Who?"

"John Wilson . . . the fellow who was with me when we caught Dupray. Dupray will want my scalp first of all now, and then he is going to want Wilson's," continued Speedy.

"Perhaps he won't want yours at all," replied Cort. "He saw me pull a gun, and he saw you knock the gun up. That ought to wipe out all old scores."

"My score can never be wiped out," answered Speedy, unmoved. "It's too long and too black. The point is that Dupray was a great legend a month ago. Now he's been dragged out into the open sunshine. People know what he looks like. They know that he can be deceived and beaten. They know that he's been caught once, and they know that there's a big reward on his head. They'll try to catch him, now, as they never tried before."

"I suppose you're right. No gratitude in the dog, nothing but a mouthful of teeth and poison," said Cort. "Well, Speedy, you and Wilson refused the reward money, I hear."

"Blood money, you know," said Speedy. "We couldn't take that. We got enough out of the rubies that we lifted off him. But we couldn't collect the reward."

"Look here, Speedy," said the other.

"Well?"

"When you ride out to see the Wilsons, I've an idea that I'd like to go along."

"You?" exclaimed Speedy, surprised.

Cort nodded. "I don't want that frog-faced beast to take after me," argued the gambler. "And I'd rather be with you than with anybody else in the world, when it comes to facing Dupray. Will you take me along?"

Speedy, frowning, drew out the money he had just received and fingered it, his mood impatient.

"It's all right if you don't want me," said Cort frankly. "I know how it is. You don't have much to do with crooks and you know that I'm a crooked gambler. Well, so is every other gambler in the world. You fleece the crooks, and we fleece the honest men, if you want to put it that way. Besides, Speedy, I'm not such a bad bargain. I can ride with most people. I can shoot a good deal better than average, a whole lot better than average. I think my nerves are pretty steady, most of the time. Only, that greasy-gray frog-face is lodged in the back of my mind, and it won't rub out. Let me ride along with you, will you?"

"Why not?" muttered Speedy thoughtfully. "Yes, come along, old son, and we'll try this trail together, though I generally ride alone. Come on."

They bought two good, seasoned mustangs. There were finer-looking animals in the stables, but the gambler, who knew horses and had had to trust his life to their speed and endurance before this day, declared that nothing in the world can outlast a Southwestern pony in its own habitat. If they wanted speed, the mustangs were the trick.

So, quickly mounting, they loped the horses out of San Lorenzo.

They had the details of the escape some time before they left. Straight down to the edge of the San Lorenzo River, Dupray had been rushed by his escort, just as Speedy suspected, and there a boat was waiting for them, a very long, light craft, with a clumsy-looking triangular sail, ready to hoist upon a short mast, and so to take advantage of the strong wind that was nearly always blowing down the river at this time of the day. Into that long boat the whole gang had leaped and thrust her adrift. They jerked up the sail, and, as they flung themselves down into the shelter of the heavy bulwarks, the wind bellied the sail, made the boat lean over, and shot it out into the stream. A rain of rifle bullets and slugs from wide-mouthed revolvers followed, as a matter of course.

258

Men said that 1,000 holes must have been knocked in the bottom of the little ship, as it heeled over in the wind. For all that, it did not sink, but safely turned the corner of the next river bend. The townsmen, following in swiftly paddled craft or straining at long oars, reached the bend of the river, rounded it, found the boat stranded and the crew gone, and in their ears beat the noise of pounding hoofs.

So Dupray and his men departed, and the peculiar feature of that eventful day, as men remembered it afterward, was that not a drop of blood had been shed by all the bullets that were aimed at the fugitives.

The townsmen came gloomily, silently back. The six guards were not particularly blamed. It was felt that the entire town of San Lorenzo, the brown population as well as the white, had been fooled and deceived to the utmost. Dupray was gone and there an end of it.

When they got to the big wagon, which had been overturned by the backward rush of the mules and the tongue of the wagon broken, they found that its load consisted of nothing more than heavy rocks, with a few logs placed on top of these. The whole thing had been a sham, effective in its simplicity, wonderfully effective in its perfect timing.

As Speedy said, when he heard the final details: "You see how it is, Bill. In Dupray, yonder, you have a fellow with the brains of a philosopher and the heart of a grizzly bear. No . . . a bear is a big, warm, affectionate beast compared to that snake of a Dupray."

259

"And you, Speedy," cried out his companion, "you stood by and looked on, when you might have stopped him! You could have stopped him, if you'd wanted to."

"Not after the rush began," argued Speedy. "There were too many of 'em."

"You could have done it, if your heart had been in the business," insisted Cort. "Instead of that, you've turned the devil loose on the world again."

"Not I," said Speedy. "Six strong-armed guards turned him loose, when a team of mules charged 'em."

"And now that he's free, you are in danger of your life."

They had talked like this as they labored into the dusky, thick light of the evening, up a long slope, their horses fairly staggering beneath them, for they had ridden them out as they approached the end of their journey.

Now, at the top of the hill, they saw a house in the hollow beyond — a wide valley whose shimmer of green was not yet entirely overshadowed by the coming of night. Lights gleamed from the windows, and Speedy murmured: "Bill, I blame myself, but I can't change myself. When I see a hunt, my heart is with the fox, not with the hunters."

CHAPTER
FOUR

"That's peaceful," said William Cort as they rode their horses down the slope.

"It is," agreed Speedy, "but every minute now, you'd better act as though the witches were just around the corner."

"You mean, you think Dupray could get out here as soon as this?"

"I don't know," said Speedy. "Whatever we've done, he can probably do. If we have good horses, he has better ones, and, if we've hurried to help people, he may have hurried all the faster to murder 'em. He's some gunman, that one." Then he added: "I don't know. Of course, he may decide on a few little robberies to make up for lost time before he goes after John Wilson and me. But I doubt it. I imagine that what's nearest and dearest to his heart is the thought of taking our scalps. That house looks peaceful, as you say, but, for all we know, those lights down there may be shining in dead faces."

"Quit it, Speedy," his companion said, his voice half choked. "You chill my blood and bone to the marrow."

"Dupray would murder a whole household as soon as not," answered Speedy, "and we've got to keep that in mind, partner."

"Back there in San Lorenzo we had him in point-blank shooting distance," groaned Cort.

"I've told you that I couldn't help myself back there," said Speedy. "I'm sorry, but I couldn't."

They came up to the house through a valley road that ran, winding, through several groves of trees and so came to the house itself. As far as could be told, it was like most other ranch houses, being long and low throughout, except for one wing, which was of two stories. It had a hitching rack in front and a dim tangle of corral fencing to the rear, with a few sheds nearby and a great square-shouldered barn.

"Ranching and farming," Speedy said, pointing to a field of grain that swept up almost to the edge of the house on one side. "I didn't know that Wilson would make such a good man in the open."

He tethered his horse at the rack in front of the house, and went to the door, not in front, but in the rear, opening apparently into the kitchen. A woman's voice, singing, came out as if to welcome them on purpose.

Speedy laid a hand on the shoulder of his companion, stopping him to say: "I'd rather hear that voice than opera, Cort. A lot rather. I've been thinking of her lying in a pool of blood and that same throat cut from ear to ear. And now . . ." He went on again, hastily, and knocked at the door.

"Come in!" cried out the singer, breaking off.

Speedy pushed open the door on a typical ranch kitchen, under a slanting roof, as though the shed that housed this important room had been added to the whole as an after-thought. There was a big range at one side, the sort of stove that is needed when a score of hungry men have to be cooked for at certain seasons of the year.

In the center of the room there was a long, capacious table and, near one end of it, the sink, with a big wooden draining board. It was at that end of the table that Jessica Wilson was standing, rolling out a slab of dough for biscuits. Her face was reddened from the heat; she was covered with flour to the bare elbows, and she dropped the rolling pin to throw up the whitened hands and clap them together.

"Speedy!" she cried, running to him. She drew him in by both hands, released him only for an instant to greet Will Cort, and then caught at the smaller man again. "You've come at last!" she exclaimed. "And for how long, Speedy? A month, a week, a day? Your room is upstairs, ready and waiting. We planned it 'specially when we built the house, you know. No one has ever slept in it. We vowed that it would be kept for you, and you've never been near us. Speedy, how long will you stay?"

"I don't know," he said. "The fact is, Jessica, that I'm just loafing across country with my friend, Cort. We're not in any great hurry. We're just drifting as the fancy moves us."

"Then let your fancy move you to stay here. There's wonderful fishing."

"I never caught a fish in my life," said Speedy.

"There's perfect shooting, though. Deer, Speedy. The woods are full of deer. It's a regular preserve."

"Never shot a deer. I'm no hunter," said Speedy.

She drew back a little and regarded him with a slight cloud on her face. "No, Speedy," she agreed. "I forgot about that. I forgot that you don't hunt dumb animals." Still frowning a little, she added: "Are you on a trail now?"

"No," he said frankly. "I'm on no man trail, if that's what you want to know. But I've got something to talk over with John. Where is he?"

"He's out in the barn. He'll be in, in a moment. He's feeding the horses, the plow team. All the men went off today. The cook, too."

"All quit on you?"

"No, they had a day off, to celebrate. It's the anniversary of our buying of the farm, and we turned all the boys loose with a little extra money. They scooted off this morning, and they won't be back till the morning, I suppose. We're doing our celebrating by having a quiet evening alone. And now you come to make it a real party."

"I'll step out to the barn," said Speedy, "and see John."

"Bring in your pack and come up to look at your room first," she urged. "It's all planned and made for you. Come along, Speedy."

She led the way cheerfully, laughing and chatting, through a big dining room, out into a hall that opened on a flight of stairs, and this they climbed to the second story.

"Here you are," she said, throwing open a door.

They stepped into a long room, with rather a low ceiling. It was divided into three parts, and there were curtains drawn back to the walls, indicating that the sections could be shut off from one another. At a glance, the parts seemed to be the bedroom, a library where the walls were lined with bookshelves, and at the farthest end of the room there was a big fireplace built into the wall, with great easy chairs drawn up before it.

The girl put down the lamp she had been carrying and hurried to draw down a great hanging lamp in the center of the chamber, suspended by chains from the ceiling. "If only I'd known that you were coming!" she cried. "The fire should be going. But a match will remedy that."

She scratched a match and touched it to the tinder under the wood that was corded up on the andirons, ready to burn. As the flames crackled and rose, thrusting up coiling masses of white wood smoke, she stepped back and dusted her hands. "It ought to be dry enough to burn," said Jessica. "It's been waiting there long enough, ready to make its master happy. Look! Look at those pots and kettles at the side. John knows how you love to be alone, a lot of the time, and it was his idea to make this room of yours as complete as a ship, so that you could lock yourself up in the place and stay a year, if you wanted to. You could do all your cooking right here, if you wanted to. Look, here's a whole cupboard let into the wall on this side of the fire. Some of those canned goods ought to be changed, I suppose. They've been there so long, waiting for you."

It was a complete kitchenette, almost as convenient as the contrivances that are put in the most modern apartment houses. There was a sink with running water, and at the sides and back were shelves crowded with all sorts of groceries and cooking utensils.

They had hardly admired this, when she had them examining the other features.

There was a big clothes closet, filled with clothes all cut exactly to the measure of Speedy — boots, hats, gloves, everything complete. There was a study table in the library section, and in the drawers sets of magnifying glasses and fine microscopes, besides a whole battery of test tubes and a thousand little vials of acids, powders, and poisons.

"There's a Bunsen burner, yonder," said the girl, "so that when you want to start experimenting, you can fill the room with as many bad odors as you please. That's not all. When you want to air it out again, you have this." She opened a door onto a balcony that ran half the length of the room, corbelled well out from the wall of the house and set with deep boxes with flowering plants.

"You like to walk under the open sky, Speedy," said the girl, "and here's the place for you to do it. Nobody'll disturb you on this garden walk."

"Jessica," said Speedy, "I never thought that I'd ever find a place where I'd want to sit still to the end of time. But this is the place for me. I'm going to come to it, sometime before I'm too old. This door is heavy, though . . . wh . . . ?" He tapped the inside of it with his knuckles, and there followed a ringing sound.

The girl laughed, triumphant. "Of course! It's bullet-proof steel, and every window shutter and every door in your room is lined with it. When you want to make sure that gunmen can't look in on you, here it's been perfectly arranged for you, Speedy."

He looked at Bill Cort. "Ever hear of anything like it?" he demanded.

"Never," agreed Cort. "You could sit in here and laugh at the world."

"Jessica," said Speedy, "everything's perfect. Nothing's been left out, and I thank you from my heart."

"But," she suggested, "but, of course, you'll never spend more than a day in your whole life here?"

"Slander, Jessica," said Speedy. "But I've got to break away to the barn, now, and give my news to John. Bill, you stay with Jessica in the kitchen."

The girl had picked up her lamp and now she looked hard at Speedy, saying: "There's something wrong . . . there's something important."

"Something that would be important, if I didn't get the news to John right away," Speedy said, and hurried before them downstairs.

"What is it?" asked the girl of Cort. "Have you any idea?"

"Even if a fellow has an idea," parried Bill Cort, "it's generally a lot better to let Speedy do his own talking."

"I know," said the girl. "Only, I can feel something in the air. Did you see how he went down the stairs?"

"I saw he was hurrying," said Cort.

"Was that all you saw?"

"Well, yes, that's all. He went down the steps pretty fast."

She paused on the landing and turned with the lamp toward Cort as though she doubted what she had just heard and wished to make sure, by examining his face more carefully as he spoke.

"Perhaps you don't know Speedy very well?" she queried.

He was stirred to answer: "I don't suppose that anybody knows him very well, except people who've had a lot of trouble."

She was willing to nod her head gravely, when she heard this. "Yes, that's true. I've had enough trouble and enough need of Speedy's help. And I've seen him in action, enough, to know some of the important signs."

He was curious when he heard her say this. And he asked: "What signs did you notice when you saw him run down the stairs?"

She smiled. "Well, he was running, wasn't he?"

"Yes."

"Tell me, then, did you hear a sound?"

"When he ran down the stairs?"

"Yes."

"No, now that I think of it, I don't think that I did."

"That's it," said Jessica Wilson. "When there's trouble in the air, he moves like a cat, with velvet paws."

CHAPTER
FIVE

Out to the barn ran Speedy, and, pushing back the sliding door, he heard a man whistling softly, while he pitched down quantities of hay into the long row of mangers.

"It's a musical family," Speedy said gloomily to himself. "I hope that they don't have to howl for it, before long." Then he raised his voice. "John!" he called.

There was a shout of joyful astonishment. Then big John Wilson came climbing down a ladder from the top of the mow and grasped the hand of his friend.

Yet his first question was: "Is there anything wrong?"

"Dupray was sentenced to death today," said Speedy, "and, on the way out of the judge's court, he was rescued and taken safely away from the town."

The head of Wilson went back, and his eyes closed as he groaned in dismay. "That's the worst news of a lifetime," he said. "You came out to warn me. You think that he'll take the trail for this place?"

"I more than think it," said Speedy. "There's more poison in him than in any snake. He's sure to come, John."

"I haven't a man on the place," said Wilson.

"There's yourself and me," said Speedy, "and I've brought a good fighting man along with me. I don't know how far he's to be trusted, but he'll fight."

"I have you," said Wilson, "and that's a lot more to me than to have a whole army of other men. Where's the other fellow?"

"He's at the house with Jessica."

"Have you told her?"

"No, I haven't told her yet. There's no need to torture her until the last minute."

They stood and regarded one another silently for a moment. A rising wind went softly, drearily, through the top of the haymow of the barn.

"You're getting fat and brown," Speedy said, nodding and smiling.

John Wilson made a gesture that banished such small considerations. "We'd better get back to the house," he said.

"Yes, we'd better," Speedy agreed, nodding his head. "The moon's coming up . . . I saw the glow of it like a fire between the mountains as I came out to the barn. It's better to get back now, before . . . well, Dupray has men who shoot pretty straight by moonlight, even."

Wilson nodded, and moved a hand back to his hip.

"Still carrying a gun, John?" asked Speedy.

"I've formed the habit," said Wilson. "Even with Dupray in jail, I've had my worries. I've always wondered when some of the Dupray gang would turn loose on me."

"Dupray wouldn't let 'em," said Speedy.

"Wouldn't let 'em? Why not?"

"He wants to save you and me for his own handiwork. I imagine that's what's in him." He pulled back the sliding door of that side of the barn as he spoke.

"How about you?" asked Wilson. "Still carrying no guns?"

"People who carry guns are always tempted to use 'em, sooner or later," answered Speedy rather shortly.

They stepped out into the night, and Wilson, putting out his lantern and hanging it up on a nail, closed the door after them. The moon was up, as Speedy had said, but its softly slanting light gave more shadow than illumination, as it seemed, and the stars were still bright in the center of the sky above them.

They walked past the long watering troughs down the side of the corral, and toward the house, Speedy half a step in the lead, Wilson, with a high head, keeping a look-out on every side.

Yet it was Speedy who said: "Be ready to run for it. There's something yonder in that grain field . . . now!"

As he finished, several dark forms rose out of the grain, only their heads and shoulders looming, and guns began to chatter. The air about Wilson and Speedy was filled with sounds like the buzzing of wasp wings blown down an incredibly swift wind. The two broke into a run and shot for the house.

A very fast man was big John Wilson, but, despite his length of leg, he saw Speedy drift out ahead of him. Yet the smaller man was not running straight, but wavering from side to side, like a snipe flying from danger.

It looked as if it were going to be impossible for them to gain the safety of the house, when from a back window of the place a revolver commenced barking rapidly. At the first sound of it, the shadowy forms disappeared into the grain from which they had risen.

The two fugitives reached the kitchen door. It was jerked open before them, and they ran in past the white face of Jessica Wilson.

Bill Cort was stepping back from a window in the kitchen and reloading his emptied revolver. He could not help noticing that the girl made no outcry, although her first intimation of the trouble had come from the noise of the guns. She was as steady as a man.

"We have four here," said Cort, "and there's moonlight to keep watch by. One of us must take, each, a side of the house and we'd better have rifles."

"That's the only thing to do," agreed Wilson. "Jessica may not do much shooting, but she can keep watch as well as any of us and give an alarm."

"It's no good," said Speedy.

"What's no good?" asked Wilson.

"It's Dupray's gang?" Jessica said quietly.

"And Dupray with it," said Speedy. "He got away after his condemnation in court today." He went on, having disposed of that subject: "The house is too big to guard all four sides of it."

"The four of us could take your room, Speedy," said the girl. "It's strong as a fort."

"While they touch a match to the house and see us all go up in smoke?" asked Speedy.

All three of the others groaned. "What's to be done then, Speedy?" asked Wilson.

"The wind is carrying from the grain field toward the house," said Speedy. "We can't backfire the ground about it, for that reason. There's nothing to be done."

"Are we to wait here, sitting helpless?" asked Bill Cort, the sweat standing out on his white face.

"There's nothing else to do," said Speedy, "except to break out and try to fight through, but that's no good, either. They have a close circle around the house by this time. And the moon is getting brighter. They'd shoot down a hundred like us, now, if we tried to get away."

"You mean that we're lost, Speedy," said the girl.

"We're lost," said Speedy.

"You mean that there's nothing for us to do!" exclaimed Wilson.

"There's supper to eat," said Speedy, "and we might as well have it in here. It's warmer in here than in the dining room."

The others exchanged stony glances. But each one of them felt that a final judgment had been spoken. While there was hope, Speedy would be the man who would find the way of deliverance. When he surrendered, it meant that nothing could be attempted.

Jessica went to the stove, opened the oven door, and took out a steaming pan of biscuits. She started to lay out food on the long kitchen table, and Speedy assisted her. Wilson and Cort were too stunned to move. All the cold speculations of death were in their eyes.

Then they sat down. Wilson and Cort could not eat. But Speedy and the girl went steadily on with the meal.

They talked to one another. He asked about the farm. She told him the story of it cheerfully. Good luck had followed them every moment since the capture of Dupray. The money that Wilson had as his share from the sale of the jewels was lodged safely in a bank. With that as a backlog, their fire of prosperity was burning very cheerfully and promised to last long.

She began to grow enthusiastic as she described the future possibilities. The color came back into her face. But her husband sat as one hewed out of stone, his hands clasped hard together. He would fight, when the time came for it, and so would Cort, but, just now, they were both tasting the full horror of death.

Outside the house a voice called: "Speedy! Oh, Speedy!"

Speedy lifted his head, and frowned a little with critical interest. "Dupray's calling me," he said, and pushed back his chair.

CHAPTER
SIX

The mere sound of the voice had made big John Wilson snatch out his revolver, saying: "It's the devil himself."

But Jessica Wilson ran around the table, as Speedy rose, and put herself between him and the door. "You don't mean that you'll go out to him, Speedy, do you?" she asked.

He looked at her in a strange way, as she never had been looked at before, as though she were not a young and pretty woman, as though she were not human, in fact, but merely an obstacle, and his voice was cold when he answered: "John, take charge of your wife, will you?"

"Hold on, Speedy," muttered Wilson. "Are you saying that you would go out there and face Dupray and his killers?"

William Cort, staring with uncomprehending glances at the trio, was aware only that there was a curious hardness in the eyes of Speedy, and a sort of angry impatience, only partially controlled.

"Are you both going to interfere?" asked Speedy. "I'm not saying that I'll go out to them. I'm simply saying that I'll answer Dupray. John, will you keep Jessica in hand?" He glanced fiercely toward Wilson, and the latter laid his hand on the arm of the girl.

275

"Speedy knows best," said Wilson, although his face was drawn and white as he turned toward his old companion in arms.

"It's all right, John," said the girl. "I won't make a scene. I know that we can't control him . . . he'll do what he wants. You can take your hand away."

Speedy already had unbolted the rear window's shutter, and now he threw a look over his shoulder. "Put out the lamp, will you?" he commanded.

Cort stepped forward and obeyed.

Through the darkness, only the fire in the stove gleamed with a red eye through little openings.

Then Speedy pushed the window wide open. "Hello, Dupray!" he called.

The voice of the bandit answered, amazingly close at hand: "Glad to hear you so close, Speedy, old son."

"Thanks," said Speedy.

"I saw you today in San Lorenzo," said Dupray. "You and your new friend, Cort, the gambler."

"Yes, we saw you there," said Speedy.

"I saw him try to make the gun play that you stopped," said Dupray. "And he's a good shot, I hear."

"He's a good shot," agreed Speedy.

"I want to know why you played me that good turn," demanded Dupray.

"My sympathy runs with the fox, not the hounds," said Speedy.

"That's a partial answer only," said Dupray. "You must have recognized Bones, driving the team, too, didn't you?"

"Yes, that was easy."

"Why didn't you give the people a warning?"

"It was the business of the law to keep you, Dupray," said Speedy. "I'd never send a man back to wait for the hangman, if I could help it."

"That sounds like talk," said Dupray.

"I don't care what it sounds like," said Speedy.

"You're in my hand, Speedy," said the other.

"I know it," said Speedy. "You scratch a match, and the house burns."

"You have brains," said the other. "Why didn't you think the thing up before you caged yourself in the house?"

"We had to come to the two inside," said Speedy.

"Oh, loyalty, eh?" said Dupray. Then he laughed, his voice ringing with a sneer of contempt. He added: "A crook like you to talk about loyalty, eh?"

"That's what I talk about, just the same," said Speedy.

"You admit you're a crook, eh?"

"I don't admit that. No."

"Why, damn you," said the other, "did you ever do an honest stroke of work in your life? All your jobs have been stealing and crooked gambling."

"I've never stolen from an honest man," said Speedy.

"That's a lie, and a fool's lie," said Dupray.

"Go ahead and scratch your match," said Speedy.

"I won't do that," said Dupray, "for a minute or two. I still want to talk to you for a minute."

"Go ahead, then."

"I'll make a bargain with you, Speedy."

"What sort?"

"There's three more beside you in there, eh?"

"Yes, three more."

"All friends of yours?"

"Yes."

"There's Missus Wilson and there's her precious husband, among the rest."

"Yes, they're both here."

"Floating on the crest of the wave, they've been, eh?"

"They've been prosperous, if that's what you mean."

"They won't last prosperous," said the criminal, angry conviction in his voice. "But I'll make a bargain with you for them."

"I'm listening."

"Swear yourself in as my man for thirty days, and I'll let the lot of them go . . . for tonight. As long as you're working for me, I'll keep away from 'em. Does that sound to you?"

"No, no, no!" cried Jessica Wilson.

"Be still," Speedy said shortly. He added: "That sounds to me. What sort of work?"

"Any work I choose to give you," said the other.

Speedy paused, and in that pause the snarling, self-satisfied laughter of Dupray began and ended.

Then Dupray went on: "I don't much care. I'd as soon close my hand over the four of you tonight and call it quits."

"The girl, too?" asked Speedy. "You wouldn't let her leave the house?"

"Let her leave, and fill the world with talk afterward? I'm not that much of a fool, Speedy. No, it would be just one of those accidental affairs. Fire catches in the

278

grain, cause unknown. House and four souls in it burn to cinders. That's all. I might set the barn and sheds on fire, too, after we've taken out all the horses that we need to borrow."

"I see your point of view," said Speedy calmly.

"You see my point of view, but what are you going to do about it?"

"If I make the bargain with you and leave the house, I trust your word and honor not to harm anything on the place."

"You trust my honor," said Dupray, laughing brutally again. "That's all that you have to trust, Speedy. Just my word and my honor. The word and the honor of Charley Dupray." He laughed once more, for the unique idea seemed to please him.

"Well," said Speedy, "that makes a fair bargain. I take your word and step out of the house. You may shoot me down as soon as I appear and burn the house afterward. Or perhaps you only want to get your hands on me, because a quick death by bullets or fire is not exactly what you want to give me, eh?"

"That may be it," said Dupray. "You won't know. You'll simply have to take your chance. I whistle, you dog, and you've got to come and lick my hand."

"And afterward," said Speedy, "you'd trust my promise to work for you thirty days?"

"I know the kind of a fool you are, and that your word's safer than steel handcuffs on another man. Yes, I'll trust you that far."

"Very well," said Speedy, "then I'll come out." He closed the shutters of the window and bolted them. "Light the lamp," he said.

Cort lighted the lamp. Jessica Wilson began to cry out, sobbing wildly, her words almost undistinguishable.

Speedy was saying to her sternly: "This is hard enough for everybody, and you're only making it harder. I know what you want to say. You want us to stay together, and all die together in the flames. But we don't choose to do that. I know that Wilson would die fighting with me . . . so would Cort. They're both brave men. But they see what I see. It may be that this is simply a trap set by Dupray to put his hands on me and work his pleasure. But it also may be that he means what he says, and that he really needs me for some work that's not exactly in his own line. Now, be quiet."

She had fallen on her knees in a paroxysm of despair, but now she stood up. So, mastering herself, she managed to say: "You're right, Speedy. You've always been right. You've saved John for me twice. Now I suppose that you'll risk your life again, but to surrender to that fiend of a Dupray." She slipped into a chair and leaned back against the wall, suddenly very faint.

Speedy said: "You're worth it. You, Jessica, and you fellows, too. Besides, a man has to die sometime." He waved his hand, and turned abruptly to the door, saying casually: "So long, everyone." He was out in the open moonlight before anyone could interfere with his movements.

Even those steel nerves of Speedy were shaken, for an instant, as he stood there in the night, the great

280

white face of the moon seeming to drift rapidly with the wind across the face of the sky, and the heaped shadowy forms of the mountain appearing to tremble and move like waves on a gigantic sea. But he mastered himself in the space of a single breath, and, turning the corner of the house, he walked straight out through the grain field.

He waded slowly through that brittle sea of brown, with the dust rising up into his face. Then, out of the deep grain around him, half a dozen men arose suddenly and seized him, and the noose of a rope flung over his shoulders bound his arms tightly against his sides.

Dupray stepped before him, laughing, sneering, and nodding his frog-face with delight. "Now, you fool," he said, "you're in my hands at last. When will you get out of 'em?"

CHAPTER
SEVEN

He did not wait for an answer, but, turning, he led the way. The captive was to be taken behind a clump of trees and shrubbery that shielded them from the sight of the people of the house, in case any of these should understand what was happening and undertake to interrupt the procedure with a rifle bullet.

"Here, Bones and Sid," said Dupray after he had looked to the way in which the hands of Speedy were bound behind his back, his feet being secured, also. "You've got enough of a grudge to be useful now. You stay here with me. The rest of you boys, spread out and watch the house. Cort's nothing much, I hear, but I know that John Wilson can put up a fight. Watch everything. If you don't like the looks, start in and shoot as much as you please. Pass the word around. I'm pleased with the whole lot of you. We've done things before, together, but nothing that I like as well as this. We're going to write our names on the West in letters a mile high. Don't be forgetting that."

They withdrew. The tall form of Bones and the stockier silhouette of Sid remained close by, while Dupray, as though excess of triumph made it impossible for him to stand still, began to walk up and down in front of his captive.

"A bright fellow, with a brain and a pair of hands, that's what you are, Speedy," he said. "But, after all, Dupray has the poison that puts you down, eh? Charley Dupray is the man to put you down." He laughed again, not loudly, but with a muscular contraction of the throat that almost stifled him. "You're down. You're in my hand. I could only think about you dying a minute ago, but now I can see you die. I can taste the death of you."

He came close to Speedy and stood, swaying a little from side to side, his lips working, as though there were an actual flavor in his mouth.

"You're an ugly looking toad," said Speedy. "What more does it prove? You've got me. Go ahead and use me. I can't help myself, and you've got helpers enough. Start the music, Dupray, and watch me dance. I suppose you'll do enough to make me dance, even with my feet tied together."

"The devil," muttered Dupray. He stepped still closer, and peered into the face of Speedy. "You're an actor. You're a fine actor, Speedy," he said. "Some people might think that you're not even afraid now of what's going to happen to you."

"It will last a certain time, and then it'll finish," answered Speedy.

"You can do some groaning for your friends in the house, Speedy," said the other. "When the flame hits the girl . . . she's a regular rose of a girl, isn't she?"

"Yes, she's a pretty thing," Speedy said calmly.

283

"Well, when the flame hits her, she'll die fast. It'll only be ten or fifteen minutes for her, eh?" His eyes worked busily over the face of Speedy, as he strove to read the mind of his captive.

But Speedy answered: "Yes, only ten or fifteen minutes."

"You'll be howling long before that, Speedy," said Dupray.

"I won't howl, partner," Speedy said.

"No?"

"I won't howl."

"You're sure, are you?"

"I'm sure."

"I can do things that would bring the music out of a stone, I tell you!" exclaimed Dupray.

"It won't bring the music out of me," insisted Speedy.

"Damn you," said Dupray. "I'll have you screeching if I have to find your nerves one by one and tear 'em out with hot pincers."

"After you start your little game," said Speedy, "you'll never get a whisper out of me."

"You lie!" exclaimed Dupray angrily. He waved in his two assistants. "Look at him, Bones. Look at him, Sid. Look at the smile on him. That's his way of looking down on us. But I'll let you see how he'll change when I'm working on him. I'll have music out of him that'll make the howling of wolves like a fine church choir. I'll have noise out of him that'll curdle the blood of the three in the house. They'll enjoy the party with you,

Speedy." He leaned and leered at Speedy again, as he spoke.

And the other said: "It's all right, Dupray. You're a man with ideas that would make a Chinese pirate sick, but you'll never be able to make me curl up in front of you."

"Tell me," said Dupray, "what makes you so infernally sure of yourself?"

"This is what makes me sure," said Speedy. "I'm not the oldest man in the world, but I've spent my life learning how to master my body, and I've learned the trick. My body's my servant, and not my master. Whatever you do to my body, it can't make me squirm or whine, or howl or beg. Start in, Dupray. I've made a fool of you before this, and tonight I'll make a fool of you again."

"Will you?" said Dupray. "Why, damn you!" He caught a deep breath, and exclaimed: "Speedy, you're iron all the way through! I thought that I'd shake you up a little before I pushed the deal through. But tell me, you mind-reading devil you, did you guess from the first that I was only bluffing about the torture business?"

"No, I didn't guess that," said Speedy. "I thought you had all of those pretty little ideas in mind. But I didn't guess as much as that. You mean that you honestly intend to carry out the bargain that you made with me through the window of the house?"

"I mean it. It's a bitter thing to me the way that I have you here in my hand, Speedy," said Dupray. "And

285

yet I can't close my hand on you, because I need you for another job of mine." He waved to his two men. "Back up," the chief said curtly.

"Want some elbow room for the conversation?" demanded Bones. "Damn me, chief, I thought for a minute that I'd have the fun of seeing you stage a party with Speedy, here. Come along, Sid. We'll have to wait for our show."

They moved off together, and Dupray, after staring intently at his prisoner, said: "I've got your word, Speedy?"

"You've got my word," Speedy repeated.

The other drew a knife, touched the cords, and instantly the prisoner was again a free man. Dupray stood a pace and a half back from him. That was all. "You know the town of Clausen?" he asked.

"Yes. I know it."

"Tell me what it looks like, then."

"It's in a ravine wedged between two mountains, with a river running through its back yards. It has one good-size plaza, and its jail is in the center of a fine lawn."

"That's it," said Dupray, "you've hit it. The scoundrels, they wouldn't build a city hall, or some such nonsense. They had to put all of their money into a fine jail, filled with tool-proof steel and such things. Were you ever inside that jail?"

"Yes."

"Ha!" cried Dupray. "You mean to say that you escaped from it?"

"No, not that. I was just jailed as a material witness in a little crime in a saloon. That was all. I was let out the next day, fast enough."

Dupray sighed. "Anyway, you know the inside of the building?"

"Yes."

"Well," said Dupray, "inside of that jail there's a special cell, made extra strong, with a door that weighs two hundred pounds. It would take a shell from a twelve-inch gun to batter in that cell door."

"Yes?" murmured Speedy.

"And behind that door," said Dupray, "there's a nephew of mine."

"Yes?" said Speedy.

"Understand?" said Dupray, his voice growing suddenly fierce. "He's my nephew. He's my blood. He's the only blood I got in the world. He's my heir. Except for him, what would I do with my money, I ask you?"

"That's a good reason for wanting him loose," said Speedy. "What's he in for?"

"Murder," said Dupray.

"Oh, murder?" said Speedy.

"That's what they say," said the other. "But everybody knows that he's my nephew. They'd say anything about him. They'd accuse him of anything. Only because he's a Dupray. You'd think that there was poison in the name, maybe. You'd think that there was poison in the blood of a Dupray." He stamped in the height of his impatience. "They're trying him now," he continued. "It was going to be a pretty close race between us to see which of the pair would hang first.

287

But I seemed to be pushing my nose under the wire first, just by a little."

"That's true," said Speedy. "Only it's odd that I haven't heard any talk about the nephew. It's enough of a coincidence to fill the newspapers."

"You don't read the newspapers," Dupray said bluntly.

"That's true," said Speedy. "How old is this nephew?"

"Twenty-one." Then he explained: "He's the only son of my oldest brother. There were four brothers in the family. The other three of 'em died. They were all older than I. And they all died years ago. There were no children except this nephew. I've got no children. There's no chance for the Duprays, except for this boy. He's the last of the line. He's the last of the blood. If he goes, we're wiped out, because I'll never have a brat of my own. You follow me?"

"If this boy goes," agreed Speedy, "it's the last of the line of Dupray."

"A good thing, you'd say?"

"No. I'm not as swift and bitter as all that."

"Then d'you see the point I'm making?"

"I see it," said Speedy.

"What is it, then?"

"You can't help your nephew. Your face is too well known, and they're looking for you and your men every minute, every day. You're known, and I suppose that most of your best men are known, too. But you think that I might have some luck in getting him out of the jail, before he's sentenced."

288

"You've put it in a nutshell," said Dupray.

"If I turn the trick, the Wilsons get out from under your hand, is that it?"

"For thirty days," the other said bitterly. "John Wilson worked with you, Speedy, when you ran me into the jail. He has to sweat for it before I die. Cort tried to pistol me when I was breaking clear. He had nothing against me, personally, and he's got to sweat for that job."

"I made the deal. I'll stick to it," said Speedy. "But suppose that you say, if I fail to get the boy loose in the thirty days, you go after everybody. If I succeed, then you forget about 'em, and go after me with knives and guns and as many men as you please. Will that suit you?"

Dupray, through a moment of silence, stared at the other. Then slowly he nodded his head. "You beat me, Speedy," he said, "but then, you're only a freak. You're not like other people. I'll make that deal with you. If you get Al Durpray free, then everything is called off, except between you and me."

"Yes," said Speedy, "that can't be called off till one of us is dead."

"Good," said Dupray, nodding his round head again. "Now about getting you to Clausen and giving you all the help that I can."

Speedy raised his hand.

"I work alone," he said. "Even if I'm working for you, I wouldn't have your help."

CHAPTER
EIGHT

Osgood had been deputy sheriff in the town of Clausen for six months, and he was maintained in his post by the force of public opinion. Stew, as he was nicknamed, was a big young man with rather a brutal face, but, as a matter of fact, he was both good-natured and charitable, except when he saw a chance for a fight and, above all, when the fighting was with guns. Therefore, he was exactly inside the tradition of the officers who had enforced the law in the town of Clausen for the last half dozen years.

Before that time, Clausen had been a convenient dumping ground for criminals of all sorts. It was the center of a hole-in-the-wall country, and from it, when pursued, fugitives from justice could slip away into the ravines or the forests that cut up the mountains nearby and overspread them.

The people of Clausen were a hardy lot and they endured a long list of riots and gunfights before they decided to take a hand. The original mansion of Clausen, a big frame building standing in the middle of a block of lawns and trees, had just burned down. The town bought the land and built on it a fine, handsome jail with walls of solid stone and some neat cells done in

290

the most expensive and disheartening tool-proof steel. When the jail was built, Clausen elected good officials to see that the jail was kept filled, and after a few years the town became one of the most unpopular places in the world for traveling criminals who were looking for a quiet spot in which to settle down while the police of various cities looked for them. It was no longer a place of refuge for thugs; too keen a wind of investigation was constantly blowing there.

The present sheriff of the county was now flat on his back in the hospital recovering gradually from the effects of a bullet that a certain cattle rustler had put through his body. Deputy Sheriff Stew Osgood had the place in hand, and he proved his capacity at once by going out and getting that same rustler with the accurate rifle. So Stew remained sole occupant of the sheriff's place of importance, for the time being, and everyone was pleased to have him there. The town would put up with a great deal from Stew. It was known that he was a rough and hearty spirit, but Clausen was itself a rough and hearty town.

At this moment, Stew Osgood had turned from the bar of the White Wizard Saloon and was saying: "Look here, Mexico, you've been chasing me around all day. Whacha want anyway?"

"Job, señor," said the other. As he spoke, he took off his tattered straw hat and showed more clearly a young face that would have been strikingly handsome, but for a long, ragged scar that puckered one cheek, pulling hard both on the eye and the mouth, so that the poor fellow had to talk all on one side, as it were.

291

He stood bowing before the deputy sheriff.

The latter surveyed him with a mixture of contempt and amusement.

"He knows you're a big man in town, Stew," said the bartender. "That's why he's chasing you around."

"Where could I give anybody a job except over in the jail?" demanded Stew Osgood with irritation. "We need a kind of a janitor over there. And a fine thing this would be to have in the jail, wouldn't it?"

"You take greasers," said the bartender with a profound air, "and they don't do much thinking. They just got hunches. You're the hunch of that kid, now. By thunder, what a mug he's got. But that ain't his fault. Looks like a mountain lion must've clawed him in the sweet days gone by."

"He's all gummed up," observed the deputy sheriff. "I'll bet that he ain't et a square meal in three days."

The man with the scar, who had stood before the pair as though he were incapable of understanding the words, now brightened, and bowed several times, rapidly.

"*Sí, señor . . . sí, señor,*" he murmured.

"Here's a dollar, anyway," said Stew Osgood, reaching into his pocket.

The man with the scar beamed with a crooked smile and started his bowing all over again. But now a heavy voice from the corner of the barroom boomed out: "That's why the country's goin' to hell!"

"Hold on," said the deputy sheriff. "Why is it goin' that way, brother?"

A mighty youth arose from a little round corner table where he had been sipping beer and eating crackers.

"Why should money be throwed away on foreign dogs?" he demanded. "I'd like to know, when there's a lot of honest men of our own that ain't got a job."

"Honest men like who?" asked the deputy sheriff.

"Like me," said the young giant, jabbing a grimy thumb against his breast by way of further identification.

Stew Osgood started to frown, for there was always plenty of battle spirit in him. However, he controlled himself, and a wicked thought gleamed in his eye. "I promised a dollar to somebody," he said, and flicked the broad-faced coin suddenly high in the air.

It hung, spinning, close to the ceiling for an instant, and then began its descent straight over the heads of the big tramp and the man of the scar.

"Out of the way, runt," said the larger of the pair, and reached up one hand for the dollar, while with the other he swung heavily at the man of the scar.

The latter avoided the swinging fist, slid in close, and with a dexterous pressure of his knee against the leg of the giant, caused the latter to sag suddenly and miss his target.

The big silver dollar fell with a resounding spat into the palm of Mexico.

At this the deputy sheriff exclaimed aloud with pleasure and surprise. "Pretty slick!" he cried out. "Pretty neat, Mexico. What happened to you, brother?"

"The dirty hound, he played a trick on me," said the tramp. "I gotta mind to eat him."

293

"Have you?" The deputy sheriff chuckled. "I dunno that you could, though." Then he smiled and added: "Here's another dollar for the man that can jump the highest."

As he spun the coin this time, the tramp paid no attention at all to the silver twinkling spot of light above his head, but gave his full eye to his rival. A casual swing had been unavailing to overawe the smaller man, so now he fell on guard and shot a very formidable straight left at the face with the scar.

Mexico swayed in and down; the blow drove over his shoulder, and, stepping closer, he gave the rigid point of his shoulder to the short ribs of the big tramp. The latter grunted, gasped, and staggered. And Mexico stooped and picked up the silver dollar that lay on the floor.

The deputy sheriff whooped with joy.

"Two for you, Mexico!" he cried. "I've got my money on you, fellow, and here's another try."

Once more, he threw a dollar into the air, but the tramp, with a string of oaths twisting out of his snarling mouth, rushed in to batter Mexico to a pulp.

The latter drew back a little, and then waited with alertness in his poise and calm in his eyes. Only at the very last minute, he bowed his body again with the swiftness of a bird as it stoops for a grain on the ground. As he stooped, his incredibly swift hands caught an outflung arm of the tramp, and, twisting himself about, he bore down with a mighty leverage.

The inevitable happened. The hulk of the tramp shot off his feet, and, hurtling over the shoulder of the

294

smaller man, it seemed as though he were purposely diving against the wall of the saloon, which he struck with a great crash.

He fell back, with a soft, thick *thud* upon the floor, while the man of the scar calmly picked up his third dollar.

"Ah, *señor*," he said, "I knew the good face the moment my eyes saw it."

The deputy sheriff was much astonished.

"How'd he do that, Jerry?" he demanded of the bartender. "Go and throw some water on that bum and roll him out into the street, unless he's got some broken bones."

The tramp did not need the water, however. He was of a tough substance, and, picking himself up now, he cast dizzy but wrathful glances around him, then staggered out through the swinging doors of the saloon.

"How'd you do that, Mexico?" the deputy sheriff repeated.

Mexico could only answer with a little dumb show of hands and attitudes.

Said Jerry, the bartender: "Ju-jitsu . . . or something like that. That's what it was, I guess. He looks a greaser, but maybe he's a chink or something. I dunno."

"Whoever heard of a Chinaman talkin' Spanish?" asked the deputy sheriff with a superior air. "This is a greaser, all right, and he can handle himself, is what I mean to say. I dunno but what he'd look pretty good in the jail, too. He'd make some of the boys in the cells think that they had the delirium tremens, maybe, taking

295

a look at this here mug. Look here, Mexico, you want a job?"

"*Sí, sí, señor*," said the other, with more of his rapid bows.

The deputy sheriff looked him over again. "You ain't much to fill the eye," he said, "but you kind of handle yourself all right, I gotta say. I gotta admit that about you. How cheap you work, son?"

A broad, smiling gesture, made with both arms, the palms of the hands up, indicated that money was no consideration, and that the honor of serving the deputy sheriff was all the happiness that he demanded from this sad world.

Stew Osgood grunted. "We gotta have somebody to tidy up around in the jail. I don't know why the greaser kid wouldn't do. Hey, what's your name?"

"I, Pedro, *señor*," said the other, with another curtsy.

"You Pedro, eh?" repeated the deputy sheriff. "Well, Pedro, you be a good boy over there in the jail, and everything'll be fine for you, but, if you try any tricks, I'm gonna skin you alive. Savvy?"

"Ah, *señor*," said Pedro, between sadness and a smile of deprecation, as though such a possibility was forever beyond his thoughts.

CHAPTER
NINE

The deputy sheriff had been having a drink in Jerry's saloon because, when he returned to the jail, he knew that a very unpleasant task was waiting for him.

Al Dupray was getting the third degree, and he had been getting it for the last hour now.

The third degree, in Clausen, was bad enough, although it was not the refined torture that was resorted to in larger and more hurried cities. The idea of Stew Osgood was simply to keep his man awake for thirty-six hours and try, by the steady pressure of questions, to make him confess a crime that, Osgood was confident, he had committed.

It was not the sort of thing that Osgood liked. He was a rough fellow. His skin was thick enough to practice most of the brutalities of his office without a qualm. But the third degree was something that revolted him. He had been told that it had to be done. The case was clear and strong against Dupray. There was hardly a doubt that he would be convicted when the case went to trial. But it would cost the county a great deal to prosecute. For the unlucky news had come in that the great and terrible

Charles Dupray, the uncle of Al, was again free and roving. He would be certain to pour huge sums of money into the defense, and, when he did that, it meant that he could hire some of the best lawyers in the country to fight out the case. Even if they failed, pressure would be brought to bear upon the prosecuting district attorney. Extra legal help would be required. Besides costing the taxpayers of the town a round sum, the trial would also give Clausen undesired publicity as a wild Western center of gun play and all the rest. The unhappy past would surely be raked up, and the town of Clausen wished at all costs to avoid such a resurrection.

There was one way to preclude all the expense of time and dollars, and that was to secure a confession from Al Dupray. A day and a half before the questioning had started. Now it was about to end, and Deputy Stew Osgood had prepared himself to put on the final pressure.

He strode back to the jail, with the shorter-stepping Pedro hurrying behind him.

When they got to the jail, the mind of the deputy sheriff was not upon his new employee but upon the disagreeable work before him. He simply picked a cap off a nail on the wall and jammed it on the head of Mexico. He picked off a uniform coat and threw it toward him.

"There's your outfit that shows you belong to the jail," he observed. "Now get busy. Grab a broom and a mop or something and start tidying up, Mexico. All you gents south of the Río Grande know how to scrub, or you ought to."

Pedro accepted the broom as though it were the sword conferring knighthood upon him. The deputy sheriff hurried on toward his own office.

He opened the door and stepped into a thick atmosphere of cigarette smoke. Through that mist he saw two hollow-eyed men, one upon either side of a figure that slumped down in a chair between them. The hands of Al Dupray were manacled together, being chained around one arm of the chair. Just as the deputy opened the door, one of the questioners shook Dupray violently by the arm, and he raised his head with a start out of the instant of slumber into which he had fallen.

It was true that he somewhat resembled the great Charley Dupray in appearance. The long vigil had given to his face a pallor like that of his celebrated and infamous uncle, and the face was itself round. But it lacked some of the frog-like hideousness of Charley. There was more of a nose. The mouth was not so wide a slit. There were lips to observe. The forehead was respectably broad, although low.

"You killed Tom Older," croaked the questioner who had shaken the young man by the shoulder. "Why don't you tell the truth and cut short the wait?"

The answer was mere silence. Gloomily the man looked up at the deputy, who scowled back in return, then went to the window and jerked it open. A long arm of freshness reached from the outer world into that stifling atmosphere.

Then big Stew Osgood took up his place before the prisoner. He spread his legs and beat his fist on the palm of his hand. "We've got you at last, kid," he said.

"Have you?" muttered Dupray, looking up with hollow eyes.

"Yeah. We've got you," the deputy sheriff repeated. "We got your fingerprints. It don't make no difference, now, whether you confess to us or not. We got your fingerprints, all right."

"On what?" asked the young man, frowning.

"You know on what, all right," said Osgood. "We got 'em, and that winds up the case."

"What would my fingerprints be on?" asked Dupray.

"On the handle of the axe that brained poor Tom Older!" cried the deputy. He leaned a little, so as to make out more clearly the effect of this lie upon the prisoner.

Dupray merely shook his head. "I used that axe, but I used it to chop wood," he insisted. "That's all." And his chin fell upon his breast; in an instant he was snoring, open mouthed.

The deputy sheriff looked at the pair. "You been at him all the time?" he muttered.

"All the time," said one of the men. "And a hell of a dirty job it is, too."

"It's a rotten job. I hate it like you do," agreed Osgood. "But it's orders, and we've got to do what we're told. There ain't any doubt that he's the murderer, is there?"

"No," admitted one of the tormentors.

300

"Then," said Osgood, "it don't make much difference what we do to him, does it?"

"Maybe not," said the first speaker. "Only, it makes me sick to see the way the kid suffers. He may be a Dupray, but he's human, just the same."

"No Dupray's human," declared Osgood. "Wake him up."

They shook him from either side. He opened his eyes with a groan of agony, but he set his teeth at once to shut off complaint and weakness.

"I've got the whole story that'll hang you," declared Osgood.

"You lie," Dupray said wearily.

"I lie, do I?" exclaimed Osgood, pretending to be in a rage. Then he made himself laugh loudly. "We've got it hung on you at last," he said.

"You lie again."

"Do I? Here it is, all wrote out. This is the confession that you can sign, brother, and then go to bed and have a good sleep."

"I won't sign nothing," said Al Dupray.

"You fool," said the sheriff. "You think that you're not going to hang, then?"

"I know that you crooks'll hang me," said Al Dupray. "I know that as sure as I know my name's Dupray, and that Charley Dupray's my uncle. But I ain't gonna sign nothin'."

"You're a fool if you don't sign this," said Stew Osgood. "Listen. We got all the facts here. I leave out the beginning. I cut right into the middle. You're supposed to be talking. And this is what you'd say, if you'd tell the truth."

He began to read aloud: "'I kept telling Tom Older that it was no good prospecting the Clausen Hills any more, because they'd been gone over with a fine-toothed comb for years. But he kept right on. I pointed out to him that I'd paid for the grubstake, and that I was doing my share of the camp work, too. I was sick of it, and I wanted to try some new ground, where we'd have a chance. But the fool kept right on. Finally, one night in the hills, it came to a show-down, and I told him that I wouldn't stand it any longer.'

"'He told me I could get out, if I didn't like his way of prospecting. I said I'd get out, willing enough, if he'd pay me back the grubstake money that I'd spent. He damned me for that and laughed in my face. He was as mean as a rat. That's what he looked like, an old rat. I couldn't stand it. Something exploded in my mind. I'd been cutting wood for the fire, and I still had the axe in my hand. I gave it a swing and brought it down on his head. He fell on his face. He never moved after I hit him.'"

Osgood stopped reading. "There you are, brother," he said. "All that you have to do is to sign."

"By thunder," said the prisoner hoarsely, "it's almost straight, every line of it."

The sheriff started violently. But he covered up his surprise by exclaiming: "Sure, it's true. We've got everything on you."

"It's almost true, every word of it," Dupray said, still astonished. "It's true that I stood there with a load of

302

wood in one arm, and the axe in my other hand. It's true that I cursed him for an old fool and asked him how many more days we were going to stay there among the rocks and the brush. Then he told me that we'd stay there as long as pleased him, and that he was kind of sorry that he was going to make a worthless, complaining fool like me a rich man.

"When I heard him say that, I was so mad that I heaved up the axe and said that I had half a mind to brain him with it. I did have half a mind to do it. But I recollected soon enough Uncle Charley. He always comes pop into my head, whenever I get a crazy wish to do something wrong. So I threw the axe away, and I went running off into the night, half crazy. That's the true story. That's the whole story. When I come back, there was Tom Older lying dead, and the axe was there with the blood on it, and the trail of a man that had come out of the brush to the fire, and gone away again."

"That was the trail of Pete Simmons, that came along and found the old man lying dead," declared Osgood. "Are you trying to put the blame on an honest man like Simmons? Dupray, you dog, you murdered the old man . . . and then you went sneaking off. It was only later that you changed your mind and came back to bluff the job out."

"Ain't Simmons staked out the mine that Tom Older found?" shouted the prisoner. "Ain't that a fact? Why wouldn't he've killed Tom, and come rushin' down to Clausen to put the blame for the killing on me and to file his claim? That's what I wanna know."

Osgood looked with sudden weariness and disgust at the wild, white face and the red-rimmed eyes. Then he said tersely: "Take him away and slam him into the cell again. I've done my best, but the fool won't listen to reason."

CHAPTER
TEN

The two third-degree tormentors jerked open the door of the sheriff's office and thrust the prisoner in willingly enough, for they hated the dirty work of the long inquisition almost as much as Al Dupray could have hated it.

As they entered the inner corridor, they almost fell over the form of the newly hired janitor, who was down on his knees, industriously scrubbing the floor just outside the door of the sheriff's office. The two guards, looking down at the uniform coat and cap, grunted out a few oaths and went on down the hall to the aisle that led between the rows of cells.

Ten men were in those cells that night, for the deputy sheriff kept himself well occupied in Clausen, and saw to it that crime was kept in check. They pressed against the bars of their cells and looked steadily at the accused murderer, as he passed down toward his own strong place of keeping. They could hear the *clanking* of the heavy chains that were fastened on him, thus fastening him to the huge steel bolts that were worked into the wall of the prison. Then they could hear the voice of one of the guards, saying, rather too loudly:

"Look a-here, kid, you oughta have more sense. It ain't gonna buy you nothing, to keep your face shut, and lie like this. Everybody knows that you croaked Tom Older. You're gonna hang for it, all right."

"I know that I'm going to hang," said the young man, "but I won't put the rope around my own neck, maybe."

"Blockhead!" said the guard angrily. "Maybe you'd have a good shot at getting off with life, if you turned in the evidence ag'in' yourself. Ain't you gonna have no sense?"

"I stick to what I've said," persisted the other calmly.

"You're a fool, and the biggest fool that I ever heard of," said the guard. "There you are, locked up safe and sound. Stay there and rot, till they come and get you for the rope."

The guards walked out, the door was closed behind them, and the three keys were turned in the three locks. They disappeared. The two larger lights were put out. And there remained only two small, flickering night lamps, to illumine the interior of the jail. They threw into every cell only a confused blur of shadows and faint light, and the eye could make out almost nothing.

Now, down the corridor, came the form of Pedro, the new janitor's assistant, with a bucket of soapy water, a scrubbing brush, and a mop. He fell upon his knees, at the end of the aisle, and began to work.

A few of the prisoners went to the bars of their cells, and, looking out, they scoffed at and reproached the solemn, industrious worker. One of them summed up the opinion of the others.

"What's the good of bein' a free man, if you're gonna work in a jail, kid? There ain't any good in it at all. If you ain't got sense enough to stay clear of a dump like this, you might as well be doin' time yourself."

Pedro returned no answer. He continued to scrub so patiently and so hard that his whole body shook with his movements.

Finally the others turned in on their cots. One or two called good nights to companions up and down the aisle. Some others cursed the brightness of the lights; others cursed their dimness, but by degrees the voices died out, and soft sounds of snoring rose.

Pedro, by this time, had carried his careful scrubbing as far as the door of the cell of Al Dupray.

Now he stood up and walked, carrying his bucket, slowly down the length of the aisle. His feet made no sound. He seemed to look neither to right nor to left, and yet he penetrated through the shadows, and saw every form stretched out under the blankets of the cots.

He returned, as he had gone, with the same soundless steps, and, putting down the bucket and scrubbing brush, he kneeled before the door of the cell of Al Dupray. In his fingers appeared a thin length of steel spring, such as might have come out of the mechanism of a big watch or a clock. With this he began to fumble at the lowest and largest of the locks. Deftly he worked, his ear pressed close to the keyhole, his whole body tense with the effort of perfect concentration.

A number of minutes passed. Then there was a slight but rather prolonged sliding sound. Pedro drew back, and nodded his head with satisfaction.

Across the aisle, behind him, a voice said quietly: "Fine, kid. You done that pretty good. Before you open the next one, you might take a look at my door and see what you can do with it."

Pedro turned his head. He could see the dim silhouette of the prisoner, the pale gleam of the hands that clasped the bars of the cell. He said nothing, but waited.

There was no more snoring, and, looking up and down the aisle, he made out other forms, other hands. A voice said, farther away: "I'll be in on this, or I'll be damned." And another: "We all walk out together."

Pedro listened and sighed.

"Me first," said the man across the aisle, who had spoken first, "or else I'm gonna squeal. I'm gonna raise hell, I tell you . . . unless you come over here, and open this door. You're a beauty, and you can use some of your good looks on me."

The man with the scar stood up from his work and turned. How did it happen that noiseless work had awakened the prisoners? Well, there are other mysteries of instinct, never so well exemplified as inside the walls of a prison.

Some electric current of sympathy had informed them all that what they wished for themselves was being brought to pass for another, a companion — and that one, the man of the strong room.

Then said Pedro in perfectly good English: "Boys, will you listen to me?"

It was a very soft and quiet voice, and it was so exquisitely gauged that it barely carried to the farther end of the row of cells.

"We'll listen," said someone halfway up the aisle and in a voice pitched like that of the speaker.

"I'm here for Al Dupray. He's here for murder," said Pedro. "And the murder he's here for is a job he didn't do. He's being railroaded because he really didn't do the job that he's accused of. Pete Simmons murdered Tom Older, and Pete threw the blame where people would believe that it ought to rest. None of the rest of you has any such charge hanging over his head. Most of you are in for small things. Let me get Dupray out of his cell, and I'll try to help the rest of you if there's time. Is that fair?"

"Fair or not," said the man across the aisle more loudly, "you start working on my door right now, or I'm gonna raise a holler. You hear me, buddy?"

"I hear you talk," Pedro said slowly. "I don't want to believe what I hear, though. You fellows don't think that I can empty the whole jail, do you? You don't think that I've got the whole night ahead of me? In less than ten minutes, there'll be a guard walking on the rounds."

"Guard or no guard," said the man across the aisle, "you open this lock, Mister Slick, or I holler. You can count to ten. Or I'll do the counting myself."

The new janitor paused before answering, and both his hands contracted.

Then a voice spoke, the same soft voice that had spoken before, halfway up the aisle: "Buck?"

"I hear you, Slim," said the man across the aisle.

"Buck," said Slim, "you know what you are?"

"I know I'm gonna walk free out of this cell in half a minute," said Buck.

"You're a hog, is what you are," said Slim.

"What do I care what you think?" demanded Buck over loudly.

And Slim answered: "Listen to me."

"I'm listening, and be damned to you and your ideas," said Buck. "I wouldn't be in here at all, except for you and some of your fast brain work."

"Buck," said Slim, "you shut up and let the kid go on with his work. If he's got a chance, he'll turn Dupray loose and come back for the rest of us. What we got ahead of us? Maybe thirty days. No more'n that. Thirty days and it's the rope for Dupray, unless he gets loose right *pronto.*"

"You do your own thinkin'," said Buck. "I'll think for myself and do for myself, from now on."

There was a moment of silence. The man of the scar did not speak. Neither did any of the other men in the cells up and down the aisle.

Then the voice of Slim struck in again. "Buck, if you carry on, I'm gonna get hold of you, after I get out of this here jail. I'm gonna follow you and cut your rat's throat." He spoke as softly as ever. But there was all the sincerity of a prayer in his speaking.

No one broke in, but all waited, and, while they waited, they counted seconds — Pedro and all the

310

others within hearing distance. Two, three, four, five, ten counts, and then it became fairly certain that Buck was considering seriously what Slim had said.

Then the voice of Slim went on as quietly and gently as ever: "I'm Slim Malone. The rest of you birds, listen to me pipe up. The one that peeps, I'm gonna remember, and I'm gonna write him down in red. You hear me? Leave the kid a free road. Leave him be. I'm Slim Malone, and I mean what I say."

Still, for another instant, Pedro waited. There was no sound, and, dropping again upon his knees, he fell to work upon the central lock of the three. Rapidly he worked and with wonderful delicacy, also. Presently the slight sliding sound came again, and it was clear that the second lock had been mastered. He rose to his feet and began on the third and last lock. As he did so, he was aware of something like a warning whisper, not so much heard, as felt. He turned and saw that every man had disappeared from the bars of the cells, and down the aisle walked a guard, keys in one hand, a lantern in the other.

CHAPTER
ELEVEN

The new janitor removed from his hand the little bit of spring with which he was working — it had that instant turned the bolt of the lock. In its place appeared a rag of cloth, with which he started polishing the outer edge of the door.

It seemed that he had conjured the bit of rag out of the thin air. Intently he worked but aware of the approaching steps, and aware, also, of eyes that watched him intently, like the eyes of hunted things, suffering and hoping for a fellow being, when a beast of prey is stalking.

A great hand fell suddenly upon the shoulder of Pedro. He turned his head with a sudden start and a gasp. "Ah, *señor!*" he exclaimed.

The great hand lifted him to his feet. He stood agape, the pull of the scar drawing his mouth all awry.

"What's the hell's work you're doing here?" asked the guard.

"Me? *Señor*, I scrub, I polish all day long. I do it everything right, no?"

The guard scowled fiercely down at him. "It ain't for nothin' that I had a pricklin' in my bones," he said.

"You skunk, you're up to something. What you been tryin' on those locks?"

"*Señor*, and what should poor Pedro try?" said the new janitor. He clasped his hands together and looked with infinite and trembling appeal at the other.

The guard drew back a little, his scowl as black as ever, his brows drawn down in a deep shadow over his eyes.

"By the looks of you," he declared, "you ain't nothin' at all. But I ain't one to go by the looks, only. There's something more than looks, I reckon. Lemme try the key on one of those locks and see if there's been any funny business around here. That's all that I wanna see." He gritted his teeth in the very premonition of rage as he spoke, and, stepping forward, he knocked Pedro back and out of his way with a gesture of his hand.

It seemed to the new janitor that the burning of the eyes from the shadow grew fiercer every moment.

The guard, in the meantime, had fitted one of the keys into the central lock, stooping to do so. As he turned the key, finding that nothing resisted against its pressure, he exclaimed suddenly under his breath.

At that moment, it seemed that Pedro grew taller, stepping almost out of his rags into a majesty of appearance. Moving forward on a noiseless foot, he struck with the edge of his palm, as a butcher might strike with a cleaver, across the back of the guard's neck. The man slumped to the floor.

Up and down the corridor came a sigh like the whisper of wind through an opened door.

The man of the scar paid no heed to it. He knew that it was the sympathetic intake of breath by all of those who covertly and so intensely looked out upon his doings. He regarded not the fallen guard for the moment. It was as though he knew perfectly how long that man would lie still, all his body stunned and benumbed by the impact of the blow, for Pedro now ran lightly as a shadow down the aisle between the cells and passed the bunch of keys through the bars into the cell of Slim Malone.

"All right, Slim," he whispered. "You can reach your hand through, and get at the lock of your door. Don't let the keys jingle. Keep on trying till you find the right one. I'm in a hurry."

He was back at the door of Al Dupray's cell instantly and pulled it open. Then he caught the limp form of the guard under the pits of the arms, dragged him inside, into the darkness, and let him slump to the floor.

Al Dupray had long since risen from his cot; he moved now, with a slight *jingling* of steel upon steel.

The man of the scar stepped out into the aisle again, brought in the lantern of the fallen guard, and set it on the floor. He spared a half second to look up, fixedly, into the face of Dupray, and that young man saw in those dark eyes a glint of yellow fire like the gleam that will appear on the polished black of a windowpane at night when a lamp is borne past it.

Then Pedro set to work upon the three locks that secured the fetters of the prisoner. As he worked, he spoke in a voice hardly louder than a whisper: "Your uncle sent me up to you. I'm Speedy. You start. That

314

means you know about me from your uncle. We made a deal for you. I'm to work to get you free. He's to leave some friends of mine alone. That's all. If we can get out of the jail, I have horses cached."

The first lock, which was upon the hands, now yielded. At the same time, there was a loud knocking at the front door of the jail, and Speedy leaped to his feet with a muffled exclamation. Only for a moment he hesitated, then he said: "I'll be back. Take charge of this." He hauled the breathing, but still senseless guard within the grip of Al Dupray's hands, then turned and fled down the corridor between the cells.

As he passed the cell of Slim Malone, he could see the hands of the man protruding through the bars, while he patiently but clumsily tried key after key in the lock. No key, so far, had fitted.

Like a ghost, soundlessly, Speedy reached the door of the jail. He pushed back the complicated bolts and opened it a fraction of an inch.

"Who's there?" he asked.

"Telegram, mister," said the voice of a drawling, sleepy boy.

Speedy pulled the door open, took the telegram from the freckle-faced lad, and scrawled a word on the receipt book. Then he closed the door, and, as he closed it, already his supple fingers were preparing to rip the envelope open, when he heard another door open and a brighter shaft of light shone into the hall.

It was Deputy Sheriff Stewart Osgood saying loudly, sternly: "What's going on here?"

The man of the scar began his bowing, as he approached. "A message for you, *señor*, that has come." He delivered it into the hands of Stew Osgood with another bow.

"Who told you to be moochin' around here at this time of night?" asked Osgood sourly.

"I? *Señor*, I am to clean the floors and the floors are large."

"Aw, the devil," muttered Osgood, turning away. "Save it for tomorrow. The jail won't rust till tomorrow. Go on and get out of here, will you?"

"I go *señor*, with thanks," said Speedy. "I go as quickly as my feet will take me. *Señor* is to Pedro as a father."

"You talk like a fool," said the deputy sheriff bluntly. "Go on and get!" He passed through the door of his office, and closed the door behind him, while Speedy turned and raced back to the open door of the cell of Dupray. Inside, there was a faint sound of scuffling and the subdued, terrible voice of Dupray, saying to the now conscious guard: "Try that ag'in, and I'm certainly gonna throttle you."

Speedy dropped to his knees, and resumed the work that he had left off.

The second lock gave way under the magic of his small bit of wire. The third was more difficult. As he worked, a fine perspiration broke out on his forehead and began to stream down his face. He had to wink his eyes to keep the stinging sweat out of them.

Dupray, just above his shoulder, was whispering: "You're the gamest that I ever seen. I thought you were a demon. But I never seen a finer thing. I don't hardly

316

care what happens to me, after I seen a thing like this, is all I gotta say."

The third lock yielded, and Dupray stepped free from the shackles. "Now this?" he asked, gesturing toward the prostrate body of the guard, and setting his jaw savagely.

"Choke him," Speedy said calmly.

"I'll do it," said Dupray, bending over, his fingers already extending like the talons of a bird.

"Don't do it, fellows," said the guard, in a voice that was a cross between whimper and whisper. "I won't make a sound. I'll lay here like I was dead. I won't blow on you. Don't bump me off, boys. I ain't gonna do a thing to give you away."

"He lies," young Dupray said sternly. "He's a sneak, and all sneaks will lie."

"Let him go," said Speedy. "We'll at least keep our hands clean, this far."

In the meantime, the deputy sheriff had taken the telegram into his office and was in no hurry to open it. He first made himself comfortable in his chair. Then he hoisted his heels to the edge of his desk. Finally he lighted a cigar and turned it in his mouth until it found a comfortable corner to fit into. When all this had been achieved, he at last opened the missive, and read:

Deputy Sheriff Stewart Osgood:
   Word just received that Harrison Williams, alias The Doctor, alias The Slip, alias Speedy, has

undertaken to try to free Al Dupray. Informant William Cort. Be on guard. Disguises of Speedy often old man with white beard and halt in one leg, or doctor with large darkened glasses and imperial, or ragged tramp, or Mexican peon with scarred face.

The deputy sheriff, as he came to this portion of his long telegram, felt his eyes thrust out from his head. He rose from his chair, his whole body stiffening. *Speedy!* He had heard that name, a name of magic. But Speedy was supposed to be the grand enemy of the terrible Charley Dupray. Speedy had caught the outlaw; Speedy had clamped him in jail, there to await the due processes of the law. Yet, this same man was here, in that building, disguised as the Mexican peon with the scarred face.

He caught up a revolver. That choice he changed for a sawed-off shotgun, and lurched for the door of his office.

CHAPTER
TWELVE

Down the inner corridor of the cells, Speedy and Al Dupray had hardly started moving, when Slim Malone turned a key that opened his door and stepped out into the hallway. As he appeared, with Speedy and Dupray moving rapidly down the corridor, it became apparent to those hungry-eyed watchers in the other cells that they had little chance of being liberated. Now, also, the injured guard in the cell where Dupray had been confined groaned heavily. It was like a signal. From every throat of every prisoner in every cell there rose a howl of rage and envy, and Buck, in particular, leaped up and down like a baboon, screeching and shaking the bars of his cell like an animal.

It was just as the deputy sheriff opened the door of his office that this howling chorus arose and beat like a heavy wave against his brain. He looked wildly up and down as Slim Malone fitted the largest of the keys in the bunch into the lock of the side door of the building.

Three men were there, and plainly the deputy distinguished among them the slender outlines of his man of the scarred face. Speedy! He jerked up the gun and fired as the door swung open. He could have sworn that he heard the impact of the bullet as it struck flesh, but then all three were swept through the door. It slammed heavily behind them and the spring lock *clanked* home. Direct pursuit on that side of the jail was impossible.

Blinded with rage and with fear, feeling that his whole reputation was hanging on their escape, the deputy raced through the front door of the jail, shouting as he ran.

Down the corridor behind him came the guard, so recently stretched prostrate in the cell of Dupray.

But, as the two ran out into the open of the night, they heard the rattling hoofs of horses at full gallop, and guessed shrewdly enough that their quarry was off to a running start.

The deputy came to a halt. Sudden pursuit would hardly gain anything for the law. As he ran his eye over the ragged outlines of the mountains, he realized that there were 10,000 possible hiding places for the fugitives, one as good as the other. There was no chance of locating them, then, unless he could read the subtle mind of the celebrated Speedy. He could hit upon only one suggestion, and that was the house of Pete Simmons, several miles out of the town.

Again and again, Al Dupray had tried to shift the blame for the killing of Tom Older upon Simmons, who was the man, in fact, who had profited by that strike that Older had made just before his death.

The story was amusing, in spite of its dreadful aftermath. Sam Deacon, riding through the Clausen Hills, had come upon Tom Older making the camp that proved to be his last, and, dismounting to talk with the veteran prospector, Older had told him, with grim amusement, about the furious discontent of his young companion, Al Dupray.

"Al's ready to kill me," Tom Older had said, as Sam Deacon had testified in the courtroom at the trial. "Al's ready to do me up. He says that I'm a fool to play around here where every inch has been prospected a hundred times over. Al's in a terrible stew. He don't know that I've got this in my pocket."

As he spoke, he had pulled out a stone chip, and showed it to the excited eyes of Deacon, with a bright veining of yellow plainly to be seen. So much was known from Sam Deacon.

But Pete Simmons, when he found the dead man and found the chip of stone in his pocket, actually located the rock from which the chip had been taken. That was why a score of men were now moiling and toiling under his direction and in his interest. He bade fair to become a rich man, as a result of that discovery of his.

At any rate, Pete Simmons was an object of hatred to Al Dupray, perhaps simply because the man had taken up the claim that might have belonged to him and to the dead man. Whatever the reasons, it well might be, no matter where the other two went, that Dupray would hunt for Simmons; one murder leads to another, the deputy sheriff was sure. And so he said to the panting guard beside him: "What happened?"

"I seen him working at the lock of the door of Dupray. The greaser, I mean. I seen him working, and he said he was only scrubbing down the steel. I didn't think that the steel needed no scrubbing. I wondered if the fool had been tryin' to pick the locks, maybe? Anyway, I put a key in, and, sure enough, the bolt had been slipped already. Just as I was about to turn and grab him, he socked me with something. I dunno what. It felt like an axe with a dull edge. And not so dog-gone dull, neither. My neck was pretty near broke."

"That's enough yammering," said the deputy sheriff. "Get Collins and Bill Wade. Get Thayer, too, and Millmarch. Tell them to be here in five minutes with their horses and guns. You be on hand, too. We're going to ride, tonight, and there may be some fighting at the far end of the ride, too."

CHAPTER
THIRTEEN

The house of Pete Simmons was a small shack that stood up high on the side of a hill, with a little rickety verandah built across the front of it and a crooked stovepipe issuing from the top. It looked very much like some of those houses that Negroes build and live in down South.

But there was nothing Negroid about Simmons. He was a big, burly, red-headed fellow with a loud, brawling laugh, considered good company on the range, an excellent shot, a great hunter of deer. He had a little patch of ground that was of no great use to him, and he made his money, or had made it until recently, by hiring out as a cowpuncher or as a worker in the mines.

Now, however, that he was taking gold out of the hard ground of the Clausen Hills and seemed certain of becoming a rich man before long, he had not changed his mode of living in the least. He did not hire a servant. He did not enlarge or improve the old shack, but remained where he had always been and seemed rather uninterested in the luck he was having with the mine. This caused the entire countryside to respect him more than ever.

On this night, he sat on his verandah, talking to a person who was none other than the editor of the Clausen *News* and giving forth his ideas on many things, while the editor took notes.

They had an audience of three, who had come upon them, unseen and unknown, by riding to the top of the hill behind the house and so slipping silently down to the side of the verandah. There they crouched in the brush and listened to the voices close over their heads.

The editor was about to leave.

"The main thing, Simmons," he said, "is this talk going around about you building a memorial to Tom Older. What about that? That's news that's worth the front page, and a lot of it, too."

"You see," said Simmons, "it's this way. That mine ain't belonging to me, except you might say by clean accident. It was accident that I come across poor old Tom lyin' dead. It was a lot more of an accident that I happened to look in his pocket and found the chip of rock. You know, I was looking for something that might kind of explain why anybody would have done dirt to Older. And it was a third accident that I happened to stumble right onto the boulder that the chip had been taken off of. By rights, Older should've had that mine . . . him and the young fellow that murdered him. But Older ain't got any relations to claim his share of it. And I guess that Dupray's claim ain't worth a damn. What am I to do? Put all the money into my pocket like a hog? No. I wanna do something about it and I figger that the best way is to put up something for Clausen that'll be worthwhile. Maybe a hospital. Maybe a courthouse, with the name of Tom Older onto it. Understand?"

"That's the right idea. It shows that you got good stuff in you, Simmons," said the editor. "And that's a thing that none of us ever doubted. Suppose that I say it's a courthouse that you're going to build. What would you spend?"

"Why, a pretty good courthouse could be built for say twenty-five thousand dollars, maybe," suggested Simmons.

"That's mighty public-spirited," said the other. "Twenty-five thousand is a lot of thousands. But it don't look so big in print. Suppose that I push it up a little bigger and say that you're planning a fine courthouse, and that the cost would be around a hundred thousand. That'll give people something to look at and something to talk about, and it'll make you a great man in Clausen."

"Aw, you handle it the way you think is the best," Simmons said carelessly. "I dunno nothing about the way that newspapers handle things at all. You do it your own way, will you?"

"I'll do that. You leave your reputation to me, Simmons, and I'll make it grow in a way that'll surprise you. Out of a thing like that courthouse, state senatorships and all sorts of honors are likely to come eventually. You'll be the Honorable Peter Simmons, one of these days, and before you know it. Leave it all to me."

"I'll leave it all to you, because I really wouldn't know what to do about it," declared Simmons. "Go ahead and do what you please, partner."

"Good night," said the editor.

"Have another drink?"

"No, thanks. I'll get along back. The night's turning chilly. Do you mind walking down to the gate with me?"

"It's a pleasure," said Simmons.

They came clumping down the front steps, and walked down the path to the gate, beyond which was the horse and buggy of the editor. There were more agreeable messages, more good nights, and then the newspaperman drove back up the little winding trail toward Clausen.

Big Pete Simmons remained for a moment to admire the moon and the stars. His hands were deep in his pockets and his head thrown far back, as he strolled slowly up the path, and, therefore, he did not see the danger until it was just upon him. On either side of him a revolver gleamed, and three men arose out of the shadows of the brush.

Simmons said calmly: "What you want, boys? Money? I'll give you what I've got in the house, if that's it."

"Stick 'em up!" said Al Dupray. The voice staggered Simmons like the blow of a bullet over the heart. He breathed a curse. "Up with your hands!" repeated Al Dupray, through his teeth.

The hands of Simmons went swiftly up in the air. He rose on tiptoe, in his eagerness to grasp at the stars, as it seemed.

326

"Just walk up the stairs," said Speedy, "and inside the house, Simmons. This'll soon be over. Don't be nervous. I don't think that we'll have to do anything to you. Just a minute, first." Deftly he picked a long-barreled Colt and a big knife out of the clothes of the other, and then Simmons walked awkwardly up the stairs, still holding his hands stiff and high above his head. He had to lower them a little, going through the front door of the house.

Now they gathered in the small front room, where the long arms of Simmons kept the tips of his fingers touching the ceiling. He was pale, but his face was grimly set rather than unnerved and sagging from overmastering fear.

"Sit down, sit down," Speedy said, taking quiet control of the situation. "Sit down, Simmons, and we'll have a little chat together."

"All right," said Simmons. He drew in a breath as he lowered his arms, and then pulled up a chair to the table.

"I'd like to finish him off, right now," Al Dupray said suddenly. "Speedy, give him his gun, and let the two of us have it out."

"Speedy?" exclaimed Simmons. "Are you Speedy?"

"Some people call me by that name," answered Speedy.

"Well" — Simmons sighed — "I'm damned glad of that. You're never mixed up with crooked work. Speedy, what's the deal about?"

"It's about the way you murdered Tom Older and laid the blame on Dupray," replied Speedy.

The shock made Simmons close his eyes. When he opened them, they were dark with desperation. "Is that the kind of a gag that they've talked over to you, Speedy?" he complained.

"That's the gag," said Speedy. "We've got the information, Simmons, but we want your signed confession before we send you to the jail."

"Signed confession?" Simmons said, growing more and more colorless. He looked wildly about him, toward the two faded photographs of his father and mother that hung on the wall. He seemed to study the details of the tattered wallpaper, also, and then he looked down to his own great, brown hands, that lay on the edge of the table.

"Signed confession," repeated Speedy.

"I'll see you dead first!" exploded Simmons.

"I told you that you'd never get it out of him, Speedy," said Al Dupray, shaking his weary head.

"Then we'll hang him in his own house," said Speedy. "We'll hang him up to his own ceiling. And we'll do it now."

"You won't. That's not your line, Speedy," said Simmons. "I know you too well for that. You can't bluff me, boys. You wouldn't do a murder that would outlaw the lot of you."

"Murder?" said Speedy. "It will pass as a suicide. When they find you, they'll find your hands free, and your signed confession lying on the table."

"My signed confession? And how might you be getting that out of me?" asked Simmons, squinting his eyes. "Besides, I never done the job."

"Who did, then?" asked Al Dupray.

"You done it, you rat," said Simmons.

Slim Malone caught the gun hand of the young man barely in time.

Simmons, after wincing, tried to face out the situation again. "The world knows that you done it," he insisted.

"Don't be a fool, Simmons," Speedy said as calmly as ever. "The fact is that you killed Tom Older, and now conscience has got hold of you, and you'll hang yourself, you poor devil, and leave your signed confession lying here on the table."

"You're gonna drive me crazy, are you? Think I'm fool enough to write out a confession?" asked Simmons.

Speedy smiled. "I'll write it for you, brother," he said. "I'm a penman, Simmons. You seem to have heard so much about me, that perhaps you've heard that, too."

Simmons stared long and earnestly. Conviction was dawning slowly in his eyes, and now his mouth dropped open, yet it was a moment before he could speak. "What would you write down in that there confession?" he asked. "Why, nobody would believe it. Everybody knows that I was a good friend of Tom Older."

"That's the point of it," said Speedy. "When you dropped in on Tom at his camp, he was so sure that you were his friend, that he even showed you the sample and the place he chipped it. Then he sat down beside the fire and talked, warmed his hands at it, while you picked up the axe to get more wood, and, while you stood there behind him, it came into your mind that it would be an easy thing to put him out of the way. You remembered how he'd told you of Dupray's discontent. Other people knew that young Al was dissatisfied, also. Therefore, the impulse came over you in a twinkling. You're not a young man. Before long, you'd have begun to get old and stiff. So you lifted the axe and . . ."

"Stop!" gasped Simmons. "Where were you hiding, Speedy, that you seen it?" He collected himself, instantly. "I mean," he said. "I mean to say that there ain't a word of truth in that lingo."

"You can write out the confession and go to jail," said Speedy, still very calm and steady, "and there you can take your chances with the law, or else we'll hang you up here, man, and leave every sign to make the world sure that you committed suicide out of a guilty conscience." He nodded to Slim Malone. "You have the rope, Slim, I think," he said.

"It's here," said Malone. He looked up toward the ceiling, at the big iron hook projecting downward, from which a lamp had probably once been suspended.

"It's all right," said Speedy. "We won't have to use it, or will we, Simmons?"

The gentleness of his voice caused a shudder of horror to sweep through the big body of Simmons.

Suddenly he said: "I'll write it. It was the damned axe. If only I hadn't laid my hands on it."

"You'd better be drifting, Slim," Speedy said, after a time, while the pen was still scratching.

Slim Malone took off his hat and smoothed his rust-colored hair. Then he grinned. "I suppose they want me more'n ever," he suggested. "More for the jail break, now, than for what I did before, eh?"

"I suppose so," said Speedy. "That was a good turn you did me in the jail, Slim. I'll remember it."

Slim Malone drew up his slender, athletic body to its full height. "Why, Speedy, it was worth it," he said, "just for the pleasure of seein' how you handled that job there in the jail. Will you tell me one thing before I go?"

"Anything I can."

"Then, what did you do to that big stiff back there in the jail? How'd you paralyze him like that?"

"Hold out your hand," said Speedy.

Malone obeyed, and, across his upturned fingers, Speedy struck with the edge of his palm. It was as though a rattan had whipped across the fingers of Malone, and he flinched from the pain.

"Thunder and blazes!" he exclaimed.

"It takes practice, is all," Speedy explained. "Back in Japan, they have fellows who can break a stone bar an inch thick with that sort of a stroke. I didn't give the guard the full weight, at that."

Malone shook hands.

"You call it easy, you call it practice," said Malone. "I call it pretty slick. So long, old son."

"So long," said Speedy. "Remember me, partner. You and I could ride some trail together, one of these days."

"Just say my name out loud whenever you want me," answered Malone, "and I'll manage to hear it and come on the dead run. So long again. Good bye, Dupray. I'm glad you're out of this here mess."

But Dupray was asleep in his chair.

Malone did not waken him. He simply stepped through the door and sped down the steps. A moment later, they heard the snort of his horse, and the *thumping* of hoofs as it galloped away through the night.

Still the pen of Simmons scratched on and on. He canted his head to one side. He sweated, not with agony at the words that he was forced to write, but with the labor of committing them to the paper. He bit his lip and grunted, strained, and finally looked up with a sigh of relief. "That's about all, I guess," he said, and added: "Wanna read it over?"

"I've read it already," Speedy said, picking it up. "It will do well enough. I read upside down, as you scrawled it."

"You're full of tricks," muttered Simmons. "You'll trick yourself into the hottest part of hell, one of these days." He lifted his head again. Horses had swept up the road and now they stopped in front of the house.

"That's probably the deputy sheriff," said Speedy, "come to catch Dupray and me, but he'll be glad to have you, instead."

CHAPTER
FOURTEEN

Now, for a moment, silence came over that room. Al Dupray was still sunk in sleep. The hand of Simmons went up to his throat, and his eyes gradually closed as he spoke, breaking the silence: "It's kind of a funny thing . . . the way I've come into this. I mean, it was the axe, the feel of it in my hand. It was like the axe did the trick, and not my hand that had hold of it. It's kind of funny."

There was a light, crackling sound outside the house.

"They're on the verandah now, and they're going to rush in and surprise us, pretty soon," Speedy warned. He smiled at that, the smile twisting all to one side on account of the pull of the imitation scar that was on his face.

Only a moment more, then through the window came the voice of the young deputy sheriff, Stewart Osgood, saying: "Up with your hands, Speedy. We got you covered from this here window, and from the door of the hall. We got Dupray, too. Up with your hands, or I'll let you have it."

Speedy did not raise his hands. He did not turn his head, even, but said: "That's all right, Osgood. You're going to get enough out of this to make you a full

333

sheriff at the next election, but don't think that you're going to get it out of me. Keep me covered, and send your men in."

There is incalculable force in the power of quiet calm and self-control. Deputy Sheriff Osgood muttered a few orders, and his men stalked into the room, their guns ready. They covered Speedy and Dupray, but Simmons made no move to break away, for he saw that Speedy's eyes were upon him, something as the eyes of a hunting cat might be upon its prey, conveniently near.

Al Dupray was unaware of the intrusion. He simply slumped forward in his chair, and, burying his face in his arms on the top of the table, he continued to sleep the sleep of utter exhaustion.

"Pick up that paper," Speedy said to the first man who had entered, and that was none other than his friend the guard of the jail.

The man obeyed. His voice went slowly over the words of the confession; before it ended, Stewart Osgood was standing in the room, listening with a frown of wonder.

At the end, not one of them was heeding Speedy or Al Dupray, after whom they had ridden so hard and so successfully that night. Their guns were pointing toward Pete Simmons, instead.

He jumped out of his chair at last, and cried out: "It's all a lie!"

"It's wrote in your own hand," Osgood said sternly.

"I had to write it. These two devils made me at the point of a gun," said Simmons. "Speedy, he swore that otherwise they'd hang me, and he'd forge my confession, and go and leave it here, like I was a suicide."

His voice trailed away and stopped. For his own guilt closed over his throat. He could not help feeling that the confession was not more visible in his written words than in his face at that moment.

"Well," said Osgood. "I guess that's about all you wanna say now, Simmons."

"D'you mean that you'll take this serious?" demanded Simmons. "D'you mean that a thug like Speedy, and a killer like Dupray, out of murderous blood . . . ?"

Al Dupray stirred and groaned in his sleep. That sound stopped the voice of Simmons in the midst of his protest, and, looking about him, he saw contempt, disgust, horror, in every face among the posse.

"What I'm thinking of," said Osgood, "is that poor Tom Older was a friend of yours. He was an old bunkie. And yet you'd murder him with an axe. It makes me sick. You're under arrest, Simmons. Anything more that you say may be used ag'in' you in the law courts." He stepped to Simmons, and clamped the handcuffs over his big brown wrists. The man sank back in his chair with a gasping groan.

Even this did not awaken Dupray.

"You and Dupray, Speedy," said Osgood, "will have to come back to the town till I get a court order that frees you. There's gonna be some kind of a charge ag'in' you for breaking jail . . . well, and turning Slim Malone loose. I reckon that there won't be any charge, though, for makin' a fool of me. That's throwed in free and extra, I guess."

"What else could I do, Osgood, but work on you?" said Speedy. "I had to get into the jail, and how else could I do it?"

"I dunno," said Osgood. "And I ain't so sad about it, neither. I ain't the first ordinary gent that's been buffaloed by you, and I reckon that I won't be the last, neither. I'd take more than that to keep from hanging the wrong man, even if he is a Dupray." He looked down at the sleeping form of the young man and added, with a sudden compassion: "Damn me, but we used him rough. It's the last time that the third degree is ever used in Clausen, and you can believe that, if you want to."

"I believe it," said Speedy.

"Wake him up," ordered the deputy sheriff. "Let him come along with us, Speedy. You've gotta go back."

"Let him stay out on parole with me, till tomorrow," answered Speedy. "I'll promise to bring him back when he's had his sleep."

The sheriff hesitated. Then, nodding, he observed: "They say that your word is enough for any man in your part of the country, and I guess that your part of the country is as good as mine. I'll trust you to show up with him tomorrow by noon, say?"

"Right," answered Speedy.

So it was that Al Dupray slept all through that scene that removed Pete Simmons from the house and started that unhappy man back toward the town of Clausen and a life sentence.

Speedy, when he heard the hoof beats depart, roused Dupray, and got him staggering, like a child, to the bed, saw him topple over, straightened out his legs, pulled off his coat and boots without completely waking him, and then pulled a pair of blankets over him. After that, he went to the top of the hill behind the house, brought the pair of horses down to the shed, and fed them.

For his own part, he was not sleepy. There was in him an ability to store up energy and sleep in quiet times that served him well in days of need, when his reserve strength had to be drawn upon over a considerable period. It served him now, and, coming back to the shack of Simmons, he kindled a fire in the stove, boiled some coffee, fried some bacon, and sat down with this and a cold pone to an appetizing, if small meal.

Later still, he washed and scrubbed from his face, hands, and body the dark stain that had covered it, using laundry soap, hot water in a galvanized iron laundry tub, and a certain chemical that he took out of a small vial in his pocket.

The dawn came before he had finished all of this work, and he went back to look at Dupray, who was still sleeping soundly.

There was no other bed in the place. Speedy, therefore, went to the table at which Simmons had sat to write his confession, kicked off his boots, and, stretching himself on the table, without so much as a blanket under him for cushion or over him for warmth, he closed his eyes and was instantly asleep.

He slept till well on in the morning, and then awoke automatically, as though an alarm had rung in his ears.

Walking back to the other room, he found that Dupray was just waking up, yawning prodigiously as he sat up on the side of his bunk. He leaped to his feet at the sight of Speedy. "You, Speedy...," he began.

"It's all right. Take it easy," said Speedy.

"Where are we, I mean?" he said confusedly.

"We're in Simmons's house. You remember back a ways. He wrote out his confession, signed it, and Osgood and a posse came here for us, and went away with Simmons, instead."

"Great Scott!" exclaimed Dupray. "How did I manage to sleep through all of that?"

"An easy conscience, perhaps," suggested Speedy, rather dryly.

Dupray glanced sharply aside at him, but, making no answer, he sat down again to pull on his boots.

Speedy worked up a new fire and cooked a second breakfast. In silence he cooked and in silence they ate, for a great cloud seemed to have enveloped the mind of the boy.

Finally, over his second cup of coffee, he said: "Look here, Speedy, what's on your mind? You're keeping something back."

"Only that you're going back to Clausen with me today," said Speedy.

"Going back?" exclaimed young Dupray. "Why should I go back? I'm free now, if they've got Simmons for that job."

"I promised the sheriff that I'd bring you in," said Speedy.

The sight of his calm face suddenly seemed to madden Al Dupray. He grew ugly; for an instant he looked not like the nephew but the very son of that Charley Dupray who was Speedy's greatest enemy.

"The hell you did!" Al Dupray shouted out. "And who are you to promise the sheriff anything from me? I'll handle myself, thanks!"

Speedy rose from the table and went to the window, through which he stared out over the valley, glistening under the morning sun. There he waited, until presently the voice of the young man said, just at his shoulder: "I'm sorry. I was a fool. I clean forgot."

"Don't be apologizing," said Speedy. "If you're ready to go, we'll start now."

"Only," said Dupray, "I dunno about going back to Clausen. I ain't liked there. I dunno that I'm liked anywhere, but, particular in Clausen, they always hated me."

"Why should they?" asked Speedy.

"My name's Dupray. That's enough," Al said, his face wrinkling at the disagreeable thought.

"You've got a new position now," said Speedy. "They called you a murderer. Now, instead of that, they find out that you're an honest man, with something that means more than honesty."

"What's that?" Dupray asked humbly.

"Money," said Speedy. "You have the mine now. Your claim to it is as clean as a whistle."

"By thunder," said Dupray, "I'd clean forgot about that. But now that I'm gonna be cleared, why, of course, it's mine." He lifted his head with a jerk and laughed. Then he snapped his fingers. "Some of 'em can look up to me now," he said. "I'll snap my whip, and they can jump." He snapped his fingers, in token of the good time to come. Then, changing his mind quickly, he said: "Look here, Speedy."

"All right," said Speedy. "Look at what?"

"Except for you, I'd be closer to hanging by the length of one night, instead of further away from it. I owe it to you."

"You owe it to your uncle," said Speedy. "You don't owe anything to me."

The young man laughed. "You wanna put it that way," he said, "but the fact is, Speedy, that you saved me. Well, I was partners with poor Tom Older . . . though it's true that I wrangled a good bit with him, I was fond of him. He was a salty old bird, I can tell you, and honest, too. He was willing to trust a Dupray, for one thing." His face darkened, as he said this, and then he continued slowly: "But with Older out of the picture, there's something remaining, Speedy. Half of that mine belongs to me, but I want the other half to belong to you."

Speedy shook his head. "I can't take it," he said.

"Because you can't take anything from a Dupray, eh?" demanded the youth.

"I didn't say that."

"You meant it, though."

"Are you sure of that?"

"Why shouldn't I be?"

"Al," said Speedy, "it's not because you're a Dupray, but because of two things. The first is there's blood on it . . . Older's blood. It's a queer freak with me, but I hate blood money. The second thing is you don't owe any gratitude to me. You owe it to your uncle."

Al Dupray blinked, and waited for the explanation. And Speedy went on slowly and solemnly: "If I'd heard of you being in prison before, I would have been glad of it. I would have been glad to know that another Dupray was to die. You see? But your uncle came and caught me off base. Away off base and up in the air. I was in his hand, and three other friends of mine were in his hand, too. He only had to scratch a match in a grain field. And you know that he hates me, Al."

Dupray nodded. His eyes, animal bright and quick, kept playing over the face of Speedy as though trying to find a hidden solution behind his words and expression.

Then he said: "Damn me, Speedy, I can't imagine why he didn't scratch the match, then. I know that he's hated you, all right. What would keep him from bumping you off? What's the answer?" He waited eagerly, hanging upon the answer.

And Speedy said: "Because he loves you, Al, and thought I might be able to help you."

Al Dupray blinked and winced. Still his eyes roved, as though the answer were not entire and satisfying.

341

At last Speedy said: "About the mine, if you think that anything should be given away, remember Tom Older, your grubstake partner. Even that hound, Simmons, was going to give some money in the name of Older. Why don't you give fifty cents out of every dollar the mine makes for you and invest it in some charity, in Tom Older's name?"

Dupray caught in his breath. Then he gasped: "Jiminy, Speedy, everybody would think I'd gone crazy, wouldn't they? But why not? Just to give 'em a slam in the eye."

CHAPTER
FIFTEEN

They rode into the town of Clausen, shoulder to shoulder, and just before noon they entered the long, winding, main street of the town. A whisper and a rumor ran before them. People hurried to windows and doors. Little children appeared by magic and trooped about.

"Look around," Speedy said to his companion. "If those people seemed to hate you before, don't they seem to be changing their minds, just now?"

Al Dupray lifted his head, and breathed more deeply once more. "It looks kind of like a new world, that I never seen before, Speedy," he declared. "You sort of opened the door of it to me."

"Your uncle did," insisted Speedy. "He gave me up. And he'd rather have had the best blood out of my heart than anything in the world. You're the only thing that makes a bigger difference to him."

"Yeah?" murmured the boy, bewildered. "And that's a funny thing, too." He added: "You know how it is . . . I never heard from Uncle Charley much, except somebody appears in the middle of the night and drops a letter into my hand, then slides off. In the letter there's just a few words that say . . . 'Here's some of the velvet, so you can spend it fast. Good luck.' That's the way that one of his letters would go. I never seen his face, myself, more'n half a dozen times, and he was never very damn' kind, at that. Look a-here, Speedy, d'you think that I look like him?" There was a world of anxiety in him.

Speedy answered briefly: "You do."

"Do I?" groaned the young man.

"You look like the best part of him," said Speedy.

"Whacha mean by that?" said Al Dupray.

"The Duprays are an old family, and they used to be a good one," said Speedy. "And they ought to be a good one again. They've gone wild, and that's all."

Dupray stared before him with a wretched face. "Bad blood," he muttered.

Or, at least, that was what the words seemed to be to the acute ear of Speedy, who answered: "What d'you mean by bad blood?"

"Like back there in Simmon's shack . . . after all that you'd done for me," Dupray said gloomily. "But this morning, when I thought that you were sort of ordering me around, why, in another minute I could've killed you."

"Take hold of this idea, partner," said Speedy.

"Yes?" Al said eagerly.

"Listen to me, now. When you see a colt in the corral that drives the rest of the horses around, you may say to yourself that it's not the handsomest of the lot, and it's not the biggest. But you've an idea, as a rule, that that horse has bottom to it. Am I wrong?"

"No, you're dead right," muttered Al.

344

"Well, when that colt grows up, it's likely to need some handling," said Speedy, "or else it will begin to go wrong, and it'll go wrong as soon as the people that handle it think it's wrong. Because your horse is going to be as bad, or twice as bad, as you let yourself think it is."

"Yes, that's true, and I sort of see what you mean," said Dupray. "I see right through the deal. Oh, Speedy, you've got a brain in your head." His enthusiasm was growing.

"You've grown up thinking that there was bad blood in you," said Speedy. "What does that bad blood amount to?"

"Murder," broke out Al Dupray in a low, choking voice. "Damnable, black murder, and lots of it. That's what's been in my blood, and my father's blood before me, and his father before him." In the exquisite perfection of his pain, he grinned, as though squinting at the sun.

"Murder, you say? There's something else, though," Speedy said.

"What else?" groaned Al Dupray. "There's murder, Speedy, and there's been murder in me. There was murder in me this very morning, and for the only man in the world, about, that's ever tried to do a kind thing for me."

"Besides murder," said Speedy, "there's strength and courage. You, Al, you never cried 'enough' in your life, not even when a bigger boy was thumping you."

"How did you know that?" Al asked, suddenly wide of eye, like a child.

"I know it because I know that you're a Dupray," Speedy answered.

"Do you?" gasped Al.

"Yes. Besides, I know that you never will say 'enough.' No Dupray ever surrenders. Why, an army of a thousand Duprays would conquer the whole world, if they'd fight shoulder to shoulder."

"A thousand Duprays?" repeated the young man. "That'd be an ugly mess, all right." He laughed a little, with excitement in his eyes.

"Then," said Speedy, "every Dupray has endurance. He can handle his body as though it were iron. A Dupray will ride or walk farther, climb higher, stand more heat or cold, fight harder, starve longer, and never say die. The fellow who has the luck to be born a Dupray is born a thoroughbred. Between him and other people, there's the difference that there is between a Kentucky thoroughbred and a plow horse."

"Would you say that?" Al said.

"I would say it, and I *am* saying it. I'd bet on a Dupray any day."

"You'd bet on a Dupray," the boy said slowly, "to break the law, and to die before he'd let himself be put in prison for it. That's how you'd bet on a Dupray."

"It's true. The whole lot of the Duprays have been too hot under the collar all the time," said Speedy. "That's what they've been. But you, Al, have had a chance to cool off. You'll find that you've a better temper than the rest. You're the sort of diamond that can cut diamond. Use yourself right. Respect yourself as much as I respect you, and you'll surely rule the roost."

Al Dupray said nothing, but his eyes were blazing, and there was on his face such a smile as no man had seen there before.

Suddenly Speedy said: "Who was your mother, Al?"

"Mother? What's she got to do with it?" asked Al Dupray, suddenly angry.

"She's your mother," Speedy said. "That's what she has to do with you. Was a wrong thing ever whispered about her?"

"No!" Al Dupray said with vehemence. "Whacha mean?"

"Then remember that your blood is half hers, and no man ever dared to so much as whisper a wrong thing about your mother. Here's the jail, Al. We turn in here and pay a call, I think. We may even have lunch in a cell, for all I know. I hope they have a good cook."

Al Dupray was suddenly laughing as he swung down from his horse and went up toward the jail, arm in arm with his companion.

Stewart Osgood met them at the door of the jail and brought them straight to his office. "I've got the judge here," he was saying. "I dunno how far I can go, but the judge, he knows. I was watchin' the sun and kind of wondering if you'd be in, right on time, Speedy, and the kid along with you." He heaved a sigh, as though a great weight had just been removed from his mind. Then, leading the way, he opened the door and admitted them to his office, where the gray-headed judge was sitting, a stern, quiet man, with a face that had braved many troubles.

"Here they are," said the deputy sheriff. "I don't want to have you waste much of your time. I know that you're a busy man, Judge Welch . . . but I'm only wondering, after all, if it was a jail break. It's true that we were holdin' Al Dupray on a wrong charge, but a jail break's a jail break. Then, they let out Malone. We weren't holding Malone for nothing much, but he was turned loose."

"The law can go hang," said the Honorable John J. Welch. "I could have told you last night that you'd be a fool to arrest either of 'em. But I wanted to see Speedy, face to face, and here he is . . . here he is."

He nodded to Al Dupray. Speedy he gripped by the hand and deliberately turned him toward the window light, as a father might turn the face of his son. Holding the hand of the younger man still, he said: "It was a good thing and a great thing and a brave thing, Speedy . . . since you won't tell us your true name. No other man in the world, I think, could have done it. I'm glad to have seen your face. I've a boy at home, Speedy, that may grow up to look like you . . . but if he grows up to be like you in more than looks, may fate help him as much as I'll admire him."

CHAPTER
SIXTEEN

Arriving at the house of John Wilson, William Cort flung himself from his horse without tethering it. He paused only long enough to throw the reins, then he ran in through the kitchen door. There he found, not Jessica Wilson, but the amazed cook and, stamping into the front of the house, came at length upon the two Wilsons. They rose up with frightened faces before him.

"He's done it," gasped William Cort, falling exhausted into a chair. "He's freed Al Dupray from the jail. I sent the telegram we agreed on, you know. We thought that it would be a way of heading Speedy off from terrible trouble, but he was already inside the jail. I don't know just how he wangled it, but he did the job, and he's managed to get Al Dupray loose. Not only that, but it turns out that young Al was wrongly accused, and it was proved by Speedy. He found the real killer and made him confess.

"The town of Clausen is burning up with excitement. Young Al Dupray has made a talk to the best men of the town and told 'em that he's giving half the profits of his mine, and it's a rich one, too, to any charity in the place. And why d'you think he's doing it? Because, he says, Speedy has taken a rope from around his neck, but chiefly out of regard for the love and kindness . . . yes, sir, those are the words . . . the love and kindness of his uncle, Charley Dupray, who got Speedy interested in the business. It's the darnedest thing that I've ever seen in a newspaper.

"I rode my horse almost into the ground to get out here to you and tell you about it. Besides, I want to be here when we explain to Speedy why we sent a telegram that might have got him into such hot water, instead of saving him from burning his fingers, as we figured it. He ought to be here almost any time, if he rides back this way, and this is the way he's pretty sure to ride. Wilson, Jessica, did you ever hear such a yarn as this in all your life?"

Not three miles away, in a narrow glen coming out of the hills, Speedy at that moment was jogging his mustang sleepily, horse and rider hanging their heads a little, with the heat of the sun pouring down steadily upon them.

But for all the somnolence of his mood, the warmth and sleep that were soaking through his body and his spirit, he was instantly aware of the shadow that moved behind one of the trees. He checked the mustang instantly and was off its back in a flash, its body between him and possible danger.

Then said the harsh, ringing voice of Charley Dupray: "It's all right, Speedy!" Next the great Dupray in person appeared from among the trees, leading after him a lofty thoroughbred with wide, shining forehead, starred with white, and the eye of a deer, ready for flight.

350

The beauty of the animal and the ugliness of the white frog-face of the man worked strangely in the mind of Speedy. He stepped out in front of his mustang. "Hello, Dupray," he said.

Dupray waved a hand. "Speedy," he said, "we've burned up ten of the thirty-day truce. I'm thinking that I'd like to make it longer."

Speedy shrugged his shoulders. "You think so now," he suggested. "But you'll change your mind, later on. You'll remember a few of the other old days, and they'll burn you up."

"Would you trust me, Speedy, if I gave you my word?" Dupray asked curiously.

"No," Speedy said, "even if you swore on all the Bibles in the world."

"You wouldn't trust me, eh?"

"No," said Speedy.

The other nodded and seemed to take no offense. "Maybe you're right," he said. "I don't know. Just now I think that maybe I could go straight, as far as you're concerned. You've done a pretty big job for me, Speedy."

The latter waved his hand in turn to banish the suggestion of kindness. "All in the day's work," he said.

"There's something else, though, that's not in the day's work," said Charley Dupray.

"What's that?"

"This," said Dupray. "And if you're not behind the writing of the best thing that ever came to me, more than gold or diamonds, I'll eat my own heart out with my own teeth. Look at this."

351

He held out a square of paper and Speedy, unfolding it, read:

Dear Uncle Charley: By this time you know that Speedy has got me freed and put me right before the world, so right that people here in Clausen seem to think that my name may not be Dupray, after all. But I'm going to teach them that it is Dupray — only, the sort of a Dupray that they don't expect, the sort of a Dupray that you could be, if you hadn't chosen the other way of living. But, whatever I am, I'll owe it to you, and I'll never forget you while there's blood in me.

Your affectionate nephew,
Al